Ripples

A novel by

Peter Endicott

This book is a work of fiction. All characters, places and events are a product of the author's imagination, or are used in a fictitious manner. Any resemblance to actual people or events is purely coincidental.

Available at: https://www.createspace.com/3507067
and also on Amazon.com

FOR LORI DRAGONETTI

Life *is* Energy

Ripples

1
Wake Up

Jake Edison didn't want to get up so early. A seven o'clock wake up wasn't his favorite way to start the summer. But they needed bait, and like his dad said, 'the tide won't wait!' He rolled out of the bunk in the shed, stretched and yawned, then scratched his short sandy blond hair and looked around.

The shed was Jake's summer home. His dad had built it to hold a set of bunk beds for some extra sleeping room at the cottage, and Jake had moved in practically while the last shingle was going on. He loved having his own place, and all of his most important things were here. There was a shelf on the wall that held a pile of comic books and a few of his favorite novels, like *'The Sword in the Stone'* and *'The Hobbit'*. His skim board was leaning against the wall, and his snorkel, mask and diving knife hung from nails in the corner. His fishing rods hung from a couple of hooks in the rafters, and seeing them, Jake remembered why he was getting up so early - bait.

He checked the tide table hanging on a nail next to his bunk. He had checked it last night, but he was just making sure. Low tide was at seven forty five, and he knew the weather was supposed to be nice today. It would be a perfect time to get a bunch of quahogs, except it wasn't a perfect time to get out of his nice warm bunk. It was only the middle of June, and the mornings could still be cool on the coast of Massachusetts, especially if the wind was from the east.

Despite the chill, Jake was ready to start his summer. It was early to start summer vacation, but they hadn't had any snow days last winter so school had gotten out even earlier than usual. He threw off the flannel pants he wore to bed and got his bathing suit on. Now he was ready for the day. A smile crossed his lips when he thought about not going right in the shower,

1

and not getting all dressed, and not lugging his books on the half-mile walk to school. That was done with until after Labor Day.

He stepped outside and started shuffling through the sand toward the cottage when he noticed the eyes gleaming in the shadows under the house. He was squinting as he looked between the posts that held the house up when something charged out from the dark and knocked him flat. He howled with laughter and tried to get up, but his pet boxer had him pinned and it felt like she was trying to lick his face right off. She was a white boxer with a brown patch around her right eye. "Bailey! Knock it off and get offa me!" he roared. Bailey finally let him up and stood there panting and wagging her stub of a tail about a hundred miles an hour. "What are you doin' up so early?" Jake asked, but he knew the answer. Bailey was making sure she didn't miss the clamming trip. She loved the boat.

Bailey the boxer and Jake walked up the stairs to the deck together and went into the cottage. The cottage had been built in 1958, and it still looked the same now as it did back then. The main room was arranged with the fridge, the sink and the stove on the right as you walked in. There was a plank table in the middle of the room, and a couch and chair were on the left. The two far corners of the room each had a set of bunk beds. There was a curtain in the doorway in the far wall next to the bunks on the left, and that led to the one 'private' bedroom. That was Jake's parents' room. To the right of that doorway, in the center of the far wall, was the old woodstove. Between the woodstove and the bunks on the right there was another doorway that led to the small bathroom.

The old propane lights still hung on the walls, and they still worked. They provided enough light for reading or playing cards, and as an added benefit they threw a little heat to add to the warmth from the wood stove when Jake and his dad would visit in the off-season.

Jake's dad was sitting at the table having coffee. "Mornin' Jake. How'd you sleep?" Brian Edison asked.

"Good, I was tired, and the sound of the crickets puts me right out."

"Me too" his dad said. "You going clamming?"

"Yeah, I just wish it wasn't so early!" Jake said.

"Well, the tide won't wait!" his dad said for the hundredth time. Jake just smiled. "Have some cereal, and get going then" his dad said.

Jake got a box of cereal from the cabinet, and the milk from the fridge. The milk was almost frozen when he poured it. "Dad, the fridge is running pretty cold" he said.

"I'll turn it down a little," his father said, and he got down on his knees to adjust the propane valve. The fridge ran on propane because the cottage was way out on a sandy peninsula, and there was no power grid out there.

Jake ate his cereal while he thought about the day ahead and all the things he planned to do during the rest of the summer. He was looking forward to seeing his beach friends, and he knew they should start arriving in the next few days. He thought it was kind of funny that he didn't see these friends all winter, but he still felt closer to them than the kids he went to school with for nine months of the year. He'd heard his mom say 'absence makes the heart grow fonder', and he guessed that it was true. He started thinking about Michele from down the beach, and Nicky from Western Point, when the curtain opened and Kelly Edison came out of the bedroom. "Good morning" she said. "You must have big plans to be up so early."

"Good morning, Mom. I'm going to get some clams with Stevie. The Connors got in last night and he wants to go" Jake replied. "Why are you up so early?"

"I thought I'd do some cleaning to get the winter filth out of this place, and then spend some time relaxing on the beach when it warms up a little."

"Sounds like a plan" Jake's dad said. "I have to go get some shingles to patch the roof, but I'll be back in a couple of hours, and I can help you then. Help you relax, that is…."

"Very funny Brian. But don't worry. I'll have a list for you when you get back!" Kelly said as she gave him a playful slap on the shoulder.

"I can hardly wait." Brian smiled and gave her a kiss. "Love you, I'll see you later." He started toward the door, then stopped and looked at Jake. "Don't forget to wear your life jacket" he said.

"I won't Dad" Jake replied. His father nodded and thought about saying something else, but Jake told him that he'd be careful. Brian seemed satisfied then, and left for his trip into town.

Jake finished up his cereal and put the bowl in the sink. He said goodbye to his mother and she said "You be careful!"

"I know, Mom, I said I would!" he protested.

"Well I want to make sure," his mom said.

"I promise. Besides, the bay's practically empty. Love you" he said and headed toward the door.

"Love you too," she said as Jake headed out with Bailey on his heels.

2
Shove Off

Jake went into the shed and got his casting rod just in case they saw some striped bass on the way to the clam-flats. Then he headed over the dune to the front beach, and started walking down the beach to his friend Stevie's cottage. Before he got too far he saw Stevie walking down the beach toward him. Stevie also had his casting rod, just in case. He looked a little comical coming down the beach hauling a fishing rod that was twice as tall as he was. Stevie was the shortest of Jake's friends, and Nicky, who was the tallest, liked to say Stevie was compensating with his oversized casting rod.

"Hey, I thought I was gonna have to wake you up!" Jake yelled.

"No way!" Stevie yelled back, flashing a big toothy grin below his freckled cheeks. "Besides, you won't find any clams if I don't go and show you how!" Stevie bragged, but he knew that wasn't true. Jake was the one who always seemed to pick the right spots to clam, or fish, or whatever. He seemed to have a sixth sense when it came to finding stuff like that. He always tried to explain it to Stevie and the other guys, but nobody seemed to tune in like Jake.

Stevie thought that sometimes it was downright creepy how Jake could zone in. He'd go all quiet, and his eyes would get a faraway look like he was daydreaming or something, then he'd snap to attention and say something like "Let's head to the far side of the island, I think the stripers will be there" and he'd always seem to be right. Then he'd make some excuse about the tide being right, or that the birds seemed to be gathering that way, but his friends never saw it. They just knew better than to argue when Jake got that look in his eye. Even the adults were amazed at how the boys always seemed to come back with fish, even when the old timers weren't having any luck at all.

Jake and Stevie headed back over the dune toward the bay side of the peninsula where Jake's little 12-foot aluminum boat was pulled up into the marsh. Bailey gave a quick chase toward a seagull, and when it took off, she shot over the dune after them.

They walked out through the marsh grass like they were walking on glass. In June, it was tough on their bare feet. The grass didn't get any softer in July and August; it's just that their feet got tougher from not wearing shoes all summer. By summer's end, they could fly through the marsh like they were on a running track wearing sneakers.

They got to the boat and put the rods in it, then picked up the anchor and set it in the bow. The old boat was a wash-up that never got claimed, and Walter Guthrie, one of the old-timers on the beach had given it to Jake – after checking with Jake's father of course. Fixing the leaks was the easy part. All it took was some aluminum putty. The hard part was convincing Jake's mom to let him have his own boat. Jake's father had smoothed that over by making sure that Jake took the safe boating course at the Coast Guard station, and then promising that he'd make sure the little boat would never leave the back bay. Jake's mom had finally relented.

Jake had named the boat the 'Corposant'. He had stumbled across the word one rainy day at the cottage while skimming through an old hardcover about sailing around Cape Horn. 'Two Years Before the Mast' was the name of it, and while Jake had never finished the whole book, he'd asked his father what the word meant. His father had handed him another book, the dictionary, and told him to look it up.

Corposant was a Portuguese word that literally translated to 'heavenly body', but also meant 'Saint Elmo's fire'. When he looked up Saint Elmo's fire, Jake saw that it was miniature lightning bolts shooting around the masts and rigging when the old sailing ships got close to electrical storms. Saint Elmo, he found out, was the patron saint of sailors.

Jake thought that 'Corposant' would be a good name for a boat if he ever got one. When Walter had given him the boat and asked what he was going to name it, Jake had replied immediately. Walter and Jake's father had exchanged a surprised look.

6

"Ah, a static nuisance on the high seas" Walter had said and winked at Jake's dad, the twinkle in his eyes matching his smile. "Seems about right for such a formidable vessel" Walter mused. Jake didn't quite follow, but he was glad Walter liked the name he had picked.

Jake and Stevie started dragging the boat through the mud toward the channel. It was low tide so they had a way to go, but the boat was out on the farthest point in the marsh, and the island was only fifty yards away from the point. The tide running through this small gap between the island and the peninsula created a natural channel that held water even at low tide. A minute or two later they were at the channel's edge. Jake said "Hold on and let me put the plug in."

"That would be good" Stevie gasped, bending over and breathing hard. Jake found the plug in the bottom of the boat, and stuck it in the drain hole. They pulled the boat a couple more feet into the water until it was floating freely. They put on their life jackets and Jake told Stevie to hop in. Bailey didn't need to be told - she jumped into the bow and leaned forward panting with her ears laid back ready to go.

Jake pushed off and jumped in. He dropped the engine and squeezed the primer bulb on the gas line. Jake knew they had plenty of gas because his father had just put a full tank in yesterday when they had tested the old engine. He choked the engine and pulled the starter cord. On the second pull, the ancient five horsepower Johnson Sea-horse motor sputtered to life. The old motor had no neutral. It was always in gear, and if you wanted to go in reverse, you had to spin the whole motor around. They were off immediately.

Jake's mom watched from the deck of the cottage through binoculars and saw the two boys in the boat, with Bailey up front like an oversized hood ornament from a Mack truck. She watched as they putted down the back side of the peninsula toward the end of the island. Kelly said a little prayer, and then went back into the cottage. She still wasn't sure that the boat was a good idea, but she had to admit that Jake was very capable for a twelve year old. He was probably a better sailor

7

than most of the yahoos she saw blazing around in the speedboats or jet skis that showed up on the weekends, she thought. Still, she'd worry until they got back. Kelly took comfort in the fact that the back bay was almost empty, and the channels were narrow enough that the boys could swim to dry land in no time if something happened.

In the boat, Jake and Stevie felt like they were on top of the world. They didn't see the narrow ribbon of water surrounded by mud flats. They saw a deep channel that led to all the oceans of the world. They sensed the adventures of the whole summer waiting for them.

3
Clamming

They cruised down the channel between the island and
peninsula feeling the sun on their faces and the wind in their
hair. Everything was perfect. Jake was starting to picture the far
end of the island where the channel got shallow, and he could
almost imagine the quahogs in the mud at the waters edge.
Stevie looked back and saw that familiar far away look in Jake's
eyes, and he decided not to say anything. Jake was zoning
already, and it was best to just let it happen. All of a sudden
Jake snapped to, and looked off to the left. Stevie looked that
way and saw a huge coyote sitting on his haunches, staring at
them from the edge of the trees on the island.

"Holy crap! Do you see that?" Stevie blurted.

Jake didn't answer. He was staring back at the coyote, which
seemed to be looking right into Jake's eyes. Bailey sensed
Jake's change of mood and looked toward the island just as the
coyote got up and walked into the bushes under the trees. Bailey
gave a short bark and started growling in the direction of the
bushes.

"Quiet Bailey, he's gone," Jake said.

"Holy crap, he was huge!" Stevie shrieked.

"Yeah, he was huge. My dad told me there were coyotes on
the island. He said that deer can swim over across the channel,
and coyotes will follow them if they're hungry enough in the
winter. Usually you don't see them in the summer though,
'cause they head back to the mainland in the spring. I've seen
them on the beach in the winter with my dad, too." Jake decided
then to skip the adventures he had planned for the island until
he found out a little more about coyotes.

They continued on down the channel, and finally got to the
place where the bottom flattened out and the water got shallow.
They watched over the side of the boat and soon were in just a
few feet of water. They could see the bottom. It was muddy and
spotted with patches of seaweed. There were horseshoe crabs

and moon snails etching lines in the muddy bottom. Jake cut the engine and drifted a little way forward. The spot felt right and he threw the anchor over and tied it off short. Tide was still going out a little, but it was almost low.

Jake took off his life jacket and hopped out of the boat, and he started feeling the muddy bottom with his feet. They were on the island side of the channel, and Stevie didn't get out right away, but sat there looking nervously toward the shore.

"He ain't gonna come out in the water, Stevie. Are you gonna clam, or what?" Jake asked.

"How do you know he won't come out here?"

Jake thought about it, and then said, "I don't know how I know, but I just do." Stevie looked at him for a minute then slowly crawled over the side. He threw his life jacket back in the boat and started feeling in the mud, but he kept sneaking nervous glances over toward the island. Suddenly he felt something like a smooth rock in the mud under his foot. He started digging with his toes down next to it, then forced his toes under it and popped it up out of the hole. He ducked under and felt the familiar shape of a quahog. It felt like a pear that got stepped on and half-flattened, and then had turned to stone. He stood up and shook his wet hair back, opened one eye and said, "Got one!" as he held the clam up high. He looked at Jake who was smiling and holding up a quahog in each of his own hands. Stevie felt another and tried to keep his balance so his foot wouldn't lose contact, and he had to take a step against the slight current with his other foot and ended up stepping on another clam. "Holy crap! I got one under each foot! How do you find these places?"

"If I told you, I'd have to kill you!" Jake said in a gravelly voice, trying to sound like a gangster he'd seen on TV. Stevie laughed and began clamming in earnest, forgetting all about the coyote. Soon they had a bucket of quahogs, and Jake said, "That should be enough".

Stevie said "Tide's not coming yet, why don't we keep going?"

Jake said, "We don't need anymore. And besides, you want to make sure there's some for next time we come, don't you?" Stevie wasn't really inclined to leave *any* clams, but he kind of wanted to make sure there were some for next time. He wouldn't have thought of it that way. He thought Jake was just strange like that, and knew better than to argue. He also knew he wouldn't win the argument anyway, so he climbed back in the boat.

Bailey welcomed them back in with some lapping and wagging. They put their life vests back on, Stevie pulled the anchor, and Jake started the engine. It sputtered to life on the first pull now that it was warmed up. They were on their way to the rest of the summer, and now they had bait to get things started.

4
Old Man Withers

Jake steered the boat the same way that they were originally heading, and Stevie knew they'd take the long way back and go around the island. That was fine by him; he was in the mood for a little cruise. There should be enough water to get their boat around the end of the island and into the channel that ran down the other side, and even if they did get stuck in the mud, tide would be coming and they wouldn't have to wait long for the boat to float free.

Just as they were turning around the end of the island, Stevie looked back and saw a solitary figure walking along the water's edge back on the peninsula. There was a weathered dory anchored nearby. He looked to be an ancient man, with a short gray beard. He was wearing an old black watch cap, a faded denim shirt and worn out black jeans. He was looking up toward the lighthouse as he walked.

"Look, that's Old Man Withers!" Stevie hissed.

"Who's he?" Jake asked, peering toward the old man.

"You don't know Old Man Withers? I can't believe it. Everybody knows Old Man Withers!"

"I don't know him! Who is he?" Jake asked, getting a little impatient with his friend.

"You really don't know him?" Stevie said.

"Ok, now I don't know which I want to know more – who Old Man Withers is, or how long it's gonna take you to swim back home!" Jake bellowed.

"Alright, alright! I'll tell you. I just can't believe you don't know the story" Stevie said, and seeing Jake's look he continued, "which I'm gonna tell you right now."

Stevie spat over the side of the boat, and then he lay back across the bench seat against one side of the boat with his feet crossed up on the other side. Jake knew it was going to be a long story, but he didn't mind; they had time. Bailey kept leaning forward in the bow, and she didn't seem the least bit interested.

"Old Man Withers" Stevie began, "is a murderer! He lives on the island now, but he didn't always."

"Get outta here! Who did he kill?" Jake asked.

"Lots of people" Stevie said, satisfied that he had his friend's full attention. "He used to be the lighthouse keeper, back when it didn't run on automatic, and they had lighthouse keepers" he continued. "Back when my dad was a kid, old Nathaniel Withers and his wife used to live up at the lighthouse all year round. He used to take care of the lighthouse, and she used to take care of him, my dad said. All he had to do was keep the lighthouse lit, and they could do anything else they felt like doing, as long as the lighthouse stayed lit." Jake thought about this, and it sounded like the best thing in the world to him. He wished they still had lighthouse keepers. He was already dreaming of all the fishing he'd do, when Stevie continued the story.

"Everything was fine for a long time. They lived there, and they fished, and they had a boat and lobster pots. She used to have a garden. They had everything they needed, and he got paid on top of that. So what they didn't have, they could go into town and buy. He even had a truck from the Coast Guard to get to town in. And it was free! All they had to do was keep the lighthouse lit" Stevie said, and paused to let that sink in.

"Go on" Jake said, a little more interested than he wanted to show.

"Well, one night in the fall, a big storm came in. It was blowing like a hurricane, and raining like crazy. The waves were crashing off the rocks of the lighthouse cliff..." Jake looked back over the peninsula to where it bent like a backwards 'L' and he could see the lighthouse on top of the hill there. He was looking at the back side of it across the marsh, but he could imagine the waves crashing against the cliff out front. He'd been fishing out by that cliff, and knew that the base of the cliff was littered with boulders that made the waves sound huge even on a nice day. Jake could see the old man walking through the marsh grass toward the lighthouse hill now.

The lighthouse faded from view as he steered the boat around the end of the island and found the channel on the other side. The boat slowed a little, and Jake knew the tide had turned and was coming in now.

Stevie went on with the story. "They say Old Man Withers went crazy that night. They say the storm drove him nuts. He heard voices in the wind and he thought they were ghosts! He ran up the ladder and shut off the light so they couldn't find him, and he laid down and cried like a baby!" Jake got the feeling that this story got a little better every time Stevie told it. Stevie was like that. It's not that he was a liar or anything, but he did like telling stories. And if the story wasn't good enough on its own, Stevie didn't mind helping it out a little. Jake didn't mind, because Stevie did tell a good story.

"Then what happened" Jake prompted.

"Well, it turns out that he *did* hear voices in the wind, only they weren't ghosts. They were people yelling on a boat that was sinking! They were yelling for help. It was one of them charter fishing boats from Plymouth that can hold about a hundred people. They were sinking and trying to get back to the harbor, but it was so stormy they couldn't see anything but the lighthouse! Then when Old Man Withers shut off the light, they were yelling for him to turn it back on, but he wouldn't 'cause he was afraid of the ghosts!" Jake didn't believe a word of it now, but he couldn't help imagining what it would be like to be on the sinking boat in pitch black, with everyone around you screaming.

Stevie sat up, looked right at Jake, and he lowered his voice and went on to what Jake knew would be the unhappy ending of this story. "The boat crashed right into the rocks and busted into a thousand pieces. Everyone got washed up against the cliff, and back through the rocks until the water was red with their blood. There wasn't anyone who survived. The next day, they arrested Old Man Withers. He spent twenty years in jail 'cause

14

he shut off the light and murdered all the people on that boat!"
Stevie finished with a shout.

Jake sat there for a minute and then said "Good one Stevie. I
missed your stories this winter."

"It's true! Every word!" Stevie said.

"Well, it's a good story, either way" Jake said. He didn't feel
like arguing about it. It was a good story, and one that he'd
already decided to ask his dad about. His father had grown up
coming here also, and he knew most of the stories. It seemed
everyone had a story. It's just that most of the real stories
weren't as good as Stevie and his other friends liked to tell
them.

Jake was still thinking about the fishing boat crashing through
the rocks in a storm and, whether the story was real or not, that
part seemed to take on a life of it's own in his head. He sat there
letting it grow in his mind, and got that far off look in his eyes.
Then he started to *feel* like he was on that doomed boat. He
started to feel the cold spray on his face, and he could feel the
deck rumble with every wave that crashed against the hull. Then
a strange thing happened. The scene began to change. He
thought he saw ropes swinging through the air, and he heard
loud creaking and groaning sounds like trees bending and
breaking in a storm. He saw a flash of lightning that lit up the
ship, but now it wasn't a fishing boat out of Plymouth, it was an
old sailing ship. Another crack of lightning, and suddenly he got
so cold he started to shiver. The third lightning bolt hit the mast
with a blinding flash that burned the image of the scene around
him into Jake's mind like a photograph. The tremendous crack
of thunder at the exact same instant shook him to the core, and
his guts felt like jelly. He saw it was snowing sideways, like a
blizzard, and for an instant he saw scared frozen faces of a
hundred sailors holding on to anything they could find on deck,
their expressions a mix of agony and horror…."

"Holy crap!" was the next thing Jake heard, and all of a sudden
it was bright sunshine again, he was back in his own little boat
and Stevie was standing and pointing off to the starboard side.

"Look at the birds! They're pounding the water right over there!"

Jake came fully awake now, and immediately turned to starboard and headed for the terns that were diving into what looked like boiling water. Despite the sunshine, he still shivered one more time as they turned away from the island toward the diving birds.

5
Blues

Jake steered the little boat past the spot where the birds were diving. He wanted to get by them without interrupting the feeding frenzy. When he got upstream, he killed the engine and let the current start to push the boat back down to the diving terns. He grabbed his casting rod and freed the treble hook of his lure from the bracket holding the middle eye of his fishing rod. His lure looked like a mackerel. Jake held his fishing line against the base of the rod with one finger while he flipped the bale over to release the line. Then he waited and watched.

He could see the birds flapping and hovering over the water, their sharp eyes peering down into the depths. Then they'd fold their wings and dive down like missiles into the water. The birds would then launch themselves back out of the water with shiny baitfish dangling in their pointed beaks, flapping their wings to get some altitude. While they were still going up they'd crane their necks and flip the baitfish back down their throats, then level off and hover again. They were picking their spots, trying not to hit the worst of the boiling water.

The water did look like it was boiling. The surface was churning and splashing, and it was filled with the fins and tails of big fish driving the shiny little baitfish toward the surface. The baitfish didn't have a chance. Go down and get eaten by monster fish, or go up and get eaten by squawking birds – it wasn't a good place to be a shiner right now. Jake knew it was either schoolie stripers or blue fish chasing the shiners to the surface. He couldn't tell which from this distance, and it seemed like the current was pushing the school along almost as fast as it was pushing the boat. He waited patiently while the boat crept ever so slowly closer to the action.

When he finally thought he could reach with a long cast, he reared the rod back over his shoulder and whipped it forward. About halfway through the arc, he let go of the line with his finger and pointed the rod at the airborne mackerel lure so that the string would run straight through the center of the rod eyes, and not drag on the edges and slow down the cast. It was a beautiful cast. The lure plopped down right into the center of the boil, and Jake immediately took one turn on the reel to set the bale down. Almost immediately he felt a savage tug. He pulled back on the rod, and feeling nothing there he started reeling and jigging a little to make the lure look like it was a wounded fish going through the water. Bam! He got a wicked hit and pulled back to set the hook. This time the fish didn't get off, and the fight was on! Jake tried to keep steady pressure while he started to reel, and the fish jerked and pulled back savagely. Jake yelled "They're blue fish!" and he adjusted the drag on the reel so the line wouldn't snap.

The fish started to run, and Jake's line starting going out with a loud whizzing sound as the drag gave the fish some play. Jake loved the sound of a running drag! He hadn't heard it since last year and he was filled with excitement!

He tightened up the drag a little and started reeling slowly when he could, and letting the fish run when he had to. The trick was to work the fish toward the boat without pulling too hard and snapping the line. He also wanted to keep any slack out of the line so the blue wouldn't get the line in his sharp teeth and bite through. While Jake played the fish closer to the boat, he looked over to see Stevie cursing and trying to get his own lure unhooked from a boat cushion. Stevie had hooked the cushion on the back swing of his cast, and hadn't even got the lure in the water yet!

"Never mind that – grab the net!" Jake yelled. Stevie dropped the rod and grabbed the net just as a beautiful thirty-inch bluefish shot out of the water, arced over sideways and plunged back in with Jake's lure hanging from its mouth. The fish was about fifteen feet from the boat and Jake was bringing it up closer. When it got close, the fish saw the boat and took off again with a whiz, and Jake didn't fight it. A minute later when it slowed down, Jake reeled the tired fish close enough for Stevie to scoop it with the net. Stevie heaved it up and fell backwards and dropped the net and fish into the boat – the fish started flapping and snapping, Bailey started barking, Stevie started cursing when the snapping fish got too close, and Jake started to laugh so hard he got tears in his eyes and fell into the bottom of the boat with the rest of them. Still laughing, he wrestled the fish under control, careful of his snapping jaws, and the commotion finally died down. Stevie grabbed his rod and stood up and looked out toward the birds, but they were about fifty yards away now and were starting to fan out looking for the baitfish again. The water had settled down, and the feeding frenzy was over. They watched for a while, but there was no more action.

"Shit! I missed them!" Stevie wailed.

"That's 'cause you were too busy catchin' boat cushions!" Jake howled and started laughing all over again. Stevie looked hard at him, but a smile crept in, and soon he was laughing right along with Jake. Bailey forgot about the fish and lifted her ears, cocked her head and just stared at them. When the laughter died down again, they caught their breath and thought again how great it was to be back on the beach for the summer.

6
Back to the beach

Stevie held the fish down while Jake grabbed the pliers to
unhook the lure from the blue's mouth. Bluefish have razor
sharp teeth, and Jake kept pliers in the tackle box in the boat
just for them. You didn't want your fingers too close to those
jaws. They got the fish unhooked and let it lay in the bottom of
the boat, careful to keep their bare feet away. Bailey was staring
at the fish and growling low in her throat. She didn't react like
that to flounder when they caught them. Jake figured it was
because the bluefish had big eyes and teeth, and Bailey knew it
was dangerous. "Never mind, Bailey. Leave the fish alone!"
Jake said. Bailey looked sideways at him as if she was asking if
he was sure about that, and Jake said, "No, leave it." Bailey
didn't look too happy about it, but she got back to her place in
the bow, and Jake started the engine and began heading back
toward the island.

From out there in the bay behind the island, they could see all
the way back north to where their peninsula connected to the
mainland. It was just a long strip of sand, dotted here and there
with bushes nestling in the beach grass on top of the low dunes.
The fragile strip of sand continued south for roughly five miles
before it finally became more substantial, rising up out of the
ocean to form a hill upon which the lighthouse sat. Cottages
surrounded the lighthouse, and there were trees and lawns and
real dirt and rocks up there. Another strip of sandy beach
extended toward the west from the lighthouse hill, but this two-
mile stretch had cottages along its length. This stretch of beach
also ended with a hill, which the locals called the 'Head'.
Beyond the Head, the peninsula turned sandy again, before it
finally submerged at Western Point.

From where the boys were, they couldn't see the stretch of
beach where their cottages were, but they could see the whole
north side of the island now. There were only two houses
visible on this side of the island, the side you never saw from

the beach. On the end that they were heading for was a huge house sitting on a manicured lawn. The house faced Plymouth harbor out the front windows. On the left side of the house, you could look across the channel and see the length of the beach from Western Point all the way back to the light house. On the right side, you could look across the bay back to the mainland. Behind the house, the island was covered with trees all the way to the other end. The only thing you could see besides the trees was the other house on the water's edge about halfway down the island. This was also a big house, but the two houses couldn't have been more different. The house on the end of the island had solar panels covering the roof, and big fancy windows that made up most of the walls. It looked brand new, and it looked like somebody rich must live there.

The big house in the trees halfway down looked like it had been there for at least a hundred years. It's not that it was run-down; it's just that it looked old. It was three stories tall if you counted the windows in the peaks of the roof. All the windows were the old fashioned type made of individual panes of glass in a frame that looked like a tic-tac-toe game. And all the windows had faded yellowing curtains that were probably white a hundred years ago. Some of the curtains were open an inch or two, and the boys always got the feeling that someone was watching when they passed by the house in the channel.

The kids from the beach knew there were a few other houses, and even an old family graveyard in the trees in the middle of the island. They'd snuck over to explore more than once. They also went over with their parents when the islanders allowed visitors to see 'Pulpit Rock', where the Pilgrims had their first Sabbath in the New World. But in all their adventures on the island, they never seemed to go near the big house on the water on the far side of the island. The graveyard didn't seem to bother them, but none of them ever even thought about going to the old house on the far side on the water's edge.

Jake steered the boat toward the far end of the island and tried not to look at the windows in the old house. He saw that Stevie was also focused on the big modern house on the end, and he was unusually quiet. It was always like this. They liked to cruise around the island, they always got quiet and tried to ignore the house at the water's edge, but they couldn't help sneaking glances at the old curtains in the windows. Jake thought about this for a minute, and then got the crazy idea that maybe this summer they should go and explore the house on the water's edge. He shivered suddenly, and just as suddenly thought 'maybe not'.

Soon they came up to the house on the end of the island and Stevie broke the silence first. "Check it out! There's a big pool next to the house now!" Jake looked, and Stevie was right. There was a pool surrounded by a wooden deck with a pool house on it. There were also six round wooden tables with folded umbrellas sticking up from them up on the deck. "Why do you need a pool when you got the whole ocean to swim in?" Stevie asked. Jake said he didn't know, but he thought maybe rich people didn't like getting salty or something. He couldn't think of anything else, but he was glad to be puzzling about salty rich people instead of wondering if someone was on the other side of those old yellow curtains in the other house.

They rounded the end of the island and headed back down the side closest to the beach toward the point in the marsh halfway down where they kept the boat. When they got close to the edge of the channel, Bailey jumped out and chased off into the marsh after a rabbit that wasn't expecting a dog to sneak up behind him in a boat. Jake killed the engine and let the boat glide to shore. He got out and walked into the marsh while Stevie held the boat. Then Jake came out of the marsh grass carrying a wire lobster pot without any holes or nets in it because it was a lobster car, not a lobster pot. It was the keeper pot they used to keep the bait alive so they could go fishing whenever they wanted. They took the quahogs from the bucket and put them in the lobster car and fastened the bungee cords that held the lid closed. They dragged the pot out into the edge of the channel where it would stay in the water even at low tide. Then they dragged the boat back up into the marsh, which was much closer now that tide had come in some. They picked up the

22

bluefish and fishing rods and headed back through the marsh to the beach. Jake glanced over his left shoulder at some movement, and in the distance he saw the old man just as he was rowing the dory around the far end of the island. He remembered his father was off the beach, but he'd ask him later about the story Stevie had told him about Old Man Withers.

Walter Guthrie

As they walked through the marsh Jake said "My Dad's off the beach, so I'm gonna go see if Walter will help me fillet this bluefish. You comin'?"

"No way! He hates me!" Stevie said. "He thinks I'm after his granddaughter."

"Well you are" Jake replied.

"Bullshit I am!" shouted Stevie. "I wouldn't if she was the only girl on the beach!" he wailed.

Jake knew better, but he didn't feel like arguing. "Whatever, I gotta get this fish filleted before it gets all oily. You can't wait with bluefish; you gotta fillet them right away."

"No shit, Sherlock" Stevie said, even though he didn't know who the hell Sherlock was. It was one of his father's expressions.

"Well, I'm going to see Walter. I'll catch you later." Jake said.

Stevie headed down the back road between the edge of the marsh and the cottages on the back side of the beach, while Jake cut through the back row of cottages and up the dune to Walter Guthrie's cottage on the front beach.

Jake had known Walter Guthrie his whole life. Jake used to call him Mr. Guthrie, but when Jake turned about seven, Walter told him 'Mr. Guthrie was my father, but he don't answer to anything anymore, so you just call me Walter.'

From that point on, Jake felt like they were friends, even though there was close to seventy years difference in their ages. Walter never talked down to him, he always had time for Jake, and he always offered Jake a drink when he had one himself, which was fairly often. Walter's favorite beverage came from Tennessee, but he first offered Jake a Moxie, and was quite amused that Jake actually liked it. After that, Walter always made sure he had Moxie in the fridge.

Jake walked up the sandy path to the back of the Guthrie cottage. He walked under the trellis covered with trumpet vines and stepped through into the little oasis of green that was Walter's yard. There were tomato plants growing in buckets of dirt, cucumbers in a dirt filled pontoon from an old boat, and string beans climbing up an old piece of lattice leaning crookedly against the pontoon.

Walter's wife Sharon was pumping water from an old pitcher pump as Jake walked up. "Hello Jake! Are you looking for Walter? I'll get him – Walter!" She called before Jake could even answer or say hi.

Walter stepped out from the shed that used to be an outhouse before the plumbing moved indoors and said, "Well look what the cat dragged in! And look what you dragged in! Where'd you find the fish? He a wash-up? Don't tell me you caught him yourself?"

Jake smiled and said "Hi Walter. I caught him out behind the island and my Dad's off the beach. I was wondering…."

"Sure, sure! I'll help you clean him up. It'll be thirsty work, though" Walter said as he ducked into the rear door of the cottage. A minute later he came out with his fillet knife, a can of Moxie and a glass with ice filled with his own favorite beverage. Sharon paid no attention to them. She went to tend to her plants while Jake and Walter walked over to the old wooden table next to the pump. There was a sharpening stone on the table, and Walter started cleaning up the edge of the fillet knife. "So how did you get to the back side of the island so early, with your dad off the beach?"

"I went in the boat you gave me last summer. My dad and me put it in the water yesterday and he said I could go get some quahogs for bait this morning. I took Stevie Connors with me."

"And where is that little stem-winder now? And where's *his* fish?" Walter asked with a little less smile on his face.

"He went home, and he didn't catch a fish" Jake said.

"Not surprised" Walter mumbled, then brightened and said, "This is a beauty! You gonna eat him all yourself?"

"No, my mom and dad like it mostly, but I'd rather eat flounder. I like catching blues the best, but I like flounder for supper. I thought maybe you'd like to keep some?" Jake asked.

25

"Well, I guess I could take some off your hands. That's mighty nice of you, Jake" Walter said with his smile back at full throttle. Walter put the sharpening stone down and set about cleaning the fish like he did it every day. Jake leaned in close to see him work, and noticing his interest Walter repositioned and slowed down so Jake could see what he was doing.

Walter was always happy when Jake came by. He wasn't like the other kids on the beach. He paid attention. He was interested in fishing and clamming, and the old stories from the beach. Walter saw that from early on. That's why Jake was the first one Walter thought of when that old boat washed up. Walter never had a son, but he knew if he had, he would want his son to be like Jake.

Jake watched intently while Walter filleted and skinned the fish. He drank his Moxie while the fillets were washed under the pump and then put in plastic bags. When that was done, Walter sat down with his glass and said "So how was school this year?"

"It was okay" Jake said. "I'm glad it's summer though. I'd rather be here."

Walter smiled and said he understood. "I'd rather be here too," he said. Walter looked like he was always here. Here it was mid-June, and Walter was already deeply tanned. He had longish gray hair, gray whiskers in a goatee, and long bushy gray eyebrows that seemed to have a life of their own. But his eyes were a bright blue, and they always looked like he was thinking about something funny. Jake didn't know a better way to explain it. Walter's eyes always looked like he knew something funny.

"Did you get any quahogs?" Walter asked, with that look like he had something funny to say, no matter what the answer was.

"Yeah, we got a bucket full. I put them in the lobster car for now. I gotta wait for my dad before we fish for flounder out front. I can only use the boat in the back bay" Jake trailed off.

"Well, you got all summer. You'll be eating flounder soon enough, I suppose" Walter said.

"After we got clams, we went around the island to see if we saw any stripers or blues. Then Stevie saw the birds diving, and I got him" Jake said, pointing to the frame of the bluefish.

"Stevie saw the birds?" Walter asked, not quite believing it. "What were you looking at?" he asked, as one bushy eyebrow rose up, demanding an answer.

Jake remembered thinking about the shipwreck, and how it had changed to an old sailing ship in a blizzard, and he almost started to zone out again. "I was daydreaming, I guess," he said.

Walter saw his face cloud over and said simply "I guess you were" and he left it at that.

Then Jake said "The house on the end of the island has a big pool on the other side now."

"I guess they had too much money kicking around the house and had to use some of it up. The island is changing, I guess," Walter said with a sigh.

Jake thought for a minute before he replied. "Not all of it is changing. The house on the water's edge on the other side looks just the same as always." He paused and said, "It looks haunted!" and laughed like it was impossible, but he thought it wasn't. Maybe he wanted Walter to tell him it was impossible. Walter didn't oblige.

"Well, there may be some ghosts living there with Nate Withers" Walter said, more to himself than to Jake.

"Old Man Withers?" Jake blurted. "I mean, is that who lives in that house?"

"It is" Walter replied with a curious look on his face and the constant smile nowhere to be seen. "And how do you know 'Old Man' Withers?" he asked with one bushy eyebrow raised.

"I, I don't" Jake stammered. "It's just that Stevie told me a story about him when we saw him on the beach this morning" Jake recovered. "He called him Old Man Withers."

"Well, whatever that little hell-raiser told you was a bunch of crap, I'm sure" Walter said emphatically. He took a breath and softened his tone before he continued. "Nathaniel Withers never bothered anybody, but ignorant people get a charge over

27

wagging their tongues about things they know nothing about" Walter finished.

Jake and Walter both sipped their drinks in the uneasy silence that followed. Jake wanted to ask Walter about Nathaniel Withers but wasn't sure how to approach the subject. He could tell that Walter didn't despise Withers like Stevie claimed everyone else did. He couldn't very well ask if he was really a murderer, or if he really went crazy. He finally decided on a more indirect question and asked, "Does he live on the island alone?"

Walter said "Well, it's a long story, and I don't have time for it now. But maybe we'll have time for it someday – in the meantime, don't believe everything people say. Now you better get that fish home and in the fridge."

Jake knew that Walter was done talking for now, so he finished his Moxie, thanked him again, said goodbye and headed home with his plastic bag of blue fish fillets. He walked over the front dune and said goodbye to Sharon Guthrie on the way by, then turned right on the beach and started walking toward his cottage. He thought about the conversation they had just had, and he knew he wouldn't stop thinking about it until he heard the real story about Nathaniel Withers.

While he walked along the beach, Jake could have sworn that he caught a glimpse out of the corner of his eye of an old sailing ship on the water. He thought the Mayflower II must be out of the harbor for a cruise, but when he looked toward the water, there was nothing there. He shook his head, rubbed his eyes and kept walking.

8
Dragon

Jake got back to his cottage just as his mother was leaving with her beach chair and a bag holding her book, sunscreen, sunglasses, a towel and who knew what else. Jake knew that if someone on the beach ever needed anything, his mother would say 'don't go back to the cottage, I have it right here', and sure enough she'd reach into that bag and pull out a bottle of water, or a napkin or whatever else was needed. It was like she was a magician or something.

"Oh, hi Jake. I'm going to sit on the beach for a little while. How was clamming?" Kelly asked.

"Good, we got plenty. I also got a bluefish. Walter filleted it for me" he said and held up the plastic bag with the fish in it.

"That's great! I'll cook it up for supper tonight. Your father will be thrilled!" she exclaimed.

"Is dad back yet?" he asked.

"No, but he should be along anytime now" she answered. "I'll be down front if you need me. There's peanut butter and jelly, or tuna fish if you want lunch."

"Okay, I'll probably make a sandwich and then go see who else is down." Jake said.

"Make sure you're home for supper" she said and headed toward the front beach.

Jake made a couple of PB&J's and got a cup of milk. He went out to the back deck and sat down at the table there to have his lunch. Jake's cottage was on the back side of the beach, and from where he sat he looked out over the marsh toward the back bay and the island. It was called Clark's Island and was named after the first mate on the Mayflower. The Pilgrims had stopped on the island before they went into what eventually became Plymouth Harbor and landed on the mainland. Jake's dad said it was because they were exploring in the long boat from the Mayflower when they got caught in a storm at night. They almost got washed up on the front beach in huge waves, but managed to row out and around the end of the peninsula to get out of the wind, and that's when they spotted the island and went to it to ride out the storm. They stayed for a while and had their first Sabbath there. There was a huge rock in the middle of the island and the preacher had stood on it during the service. That rock was now called 'Pulpit Rock' and Jake and his friends had snuck over many times to see it. The rock had an inscription carved into it that read;

ON THE SABBOTH DAY WEE RESTED
20 DECEMBER. 1620

The old family graveyard on the island was also a spot Jake and his friends liked to explore. Their adventures would always end when one of the few islanders spotted them at which point the kids would run like hell back to the boat and row like mad back to the beach. Jake thought they could make a quicker getaway with his five-horse motor now, and the thought made him smile as he ate his sandwich.

Jake could see the point in the marsh that seemed to reach out to the island, but he couldn't see his little boat from here because of the tall marsh grass. To the left of the point, the marsh curved back toward Jake's cottage and then flattened out and faded into the higher ground of the Head, which curved back out toward the bay. The Head eventually tapered back down into an expanse of sand dunes that ended on Western Point at the bitter end of the peninsula. There was a natural cove between the point in the marsh and Western Point that held a dozen moorings that were protected between the beach and the island from the nor'easters that battered the coast. Jake's dad's boat bobbed lazily on one of the moorings there. While the cove was a safe place to keep the boat, the tide went out of it leaving the boats sitting in the mud twice a day, so his dad also had a mooring out in front of the beach. When the weather was calm, his dad kept the boat out front so they wouldn't have to wait for the tide to use it. Jake's boat was too small to leave on a mooring. A good rainstorm would sink it since it wasn't self-bailing and it didn't have a bilge pump. Jake was looking toward the bigger boats considering which kind he'd like to own when he noticed movement way out on Western Point.

There was a Chevy Suburban backed up to the dune at the last cottage Jake could see on the point, and there were specks that looked like ants carrying piles of stuff up to the cottage. "Alright, Dragon's here!" Jake said to himself as he got up to put his empty plate and cup in the sink. He practically ran out of the cottage on his way to see his friend Nicky Dragoni who must have just gotten down to the beach.

Nicky Dragoni, or Dragon as his friends called him, was Jake's oldest and best friend. They'd both grown up on the beach in the summer their whole lives. Stevie Connors got a cottage when he was seven, so he'd always be the newcomer, and Dragon would always remind him of that, but not in a mean way. Nicky was a little bigger than Jake, and a little wilder too, more reactive while Jake was more thoughtful.

Nicky lived up near Boston, and his family owned a restaurant in the city. Jake had never been there, but he loved Nicky's stories about the famous people that would go there to eat, or the parties and fireworks in the city on New Years Eve, or banks that got robbed in the neighborhood, or whatever. Jake's winter house was here on the South Shore. While it wasn't the boondocks or anything, it was boring compared to life in the city the way Dragon described it. Nicky always had good stories, and he knew how to tell them. Sometimes when things got boring in the middle of summer, they'd just hang out under Jake's cottage in the shade and ask Dragon to tell a story. Dragon would always act like he didn't want to at first, but he'd get one going and you could tell he was really enjoying himself. By the end he'd be acting out the parts of whomever he was telling about, and making up voices and accents for the gangsters or cops. The rest of them would be laughing so hard they'd be crying by the end of the story, because someone in the story was always stupid, and somehow that was hilarious to them.

Jake made his way up over the Head on the 'goat trail', which is what they called the rocky road that went up and over. If it was still low tide, he would have walked along the edge of the cove, but the water was too high for that now. He would have had to walk in the marsh, or climb on the seawalls that lined the cove along the bay side of the Head. He wished he wore his sneakers along the goat trail, but he also didn't want to look like a wimp if one of the other kids saw him. There was an unwritten rule that the kids from the beach didn't wear shoes unless they left the beach to go in town. You just had to tough it out until your feet got used to it. In a week or two, he knew he'd be running down the goat trail, but for now he was relieved when the road came down and turned into a sandy double tire track out through the dunes to Western Point. He walked along one of the tracks and pulled a long piece of beach grass from the dune and chewed on the end as he walked. As he turned the last corner around the dune by the Dragoni cottage, he saw Nicky's mother up on the deck yelling, "Where do you think you're going? You have a lot of unpacking to do!"

Dragon was already walking down the track toward Jake when he yelled back "Aw Ma, I just wanna go see if Jake's around – I'll unpack later!"

Mrs. Dragoni saw Jake then, and her voice changed instantly to a high sweet song – "Well hello Jake! How are you doing?"

"Hi Mrs. Dragoni, I'm fine!" Jake shouted back.

"And your parents?" she said.

"They're fine too. My mom's out on the beach, and my dad went to the lumber yard, but he'll be back soon."

"Tell them I said hello, and stop by for a visit!" she sang back.

"I will" Jake said.

"Now you two stay out of trouble, and Nicky, don't forget to put your things away when you get back!" she finished.

"I will, I will" Dragon said without turning back. Then he looked at Jake, his eyes so dark you couldn't even tell if he had pupils, and said 'Hey Jake, thanks for saving me" low enough that Mrs. Dragoni couldn't hear.

"No problem" Jake replied. "How's things?"

"Awesome, now that I'm down the beach" Dragon mumbled. "My old man had me working like a slave in the restaurant last week. Said it would build character, or some freakin' thing. I think he just didn't want to pay someone to clean the tables. Finally my mom said she was going to the beach, and he didn't want to be stuck with me, so here I am! He'll be down on weekends. Is your old man around this summer?" Nicky asked.

"Yeah, he'll be here the whole summer! He just got off a ship a couple of weeks ago and doesn't have to go back until the middle of September!" Jake told him. Brian Edison was an engineer in the Merchant Marines. He went away for a few months, which was hard, but then he was back for a few months, which was awesome.

Dragon was as happy about this news as Jake was because he knew that Mr. Edison would take them out in the big boat all the time, because he liked it as much as the kids did. "Awesome!" he said. "Who else is around?" Dragon asked.

"Well, Stevie is here. They just got in yesterday. We went clamming this morning and did pretty good," Jake said.

"What kind of clamming?"

"Quahogs – for bait" Jake said.

"Sweet! When are we going fishing?" Nicky asked.

"Not until my dad fixes the roof, and definitely not until you put your stuff away if you mother catches you!" Jake laughed.

"Funny" Dragon said, but he wasn't laughing.

They walked back toward the beach, and Jake and Dragon both marched along the goat trail like their feet were in mid-summer form, each afraid to show the other how much the rocks were hurting them. When they came down the other side of the Head, they turned right and headed out to the front beach. They walked along the water's edge where there was still a strip of hard sand that the incoming tide hadn't yet covered. A couple hundred yards down the beach, Jake's mom was sitting in her beach chair reading. "Hello Nicky!" she said when the boys walked up.

"Hi Mrs. E!" Dragon replied with genuine enthusiasm. Dragon liked Jake's mom a lot. All of the kids did. Kelly Edison always welcomed Jake's friends and made them feel at home. She always let them hang out at the cottage, and told them to help themselves to the drinks in the fridge or whatever was in the cabinets. There was always enough food for them to eat over, and many nights they'd sleep out in the yard or in Jake's shed. Some houses just seem to be the center of kid activity, and Jake's house was that place here on the beach. Kelly Edison was the reason why.

"When did you get down?" she asked.

"About an hour ago. My mom said hello, and stop over if you want" Dragon said, brushing his longish dark hair off his forehead with his hand.

"I will. Where are you boys heading?" she said.

"I don't know" Jake replied. "We were just going to see who was around."

"I think I saw Michele's family pulling up down the beach" Kelly said, and turned in her chair to look down the beach in the direction of the lighthouse. Jake and Nicky looked that way and saw a Jeep in front of a cottage about a quarter mile down.

"Yeah, that's them" Jake said. "We'll go down and say hello."

"Ok, have fun" she said, and the boys started down the beach.

9
Michele

Michele Malone was a tomboy. She wore her hair short and she dressed like the boys dressed – shorts and tee shirts. She played the same games as them, and she was good enough to get picked somewhere in the middle when they were choosing teams. From a distance, you would have thought she was just another one of the guys. Of course, that was last summer.

When Jake and Nicky walked up the path, they weren't quite sure they were at the right cottage. Michele was wearing a two-piece blue bathing suit and she was sitting on the railing swinging her long legs back and forth slowly. Her brown hair was long now, and hanging down over one shoulder. Her face was different somehow, with more cheekbones and less cheeks, and her dark eyes and lashes looked like they belonged to one of those models on a magazine cover. She wasn't going to be mistaken for one of the guys this year - that was for sure. Stevie Connors was sitting in a deck chair and his face looked like a puppy's. Michelle was saying something to him, and he was just nodding his head and sighing when Michele turned and noticed the others coming up the path.

"Hi!" she chirped as she hopped of the railing and danced down the steps to hug them. "How are you guys?"

"Good. How are you? You look great!" Jake said before he could think about it too much.

"Yeah, you look good" Nicky said "but you better throw on a shirt so Stevie can breathe again!"

Michele whacked him on the arm, and Nicky acted like it hurt. Stevie's eyes came into focus, he snapped his jaw back shut and then spat "Bite me Dragon!" The other three laughed and Stevie looked like he was going to say something, but then kept his mouth shut and just turned red instead.

"I'm just kidding" Nicky said. "How are ya, Stevie?"

"I'm good" he said, but didn't sound it. "When did you get down?"

"Just a little while ago. Jake came and saved me" Dragon answered. "My mother got all nice when he walked up and I got paroled for a while". They all nodded like they knew the drill. Seemed like all the mothers liked other people's kids better than their own sometimes, or at least they acted like that in front of them.

Michele said, "Well I have to unpack before I can get out" and she worked her face into a little pout that made Jake want to unpack for her. He was a little surprised by the feeling, and looked away before it showed on his face.

"How long is that gonna take?" Jake asked, like he didn't really care.

"A while. I probably won't be out 'til after supper" Michele continued, "but I better start now." She thought for a couple of seconds, and then said "Maybe we can have a fire later?"

The boys' faces brightened and they all started talking at the same time - "Sounds good!" - "We'll find some wood" - "Yeah, I'll grab a shovel to dig the hole", and it was agreed.

"Michele!" came the call from inside the cottage.

"Well, I better get going. See you later on the front beach?" she asked.

They all said see you later, and the boys started walking down the path together. Nicky was the first one to say what they were all thinking. "Wow, she changed, huh?" The others nodded, but didn't know what else to say, so they shuffled off through the sand, each lost in his own thoughts.

10
The Fire

Later on, Jake's mother noticed him heading toward the sink with his dirty supper dish while he was still chewing the last of his food, and she asked, "What's the big rush, Jake?"

He swallowed and replied, "I'm gonna go find some wood for a fire."

His father looked up and said, "There's scrap wood under the deck near the propane tanks left over from the shed. You can take that. Are you going right down front?"

"Yeah" Jake replied, "We'll be in front of the tarp."

"Ok, but keep the fire low, especially if it gets windy."

"We will" Jake said.

"And dig a good hole" his father went on.

"We will" Jake replied again.

"And come home at 9:30" his mother added.

"Aw mom, can't I stay a little later? It's not even dark 'til 8:30 now" Jake protested, and looked at his father for help.

Brian Edison looked at Kelly, and then said, "The beach is pretty quiet. They'll be ok" and trailed off.

Kelly thought for a minute and looked back and forth between them, and she finally relented. "Alright, come up at 10:00 then, but no later!"

Jake smiled and said "Thanks mom!" as he shot out the door.

Brian looked at Kelly, and knew what she was about to say, but before she could he said, "Kelly, they'll be fine. They're right out front and we can see the glow of the fire from the deck. We'll hear them if they get noisy" and he stopped to let her agree – hopefully. Kelly thought about it but said nothing, and Brian smiled and went back to eating his dinner. He was enjoying the bluefish, especially since he hadn't expected to see any until later in the summer. June was pretty early for blues.

Jake got as much wood as he could hold in his arms while carrying the shovel in one hand, and he shuffled up the path and over the dune to the front beach. Stevie was in front of the tarp near Walter Guthrie's cottage and he was already scooping sand out to make a hole for the fire.

The tarp was just a square frame covered with black landscaping cloth mounted on four poles dug into the sand. It offered some shade for the old timers and small kids on hot summer days, and it was a gathering spot for the people from the surrounding cottages. When there was a fire in front of the tarp, everyone was welcome, but this early in the season the kids knew they'd probably have it to themselves.

Jake called out, "Stevie, I got a shovel. Grab some more wood from under my deck."

Stevie stood up and started walking back up to Jake's cottage just as Michele was walking up to the tarp. Jake was going to tell her to go grab wood, but decided not to, although last summer he would have. Michele dropped a small plastic shopping bag she was carrying onto the sand under the tarp, and kept walking past the hole, following Stevie. She said, "Where's the wood?"

Jake answered "Under my deck" as she walked past him. He dropped his armload of wood and started digging.

Pretty soon the three of them were sitting around a small cozy fire as the sun was setting over the back bay and the evening chill was setting in. They were quiet for a while and just stared at the flames contentedly. Michele took a deep breath, and then let out a long sigh and said, "It is *soooo* good to be at the beach again."

"Yeah" Jake agreed, and Stevie nodded. "How was your winter?" Jake asked Michele.

"It was okay," she said, "but I miss it here, and I miss you guys."

"Yeah, me too" Jake said, and he felt a little flutter in his stomach. He looked across the flames at her. She was sitting with her long legs pulled up to her chest with her arms wrapped around them, and she was staring down at the fire. Her dark eyes shone perfect tiny reflections of the flames. He caught himself staring at her eyes, and looked down at the fire just as she looked up at him.

"How was sixth grade?" she asked, and Jake felt a slight connection, like a secret they shared. Jake and Michele had just finished sixth grade, but Stevie was a year younger, and Nicky was a year older and he wasn't even here yet. The question was all his.

"It was okay," he said. "It was different being at a new school. We go to the middle school in sixth" he said.

"Yeah, we do too. I hated it. The older kids were so mean" she said and shook her head. Jake thought about the eighth graders being mean to Michele and found himself getting angry. He found himself starting to think about what he'd like to do to them, when Nicky walked up into the firelight.

"Man, I never thought I'd get out!" Nicky exclaimed. The others turned toward him and he went on with his rant. "She had me hauling mattresses out and shaking them off, stacking firewood, dragging furniture around. It was easier working for my old man!" he gasped, and plopped down in the sand.

"Well you're here now, so quit bitchin'" Stevie said, and laughed. Nicky rolled over and whacked him on the arm, but it was a glancing blow because Stevie knew it was coming and rolled the other way.

"Anyone want to toast marshmallows?" Michele asked as she got the bag that she had dropped under the tarp earlier.

"Oh yeah" Stevie said, and grabbed one of the sticks that Michele was offering. She passed the other sticks and the marshmallows around. Naturally it turned into a contest for the perfect golden-brown marshmallow, with lots of insults directed toward the other guy's marshmallow, and occasional howls of laughter whenever Stevie got his too close and it burst into flames, turned black, and fell sputtering into the sand while Stevie blew on it furiously trying to save it.

When the first marshmallow massacre of the summer was complete, they settled back to watch the fire. Jake looked up to try to find the North Star on the end of the handle of the Little Dipper. It was full dark now, but he had to shield his eyes from the firelight. He finally located it above the tarp, right where it should be. He didn't know many of the constellations, but the

39

Big Dipper, the Little Dipper and the North Star were the first ones his father had taught him to locate. Brian Edison told Jake that if you could find the North Star, you'd always know which way you were going, especially on a boat at night. Fat chance his mom would ever let him take his boat out at night, but he liked to dream about cruising along in the Corposant, following the North Star.

Michele broke the silence first. "I missed the way the sky looks here at night. There's too many lights at home to see many stars."

Nicky added "You can't see *any* stars at my house at night."

Jake spotted a satellite cruising across the sky and pointed it out to them. It looked like a moving star, and you could spot them pretty easily at the beach once you knew how. You just had to stare at one star until your eye caught movement and was drawn to it. The satellites seemed to go over every 10 minutes or so, and sometimes you could even see two at once. Jake wondered why they never crashed into each other.

Stevie said "That's probably a spy satellite. My dad says they can read a newspaper on the ground from up there."

"Wow, that's pretty good. Maybe if you went up there you could read a newspaper too!" Nicky snapped.

"Bite me Dragon" Stevie snapped back, and Jake thought they were already in mid-summer form. Then Stevie changed the subject and said "Jake and me seen Old Man Withers today."

That got Nicky's attention and he asked, "What was he doing?"

"How do I know? He rowed over to the marsh behind the lighthouse and was walking around."

"Well that's what he was doing then" Nicky said. Stevie just gave him a sour look and shook his head.

"Probably just looking for steamers," Nicky mumbled.

"He wasn't looking for steamers! He was looking up at the lighthouse. You ever find steamers looking up at the lighthouse, dipshit?" Stevie shouted. That got him another whack in the arm from Nicky, but Stevie persisted. "He was probably looking for ghosts!"

40

"You and your friggin' ghost! There ain't any ghosts" Nicky spat with disgust.

"How do you know? Just 'cause they don't walk in and eat at your restaurant?" Stevie countered.

Nicky glared at Stevie like he was the world's biggest loser until Michele offered, "I believe in ghosts." Stevie smirked smugly at Nicky.

"Not you too!" Nicky wailed and fell back in the sand like he had passed out.

"How do you know? You don't know everything. You only believe in things you can see, but there's lots of things you can't see" Michele reasoned. "Do you believe in air?" she asked, and Nicky just groaned.

Jake watched the lighthouse beam flash by in its slow rhythm while Nicky set about trying to shoot holes in Michele's theories about ghosts. Soon Jake wasn't even hearing them, his eyes lost focus on the beam, and his thoughts began to drift toward things he couldn't see.

Jake started to imagine that charter fishing boat running up on the rocks in the blizzard – no that wasn't right. There was no blizzard, but the blizzard *felt* right. The *boat* was wrong, but soon the scene changed to that old sailing ship. *That* was right, Jake thought. As the scene took shape in Jake's mind, the lightning flashed through the flying snow and Jake could see that the ship was filled with terrified sailors, and he could see their agonized faces. Then the lightning rippled again like a flickering candle, and Jake saw that one of the sailors was staring right back at him! It was different from the rest of the picture. This man seemed to be aware that Jake was seeing them, and he was the only sailor that seemed to be able to see Jake. The sailor had a scar on his cheek, and he was staring at Jake with burning green eyes, and he seemed to be uninterested in the mayhem happening all around him. All his attention was on Jake. Suddenly it went pitch dark and a huge roar of thunder shook Jake out of his trance, but the image of the man's face lingered as if it was burned into Jake's brain.

41

Jake shivered and looked at Michele who was pleading, "Are you alright? Jake! Are you ok?"

"Huh? Yeah, I'm fine" Jake lied.

"You don't look fine. I asked you if you believe in ghosts, and you look like you just saw one" she said with real concern.

"No, I was just daydreaming" he mumbled.

"Well, do you?" she asked.

"Do I what?" Jake said, puzzled.

"Do you believe in ghosts?" she said, a little impatiently.

"I don't know," he said. "I suppose it's possible. My dad says almost anything is possible."

Nicky was staring at Jake during this exchange and interrupted. "She's right, Jake. You don't look so good."

Jake was already tired of the questions. "Well, I do feel a little sick. Maybe I ate too much bluefish or something. I think I'll head up to the cottage."

"It's almost ten. I gotta go too," Stevie said.

"Me too" added Michele. "I hope you feel better Jake" she said as she stood up.

"Thanks," he answered, "and thanks for the marshmallows."

"You're welcome, Jake. And so are you two" she said and gave Nicky and Stevie a look that she must have learned from her mother.

"Thanks" they mumbled in unison.

Jake smiled at the little guilt trip she had sent them on. Then he said, "Dragon, will you take care of the fire?"

"Yeah, I'm gonna stay for a little while, I'll let it burn down. I'll leave your shovel under the tarp when I go" Nicky said.

"Ok, I'll see you all tomorrow" Jake said as he turned to leave. They probably said it back, but he didn't hear. He was already trying to stop seeing the face of the sailor with the burning green eyes as he walked off into the darkness toward the dunes and his bunk in the shed. He thought about sleeping in the cottage tonight, but rejected that idea when he thought of the questions he'd get from his mother in the morning. He'd let Bailey bunk with him tonight, though.

42

11
Ripples

The next morning, Bailey woke Jake when she jerked to her feet in the bunk and peered through the screen door with her stub of a tail whipping back and forth like a flag on a speedboat. Jake looked out and saw his father walking up to the door. He opened the door, and Bailey pushed out and began hopping and panting as Brian patted her. "Good girl, settle down" he said to her, then to Jake, "I was going to patch the roof, and I could use some help after breakfast."

"Sure, I'll help" Jake yawned.

"Okay, thanks. I'd like to get it done early, so…"

"I'll get up now," Jake said.

Satisfied, Brian went back to the house with Bailey on his heels, still hopping up for attention.

Jake lied there for another minute while he came fully awake. Last night it had taken him a long time to nod off, but Bailey's slow breathing had eventually lulled him to sleep. He couldn't remember having any dreams, and thankfully no nightmares. He could still see the sailor with the green eyes if he thought about it, but the light of day seemed to make the vision less real. He climbed out of his bunk, changed into his shorts and headed up for breakfast.

It was warmer this morning, and the flag on the pole on the corner of the deck hung straight down. There wasn't even a hint of a breeze, and it would get hot on the roof later if it stayed like this.

Jake went inside and said good morning to his mother, who was drinking coffee and reading the paper that Brian had brought back from town yesterday. He got a bowl of cereal and sat down and ate in silence.

He finished his cereal and went out to find his father who was already carrying a bundle of shingles up the ladder. When Jake got there, he passed a bundle to Brian before he came all the way back down the ladder. There was one more bundle of shingles, but Brian said to leave it for now.

Brian climbed the ladder carrying a rope that was tied to a bucket with tools in it. When he got to the roof, he hauled it up, emptied the tools and lowered it back down so Jake could put the box of roofing nails and the caulking gun in the bucket. When everything was up, Jake climbed the ladder and joined his father on the roof.

The roof was practically flat, with no peak and a slope of about two feet from one side of the house to the other. Brian wanted to put a roof deck on sometime, because the view from up here was spectacular. You could see over the dune to the water on the front beach on one side, and the entire back bay and the island on the other. For now, he just wanted to repair the shingles that had gotten damaged in the winter nor'easters, but a roof deck was definitely on the 'someday' list.

As Brian worked the damaged shingles loose with the flat bar, Jake looked out over the dunes to the beach. He could see that the ocean was flat calm, but the waves seemed to rise up from nowhere at the water's edge and rumble onto shore. He thought about this for a minute and then asked his father about it. "Dad, how come the waves are so big near shore, but there's no waves at all out past the moorings?"

Brian thought once again how observant Jake really was. Most people that he knew would just walk on by, and never even notice the ocean that never stopped in its restless back and forth. But not Jake, he noticed things and he wanted to know about them. Brian sometimes wished he could explain things better, because Jake wasn't a little kid anymore. He wanted details now, and Brian didn't always have them. Funny, he thought, but Jake wanted to know more than Brian could tell him.

"Well Jake, I can tell you what I think is going on" Brian began. He thought back to the wave pools that they had studied back at the maritime academy, and started sorting through the rusty knowledge that was packed away in his head, down deep, like the little used articles relegated to a dusty attic. This was a subject for a 'deckie', or an officer of the deck as they're

44

properly called. Brian had learned the basics of seamanship during his freshman year, but then he had turned toward engineering. Engineers tended to focus on keeping the machinery of the ship going, while the deckies worried about waves and driving the ship. He thought back to the rivalry between the two groups at school. Engineers liked to say that the deckies got to drive, but the engineers did everything else. Deckies naturally saw it differently. Brian wished that he had a deckie nearby now, but he forged ahead.

"Everything that comes into contact with the water makes ripples. Whether it's fish making little ripples, or boats or wind making waves, or the pull of the moon that makes the tides turn, everything makes ripples. Those ripples contain energy, and energy can never be created or destroyed, it just changes from one form to another. That's a proven fact of engineering called the first law of thermodynamics…" Brian stopped, realizing he was about to start babbling about engineering principles, which would only confuse Jake at this point. He searched for the right tack, and then he figured Jake could handle the basic concepts, and he went on. "Waves have a top, called a crest, and a bottom, called a trough. If you have two waves going in opposite directions, when they meet, the trough of one will cancel out the crest of the other and the water will be exactly level for a second, just like before the waves came. But a second later when the two crests meet, the wave will be twice as tall. Can you understand that?"

"I think so" Jake said in a tone of voice that made Brian think that he truly did understand.

"If you looked at the water right where the trough and crest met, you wouldn't see anything but flat water. You wouldn't know there was anything there. You wouldn't know there was any energy at all. But the energy is still in the water, and a second later when the two peaks meet, you'd see it right away." He looked at Jake and saw that he was following. "The ocean is full of energy, Jake. It's always there. It's been moving for millions of years before people got here, and it'll be moving long after we're gone. Sometimes it's easy to see, like in a

45

hurricane when the wind is slamming, and it's churning out huge waves and spray. Other times it looks like it's not there at all, but it is still there. The energy is still there after the hurricane passes, but it's not all gathered on the surface. It settles deeper into the ocean, and the surface calms down. You can't see the energy anymore, but it's still there." Jake thought back to Michele's comments about believing in things even if you don't see them, then he shook that thought off before it could take him somewhere he didn't want to go right now.

Brian went on. "When all the energy below the surface gets near the edge of the ocean where it gets shallow, there's nowhere for it to go, and it gets squeezed out as waves along the shore." Brian paused for a minute thinking about potential and kinetic energy and the changing states, but decided to hold off. He himself didn't understand it until he was much older than Jake, but he thought that if he had the ability to explain it well (which he didn't), Jake would probably understand at the ripe old age of twelve. Instead he just asked, "You get what I'm saying?"

Jake was still looking out toward the water and he nodded. "Yeah, I think so. Everything makes ripples, and they never really go away. You just can't see them all the time." He paused for a few seconds, still looking seaward, then he finished "But they leak out when they get close to the edges."

Brian looked at Jake gazing at the ocean, and he saw true understanding in his son's eyes. He thought again how perceptive Jake was, and how much he grasped despite Brian's stumbling guidance. Brian whispered a silent 'Thank you, God" and went back to work.

12
The Lighthouse

Later that day, while Jake and Brian were finishing putting the tools away, Michele showed up at the cottage. "Hi Jake – hi Mr. Edison!" she called out as she walked up.

Jake turned to say hello, and was shocked again at how different Michele looked this year. His mouth opened, but he froze for just a second like a deer in the headlights. Michele was wearing denim jeans that weren't quite long pants, but weren't shorts either. His mother would have called them capris. Her shirt was a funky pattern of browns and black with hints of different colors mixed in that was buttoned half way up. It had flowing sleeves and flared out below the waist, and it seemed to have a life of its own in the small breeze that had come up around noon. It was made of a sheer material that showed the black bikini top she wore beneath the shirt.

Brian looked first at Jake's expression, and then toward Michele. He saw immediately why Jake had gotten brain freeze. The little tomboy in the shorts and tee shirts was gone for good. "Hey Michelle, good to see you. Jake told me you were down. How was school this year?" Brian said to buy Jake some recovery time. The things you do for your kids that they never know about, he thought to himself.

"School was good" she lied. She paused for a bit, looking down and shuffling her feet slightly. "Are you guys done with the roof?" she asked, hoping to sound like she had no agenda at all.

Brian said, "Yeah, we just finished up" with just the hint of a smile.

Jake finally found his voice. "Yeah, we're all done. What's going on?"

"The kids from the Head are starting a wiffle ball game out on the beach. Dragon and Stevie are there too, but I thought I might take a walk up to the lighthouse. It's a nice day," she said. "Do you want to go?"

47

Jake thought for a minute, Brian held his breath, then Jake said "Sure, I'll go", and Brian thought 'that's my boy' as one of his eyebrows and the corner of his mouth rose slightly.

Kelly Edison came around the corner of the house then. She saw Michele and gave her a big hug, and soon they were in a lengthy conversation, including some details about why school really wasn't so good. Jake went in to wash up, then came out and hovered for what seemed like a couple of hours while Kelly and Michele kept talking. Finally, Jake pried Michele away from the endless conversation and they started out along the back road toward the lighthouse.

Brian put his arm around Kelly and walked her toward the house before she could tell Jake not to climb the ladder at the lighthouse, and not to go too close to the edge of the cliff. Sometimes kids had to be a little more carefree than careful, he thought, as he steered Kelly away from the kids.

"Do you want to go the back road the whole way?" Michele asked Jake as they walked along.

"No, we don't have to. We can go out front at the next cut-off. I just want to get past the wiffle ball game so I don't get sucked in" Jake said. Michele smiled a little and nodded as they continued down the back road toward the 'cut-off', which in the local lingo meant a road over the dune to the front beach.

"There's lots of heather in the marsh this year, and it's way too early for it" Michele commented as they walked along. Jake glanced over at the tiny purple flowers on what looked like miniature shrubs poking up through the marsh grass. He knew he could have walked all the way to the lighthouse without seeing it if Michele hadn't pointed it out to him. He'd notice tiny holes in the sand from steamer clams from twenty feet away, but a marsh full of heather didn't interest him.

"Yeah, there's tons. It must be 'cause of all the rain this spring" he said, with what he hoped was enough enthusiasm.

Suddenly they felt the hard packed sand of the back road vibrate like a stampede was coming, and a white flash shot by Michele. She shrieked and jumped into Jake, and he caught her instinctively. He looked up the road just as his dog turned

48

around and ran back toward them for another fly-by. "It's just Bailey" he said. "She must want to go for a walk too."

Michele looked at him and said, "She scared me" and stepped away slowly. Jake reluctantly released his hold on her and felt that little flutter in his stomach again. He thought how nice Michele's hair had smelled. They walked on, and Jake thought about saying that her hair smelled nice, but as he thought more about it, trying to say those words scared the hell out of him for some reason. Bailey ran back and forth, sniffing at the edges of the road, and chasing every rustle in the bushes while Jake wished she'd spook Michele again.

They got to the cut-off and walked up over the dunes to the beach. The wiffle ball game was in full swing to their right, but it was far enough away so that they could hear the voices but not make out the words as the players argued about a call without the benefit of an umpire. Fair or foul, ball or strike, safe or out; there'd be a few more disputes before this summer was over. They'd work it out though, and the games would go on. They'd work it out quicker if there were no adults involved.

Jake and Michele turned left toward the lighthouse and started down the beach. It was still a couple of hours until high tide, so they walked in the hard sand that would be the tide pool when the water came all the way in. The sand was dry and packed down now, and it was covered with ripples. It looked to Jake like an ocean frozen in time. He thought about the conversation he'd had on the roof earlier, and he pictured the energy leaking out of the ocean and carving a picture of itself in the sand as it receded back toward low tide.

Michele broke the silence when she asked, "Do you think there'll be any seals up there?"

Jake pictured the seals that hung out near the lighthouse in the cold weather. You could stand on the cliff in the winter and early spring and watch them sunning themselves on the rocks, and if the sun was right you could see them swimming below the surface of the water looking for fish.

Jake knew the seals were usually gone to wherever they go to by the end of April, but he remembered occasionally seeing them later in the year. He thought about that one time in the middle of August when they were out fishing. A baby seal had popped its head up right next to the boat and looked up at Bailey, who stared right back at it with a look of astonishment. Jake remembered thinking how much the seal had resembled his pet boxer, except for the floppy ears. It was like they each saw their own reflection in a fun-house mirror. They were both so surprised that neither one of them barked. Then Bailey had leaned over like she was going to dive into the water, and Jake grabbed her as the seal went back under and disappeared. They had seen the seal again later from a distance, but luckily Bailey hadn't noticed.

"Yeah, we may see some seals" Jake said trying to sound optimistic. "It's been so cold and rainy this spring, they might have hung around late this year" he said, but he really didn't think so. It could happen, but it would be unusual, kind of like the heather in June.

"You're lying" Michele said, looking him hard in the face, but smiling while she did. "You don't think there'll be any seals. You're just saying that to make me feel good. What's up with you?"

Jake felt trapped, and got a little angry at first, but then he laughed and felt relieved for some reason. "I just thought I'd be nice to you to start the summer off, but I forgot what a pain in the ass you can be. It won't happen again".

"Good" she said, "I don't want to hang out with liars. There're enough of them back at the wiffle ball game. I'm not wasting my time with them this year" she finished, but she didn't sound finished. There was something bothering her, and even Jake could figure that out, because she wasn't smiling now.

"What's the matter, Michele? What's bothering you?" he asked with real concern this time.

She walked along slowly and looked straight down at her feet as she did. Finally she said, "It's just that I'm sick of liars. My new school's full of them, especially the eighth-graders." Jake didn't say anything. He didn't know what to say. "There's this one kid named Dennis McQuaid there who started rumors about me. He started saying how I like him, but that he told me to get lost. He said I'm a spoiled little bitch, and he wouldn't touch me if I were the only girl in school. He said other things too.." she faltered, and Jake saw that she was tearing up. His first thought was to ask if she did like him, but he decided not to. The question seemed dangerous, but he didn't know how he knew that.

It turned out he didn't have to ask, because Michele went on in a shout. "That asshole asked *me* out! I told him no, but he kept pushing until I told him to go aggravate someone else, and that I couldn't stand him. I tried to tell him nicely, but he kept pushing and pushing until I had no choice! Now he's spreading lies about me!" she finished, and now she was crying.

Jake reached over and put his arm around her. "What an asshole" was all he could say. Michele stopped, turned to Jake and buried her face in his shoulder as he held her. Finally she took a few deep breaths and got control. She wiped her eyes on her shirtsleeves and started walking again. Jake walked next to her and after a little time he asked, "Are you okay now?" Michele nodded, and Jake said "You want me to hunt down this McQuaid kid and stuff him in a lobster pot?" and she finally laughed. It was like music to Jake. Michele felt better, he felt better, but he really would like to bait some pots with the McQuaid kid. He didn't even know him, but he hated him already. He knew he wasn't supposed to hate, but it really felt right, somehow.

They walked in silence for a while, and then Michele said "Thanks, Jake."

"Thanks for what? I haven't even found the kid, never mind baited the pots with him yet" he joked. She smiled and pushed him playfully toward the water's edge.

"I'm not kidding. Thanks for listening" she said.

"You're welcome" he responded, "I like listening to you." Michele smiled at him, and then looked away. Jake walked along, and he felt as though a storm had lifted. The sun felt stronger, he could hear the waves and some seagulls crying, he could smell the ocean, and none of those things seemed to have been there a few minutes ago when Michele was crying.

They came to the end of the beach where it met the higher ground of Gurnet Point. Plymouth Light sat atop Gurnet Point staring out over the cliff toward Cape Cod Bay and the Atlantic Ocean. They walked up the road between the bushes and cottages and made their way to the grassy field surrounding the lighthouse. As they entered, three wild rabbits that were munching on the grass flicked their long ears up, and then hopped off into the bushes at the edge of the field. Bailey saw the last one go, and shot off after it.

They walked across the field to the small hill on which the lighthouse sat. They climbed the hill, looking first up at the light tower, and then at the view surrounding them. They could see their entire summer world from up here. Looking north, they could see the five mile long sandy strip that connected them to the mainland, and then turning to the left, they could see the two mile long beach dotted with cottages surrounded by bushes and dune grass, and finally, the Head at the end of the beach. They couldn't see over the Head to Western Point from here, but beyond the Head they could see the waters of Plymouth Harbor. From here it was obvious that the two-mile stretch of beach was slightly curved, like a crescent moon, and the curve of the waves rolling in was a perfect match to that of the beach. Behind the curved beach, the island floated serenely in the bay.

They turned toward the ocean but couldn't see down over the cliff from here, because the lighthouse had been moved back from the edge in 1998. They could still see the little hill closer to the edge of the cliff where this lighthouse used to be. That hill had two octagonal bare patches in the grass, matching the shape of the lighthouse. Originally, there were twin lighthouses there, and the granite foundation of one still sat atop the old hill in one of the bare spots of the figure eight, waiting patiently for erosion to take it down to the sea below. The lighthouse that had been on that foundation had been torn down in 1924, but the second light had been refurbished and sat there alone for the next seventy four years, until they finally moved it back, foundation and all, because the cliff was creeping closer and closer.

Jake's mom had pictures of him as a baby, with the lighthouse up on girders being slowly rolled to safety in the background. Jake looked toward the old hill and was imagining the lighthouse still there when he noticed a spot of red sitting on the gray granite foundation. Before he could figure out what it was, Michele yelled, "Race ya!" and ran down the hill and across the field toward the fence at the edge of the cliff.

Jake took off after her and just passed her by the time they got to the other side. He had to do a baseball slide to keep from crashing through the wooden rail fence and over the cliff, but he stopped in time with the help of one of the fence posts. He stood up, and they looked over the edge at the rocks and waves below. Michele pointed and said "Ha! I told you so!". Jake looked where she was pointing toward the rocks poking out of the water, and he saw two seals sitting there. They were mostly black but had patches of gray on their bellies. They were sunning themselves on their little temporary islands until the tide came fully in to reclaim them. One seal was much smaller, and the other looked like the mother by the way she kept watch on the little one.

"Wow, they're here late" Jake said.

"It must be because of all the cold and rain we had this spring" Michele said in the best 'Jake voice' she could muster. She laughed and Jake joined her, glad she was back to being in a good mood.

Then Jake sensed, more than saw, movement down at the base of the cliff. He looked down and saw another small seal huddled in the sand against the bottom of the precipice behind one of the larger rocks. The seal had blood on its head and was almost motionless. The little creature craned its neck to peer around the boulder it hid behind, then laid its head slowly back down. Michele followed Jake's gaze down and saw the seal. "Oh, the poor thing, he's hurt! Can we help him?" she asked.

53

"There's not much we can do now. The tide's almost in. He'll have to swim in a few minutes" Jake said. He saw that Michele didn't like that answer, and he didn't like it much either. He liked the seals, and last winter he'd tried to imagine what it was like to be one while he'd been reading 'The Sword In The Stone'. In that book, the magician Merlin had turned young Arthur into different animals so he could see what it was like. When Jake had read that, he'd imagined himself swimming like a seal, and flying like a seagull. Those were the animals that he knew, and it was pretty easy to paint the picture in his head. It was funny, but if he imagined hard enough, it really seemed like he could feel what those animals felt. He felt like the little seal was scared now, because he was *sure* someone had hurt it on purpose. He'd heard that some commercial fishermen would kill seals so they wouldn't eat the fish, and Jake thought this seal was lucky to have escaped at all.

"Can't we do anything?" Michele pleaded.

Jake considered for a moment, and then said "We can come back tomorrow morning when the tide is out and check on him, if you want." Michele accepted that, and made Jake promise to come back with her.

They turned and walked to the old lighthouse hill at the cliff's edge. They climbed to the top and Michele walked over to the side closest to the cliff to look down at the seal. Jake looked down at the foundation for the spot of red he'd seen from the lighthouse.

Jake saw a single red rose, slightly wilted, lying there on the granite slab. He walked towards it and Michele glanced back at him. Jake had that far away look on his face as he looked down at the flower.

The rose had obviously been there for at least a day, because Jake could still see dew from last night lying in the little shadow cast by the flower on the granite slab. Wilted or not, it seemed to Jake to be very alive somehow, and inviting, and begging to be picked up.

Jake bent and grasped the stem, and he felt a slight vibration in his fingertips. The vibration grew as he straightened up, and it

54

pulsed up his arm and rippled through his whole body. His vision darkened, and he heard the blood pumping through his veins. The rush of his blood got louder in his ears until the sound was deafening, then it slowed and took on the rhythm of giant crashing waves. He couldn't see anything but darkness now. Slowly, his sight returned, but it was full night now. Driving rain was pelting him. He heard a tremendous crash and screeching sound like giant fingernails on a giant blackboard, and he looked down and saw a huge blue and white hull being torn apart on the rocks below. The boat was spilling its cargo through the gashes in its battered metal corpse, and the cargo was a mix of fishing rods and ropes and boxes, and screaming people. Some were wearing life jackets, some were not. Some were screaming and flailing, some were silent and floating limply, and all were being slammed against the cliff with brutal force with each tremendous wave whose sound rushed through Jake's ears like a locomotive, and then they were dragged back through the tearing rocks as the mighty ocean took another breath, and then slammed into the cliff once more.

As he stared in horror, he noticed an oil lantern sitting on the edge of the cliff to his left, and next to it was a rain drenched woman crouched down and holding a rope that dangled down to the chaos below, dangled like false hope. She wore a black raincoat, but it was unbuttoned and the hood was hanging down, as if she'd just thrown it on and ran to the cliff. A silver medal swung from a chain around her neck, reflecting the light of the oil lantern like a hypnotist's trinket. She was on the edge outside of the fence, reaching back and trying to tie the rope around the base of the fence post, the same post that Jake had slid into a moment ago on a bright sunny day. Before she could secure it, the rope went taught, and she grabbed the rope with two hands and pulled with all her might. She almost seemed to gain a little ground as the rumble of the wave subsided, but as the ocean drew its next breath, she was dragged slowly through the wet grass. She went silently over the edge still holding the rope with both hands, and a moment later the tremendous crash of the next wave shook the cliff again. The lantern sat there with its little spot of light and warmth amidst the chaos, until it too slowly faded and went dark.

Jake saw nothing, and then the lantern seemed to be lighting again, and then glowing brilliantly so that he had to shade his eyes. He was shaking – no he was being shaken and when he took his hand away from his eyes he was staring up into the bright sunshine. Michele was shaking him, and calling his name as he blinked and sat upright.

"Oh my God, Jake, what happened? You passed out! What happened?" she was stammering.

"I – I don't know" Jake said groggily. He sat with his head hanging between his knees and took some deep breaths while his mind cleared and Michele fussed around him.

"Are you alright? What happened? You picked up the flower, and then your eyes rolled back and you passed out and fell down. You laid there shaking and mumbling while I tried to wake you! What happened?" she cried.

"I must have stood up too quick" he half whispered.

"Don't lie to me!" she screamed. "Something happened! What happened to you Jake? You just passed out, and you looked like you were going to pass out at the fire last night too. Remember? What's happening to you Jake? Tell me!" she pleaded.

He wished he could tell her, he really did. But he didn't know what was happening, not really. Should he say he was having bad daydreams, not nightmares but 'daymares'? Should he tell her about the things he was seeing? Would she think he was going crazy?

He was having this little debate in his head when Michele said "Jake, whatever it is, you can tell me. Even if you don't understand it, tell me what you do know and I'll help you figure it out. Something's happening, and if you won't talk about it, I have to tell your parents. I'm worried about you, so I'll have to tell them something's wrong if you don't talk to me."

Michele stared at him, and he knew she was right. He had to figure out what was going on, because something was definitely going on. If he told his parents, he'd be off the beach in a hurry and waiting in some hospital or doctor's office for who knew

56

how long. And if they couldn't figure it out, they'd probably say something stupid like 'keep him out of the hot sun' or 'he needs more rest' and before you knew it, his time at the beach would be over. He'd be at home in the shade sitting in a rocking chair with a blanket on like an old lady, while his mother made him soup. This image at least made him laugh a little, and that brought a little relief to Michele's worried face.

"Listen Michele, I'm not sure what happened. Maybe I am a little sick or something. I – I'm blanking out a little bit, like a daydream in math class. You know how you can sit there for half an hour with your eyes open, and be somewhere else in your head the whole time? It's kind of like that, but harder to wake up from." It wasn't everything, but it was a start. And it wasn't a lie. He wasn't lying to her.

Michele wasn't letting it go so easy. "When you're daydreaming in math class, and you're somewhere else in your head, you're at the beach. And you're fishing, or riding around in your boat. I know you Jake. When you were 'daydreaming'" she went on, making little quotation signs with her fingers, "just now, you weren't fishing. Where were you? What did you see?" she finished.

Jake thought for a minute, and he knew he wasn't going to lie to her. But he wasn't ready to talk about it yet. He made a decision then, that he would trust her. She'd understand better than any grown up would, he thought, but he still didn't want to freak her out. "You're right, I wasn't fishing." Jake said. "It was more like a nightmare, but more like *being* there than dreaming it. I mean, it was more like being *then* than being *there*, because I'm seeing stuff that happens *here*, but not *now*. I can't explain it any better, and I'm not sure what I'm seeing. I gotta think about it some more, and figure it out. Let me think about it, sort it out a little, and I'll talk to you later when I figure it out some more."

Michele looked at him and thought about what he'd said. She knew he was telling the truth, she could see it in his face. He was scared, and he didn't want to scare her. She decided not to push him right now. She was scared for him too. "Okay" she

57

said, "but you promise, right? You'll tell me later? After you think about it some more, even if it doesn't make sense? You'll still talk to me about it? You promise?" Michele held his gaze, waiting for an answer.

"I promise" Jake finally said, and he meant it. It was a relief to make the promise. He wasn't sure why, but he felt like he wasn't alone in this anymore.

And he *had* been scared.

13
Jenny

The walk back to the beach was quiet, even by Jake's standards. He wasn't one for endless conversation anyway, but the events at the lighthouse had him especially somber. Michele gave him space by collecting sea glass on the walk back, but there was precious little of that because the tide was all the way up now. Bailey hadn't seen him pass out because she had been in the bushes after rabbits, so she wasn't concerned with anything but chasing seagulls on the way home.

When they got close to their end of the beach, Michele saw a familiar figure by the tarp. "Is that Jenny?" she asked.

Jake looked, and seeing that Stevie was also there, he was sure that Walter's granddaughter had arrived. "Yeah, that's her. She must have just gotten down" he said. As they approached, Jenny hopped off of the wooden cable spool that doubled as a table that she'd been sitting on. She ran up to Michele and hugged her.

"It's great to see you guys!" she said. Jenny had blue-green eyes and wavy strawberry blond hair that was always a little wild. It sort of matched her personality, at times.

"It's great to see you too!" Michele answered. "I didn't know you were coming so early. Don't you usually come in July?"

"Yup, always July. But not this year. My mom got a new job and she travels a lot. I'm staying with my grandparents. I'm here for the whole summer!" Jenny squealed.

"That's awesome!" Michele said. "Isn't that awesome Jake?"

"Yeah, that's great" he replied. Although he didn't sound too excited, he really was happy for her. Michele could see he was still distracted though, and that worried her.

Jenny's mom was a single parent; Jenny's father had been a sailor, but he had been killed overseas while her mom was pregnant with Jenny. Jenny had never even known her dad. Despite the fact that Jenny's mom did everything to give her a normal family life, Jenny still felt different sometimes, and when you're a kid, different isn't a good thing.

One of the differences was that Jenny only got to come to the beach for two weeks in the summer. She spent the rest of the time back home in day camps, or hanging out with her 'other' friends while her mother worked. She'd always said she wished she could stay for a whole summer, but when she was younger her mother hadn't felt comfortable leaving her with her grandparents because it was too much to ask of them. Jenny told them that this year, with the new job and all, Sharon Guthrie had insisted that Jenny stay at the beach.

While Jenny told them her good news, Stevie stood there, head tilted, staring at her like a basset hound at dinnertime. Jake noticed his look and imagined little hearts and bluebirds floating around Stevie's head, and that image brought him fully back to the present. He laughed and said, "That's great!" again, this time like he meant it.

"Yeah, it is great. My mom dropped me off about an hour ago, but Mr. Wither's was visiting my grandparents, so I came out front to see what was going on. But I have to go unpack pretty soon." Jenny explained.

When Jenny mentioned Mr. Withers, Stevie looked at Jake like his ass had just caught on fire. Jake gave him a look that said pretty clearly that Stevie ought to keep his mouth shut for once. Thankfully, Stevie got the message and looked down at his feet.

"Oh yeah," Jenny remembered, "Gramps said he cleaned a fish that you caught yesterday, and he wants you to come get what's left of it and put it in your lobster pots, or give it to the seagulls, or whatever. He said you forgot it yesterday."

"Yeah, I got a bluefish out back. I'll go get it when you go up" Jake said.

"Let's go" Jenny said, "You guys can all come up and hang out while I put my stuff away."

Michele and Jake followed her up the sandy path, while Stevie stood there looking absolutely torn. Finally, his fear of Old Man Withers won, and he said he had to go help his mother, but he'd see them later. Jake just chuckled to himself and followed the girls up to the Guthrie cottage.

As they entered the cottage, Jake noticed that Mr. Withers was already gone. Walter Guthrie was putting a bottle and two shot glasses into the roll-up desk in the corner. "It would have been Rose's seventy fifth birthday yesterday. That's why he was so broken up. If you hadn't noticed, he comes by every year around this time" Walter was calling to Sharon in the kitchen.

Jenny said "Who's Rose?" as they walked in.

Walter looked toward her, smiled and said "Well, little miss, I forgot what big ears you had. I'm gonna have to watch what I say this summer." His blue eyes twinkled as he waited for her response, and he knew it wouldn't be a long wait, not from his Jenny.

"Gramps, I'd have to be deaf not to hear you. You weren't exactly whispering. Who's Rose?" she asked again, undaunted.

Walter chuckled and said "Ahh, a woman just has to know" more to himself than to Jenny. "Rose, my dear girl, was Nate Withers wife. Yesterday she would have been seventy five years old, and Nate's still missing her, if you can believe it" he said, and there was no gleam in his eye now. He leaned on the table and stared for a moment with his eyes unfocused, looking all of his seventy-nine years old. Then as if someone hit his 'on' button, he stood straight up, clapped his hands once and said, "Now you've got some work to do, little miss. Take your things off of my couch and put them in the bunkroom. And I'll not have your unmentionables decorating my furniture this summer, so keep them in the bunk room!" and just like that Walter was his old self. "Jake, Miss Malone, would you care for a beverage while Miss Jenny takes care of her business?" he asked them.

"No thanks" they said in unison.

"Well have a seat then, make yourself at home" he said.

They sat down at the table while Jenny gathered her bags and hauled them to the bunkroom.

Jake's curiosity got the best of him, and before he could stop himself he said, "Walter, what happened to Rose Withers?"

14
Rose

Walter hesitated, and by his look Jake thought he was trying to figure out how best to answer the question. Walter was actually considering whether to answer him at all. He remembered Jake's questions about Nate Withers on the porch yesterday. He remembered that Jake had said that Stevie Collins had told him a 'story' about 'Old Man Withers'. While Walter hadn't heard the details, he could imagine what kind of story it had been. Walter had heard other bits and pieces of stories floating around the beach for the longest time, mostly from the mouths of ignorant people who not only had never met Nate Withers, but weren't even alive when it all had happened. His first impulse was to tell Jake to mind his own business, but he looked at Jake and saw that he was just a curious young boy, and Walter's anger subsided. Jake wasn't one of those thoughtless busybodies who spread rumors that tear down other people in the hope that it will make them feel bigger somehow. Jake was just a curious boy, and Walter knew that despite his youth, Jake understood what you told him, and he made sure he understood things before he felt comfortable telling someone else. Walter knew plenty of 'adults' on the beach who heard one little thing, and went around shooting their mouths off like they were the resident experts on the subject. Those 'adults' could learn plenty from Jake, Walter thought. He decided then to answer the question. He didn't know how much he'd say, but he didn't want to put Jake off again, like he'd done yesterday. And maybe, he thought, it was time to end the rumors in the next generation.

"Well Jake," Walter began, "nobody really knows what happened to Rose, and that's the shame of it." He paused, and thought back about a half a century. Funny how it could seem like only yesterday when you looked right at it, he thought. "Rose was a pretty young girl, years ago. She lived on the island with her father, in the old house on the other side that you asked about. The house that Nate lives in now. Her mother died when she was a child, and Rose took care of her father in his later years."

Walter glanced out the window toward the distant lighthouse, and he seemed to be looking back in time. Now that he'd started, the words and memories came easier. "The beach was different. There were only a handful of cottages back then, and not many people on the beach, you can imagine. This cottage was here, and another pretty young lady named Sharon spent her summers here" Walter said, loud enough for his wife to hear him in the kitchen. The twinkle was back in his eyes as he talked. "Well naturally Rose and Sharon became friends. Rose used to come over to the beach to visit my future bride often when the weather turned warm." Sharon came into the living room then, and set a cup of coffee down in front of Walter. "And did I mention that Sharon was a mind-reader?" Walter joked, as Sharon smiled and went back into the kitchen shaking her head.

Walter sipped his coffee and continued. "Nathaniel Withers came to the beach in 1955. He was with the US Coast Guard, and his job was to take care of the lighthouse. I was a carpenter, and I happened to be working on the light keeper's house when Nate first showed up. I had done work on the lighthouse and most of the cottages here for a few years, and I sort of showed Nate around. Well, we became friends. One day, Nate and I were riding along the beach in my old Willy's pickup, and we came upon Sharon and Rose, who were walking along collecting shells." He paused then, lost in the memory. "Ah, two tanned beauties in bathing suits walking along the beach alone, and two strapping young men with nothing but time." He shook himself back to the present as he remembered his audience.

Michele smiled at Jake as Walter resumed. "To make a long story short, Nate and I had met our matches, both figuratively and literally. We'd all be married within a year. Rose's father had passed on that summer, and she moved to the light keeper's house with Nate when they got married. They kept the house on the island, but just closed it up and checked on it occasionally.

Sharon and I lived in an apartment off the beach, but we spent most weekends in the summer here, and we visited Nate and Rose in the off-season. Those were happy times.." he trailed off.

Walter sipped his coffee, and his eyes grew distant again. "A few years went by, and life was good. Sharon and I bought our first house, while Rose and Nate made the keeper's house a home. Then, in 1960 it all changed." Walter struggled with the memories now. It was still all a blur when he thought about those days following the awful news. He glanced across the table at Jake, who waited patiently for him to continue.

"Nate was off the beach getting supplies one day. It was a routine trip he made every week when the weather was nice. The only difference this time was that he needed the brakes fixed on the truck, but he'd planned it and they were expecting him at the garage in Plymouth. Even if he was going to be a little late getting back to the beach, he wasn't worried because Rose knew the lighthouse as well as he did, and she said she'd take care of things while he was gone. Remember, Rose grew up on the island, and she was used to taking care of things herself...." Walter paused and swirled the coffee around in the bottom of his cup, and looked at the miniature maelstrom spinning there. Then he looked up at Jake and said "Walter *was* late that night. Very late. The mechanic at the garage broke a part while repairing the truck, it took hours to get a replacement, and the truck wasn't put back together until well after dark. And to make things worse, there was a terrible storm that seemed to grow out of nowhere that night."

He paused again, and Jake could see how much the memories were hurting him. Finally Walter looked up and said, "When Nate finally got back here, the lighthouse was dark and the light was missing from the tower, there had been a terrible shipwreck with forty people killed, and Rose was gone."

15

The Lens

Michele was shocked, and Jake was even worse. Michele asked, "He never found out what happened to Rose? He never found her?"

Walter shook his head slowly. "No, he never did."

"That's so sad" Michele said.

Jenny came out of the bunkroom then, and Sharon met her at the door. "Did you get your things put away?" Sharon asked.

"Yup" Jenny replied.

"Good, now I could use a little help in the garden before you run off" Sharon said.

"Gram, but…" Jenny started, but Sharon stopped her.

"It won't take long, just a little weeding while I have an extra set of hands" Sharon said. Her raised eyebrow and crossed arms said the rest.

"Okay, okay" Jenny relented. "Michele, do you feel like doing a little gardening?" Jenny asked with a pleading look.

"Sure, I'll help" Michele answered, and they followed Sharon out to the porch.

Jake and Walter were left sitting alone at the table, and Jake was thinking about what Walter had said. Jake didn't trust himself to speak right then, but he still had a lot of questions.

Walter leaned back and took an old newspaper clipping out of one of the compartments in the ancient roll-top desk and handed it to Jake. It was yellowed and ragged, and Jake saw that it was from the *Plymouth Sentinel* from September of 1960. Jake read the article.

Storm Claims 38 lives, Others Missing
Plymouth – The violent storm that surprised forecasters last Friday caused the deaths of 38 people when the boat they were on was forced onto the rocks at the base of Gurnet Point. The fishing boat 'Sea Witch' was

returning to Plymouth Harbor following a day of charter fishing. Authorities are unsure if mechanical problems contributed to the disaster as none of the passengers or crew survived. The eighty-foot vessel was inspected in May of this year with no major deficiencies noted.

There is speculation that the radio was inoperable as no Mayday call was received. It was the worst maritime disaster in Plymouth waters in the last one hundred and eighty two years.

Another vessel from Plymouth is also missing. The 'Wanderer', a thirty-two foot lobster boat left port on Friday morning and has not been heard from since. Local lobsterman Malcolm Higgs was the only person on board.

The seventy-foot fishing vessel 'Maria' out of New Bedford has also gone missing. The vessel was captained by Manual Santiago. His brother Jose and crewman Miguel Rodriguez were also onboard the vessel.

The Coast Guard continues to search for the two missing vessels.

Jake looked up and handed the newspaper clipping back to Walter. He was still shaken by the story, and the article only raised more questions. "It..it doesn't say anything about Rose or the light bulb being missing" he managed to say.

Walter laughed at this, and then stopped when he saw the look of confusion on Jake's face. "Sorry Jake. I don't mean to laugh. When you said 'light bulb' I pictured a 60-watt Sylvania like you put in a lamp. Sounds pretty trivial when you put it like that. That's my fault – let me explain."

"A lighthouse doesn't have a 'light bulb' like you're thinking of it. Especially an old lighthouse, like the one up at Gurnet. That lighthouse had what's called a 'Fresnel Lens'." Walter paused and considered how much he needed to say to make

Jake understand. He'd worked at the lighthouse many times over the years, and he'd heard the history of the light more than once. He also knew about Nate's suspicions concerning the fate of the lens.

"The Fresnel Lens is named after the man who invented it. He was a Frenchman, but we don't hold that against him." No response from Jake, and Walter decided to tell it straight. "He invented the lens in the early 1800's, and it worked so well that folks started using them in lighthouses all over the world. You could see the light from a Fresnel lens twenty miles or more out to sea – they were much better than the original lenses. That's why they ended up replacing the lens in the Gurnet Lighthouse with the Fresnel lens."

Jake interrupted him here. "The lighthouse at Gurnet says 1842 on it. Why didn't they put the Fresnel Lens in at the beginning if they were already invented?"

Walter was impressed. He thought once again how perceptive Jake was. He was like no other boy Walter had ever met.

"Well Jake, the lighthouse that's up there *now* was built in 1842. But the original lighthouses were built in 1768, before there was any such thing as a Fresnel lens. Well, there were fires, and other damage that caused the towers to be rebuilt over the years, but they used the same lenses. In 1871 they finally replaced them with Fourth Order Fresnel Lenses because Plymouth Harbor was such a busy port, and they wanted to make sure it was clearly visible to ships at sea. You know that there used to be two lighthouses at the Gurnet?"

"Yeah, you can still see the outline of both of them on the old hill" Jake said. He thought of his 'daymare' earlier that day, and shook off the thought. Didn't want to go there, no sir.

Of course Jake knew there were two lighthouses, Walter thought. "There were two lighthouses until 1924 when they tore one down and decided to maintain just the one light" Walter said. "But enough of that. The thing you have to understand is that the Fresnel lens was hand made. It's really a whole bunch of hand made glass lenses set in a brass frame. And they're worth a boatload of money, because they don't make them anymore. They haven't been made in years, so the ones that are still around are that much more valuable, to the right person that is. You understand?" Walter asked.

"Yeah, it's like real old cars. My dad says the good ones are worth more now than when they were made" Jake said.

"It's just like that Jake, it's just like that" Walter replied. "Well, that day after the storm, that Fresnel Lens was missing."

"But why wasn't that in the paper? If it was worth a bunch of money, they should have put it in the paper, like if you robbed a bank, shouldn't they?" Jake asked.

Walter shook his head and thought to himself, this boy is relentless. When he's interested in something, he's sure going to find out about it. Incredible. "Well Jake, the simple fact is they were embarrassed. The United States Coast Guard was embarrassed. They also didn't want to get blamed for the shipwreck. They didn't even have to lie about what had happened, like most government agencies, they just never mentioned it, and nobody asked. After all, the lighthouse had been lit for a couple hundred years. Who would expect it to ever not be lit? The District Commander and his gang were down from Boston, and they grilled poor old Nate about what happened that night. And Nate wasn't very helpful because he wanted to find out what happened to Rose, and all the big wigs wanted to know about was what happened to the lens." This part of the story still got Walter's blood boiling. "Those bastards hushed the story up, and they were able to do it. Back then, you didn't have TV news trucks all over the place filmin' every car accident. The newspapers didn't even know about what happened until late on Saturday." A different world, that's what it was, Walter thought.

"Didn't people know when it got dark that night and the lighthouse didn't come on?" Jake asked.

Bingo, Walter thought. It was like talking to that TV detective 'Columbo'. The boy didn't miss anything. "Well, they would have known Jake, they surely would have. But the light wasn't dark that night. Remember there used to be two lighthouses? Well, when they tore down the second light in 1924, they put the other lens in the storage shed. That lens sat there covered with a tarp for almost forty years collectin' dust. Nate knew it was there, and the District Commander knew it was there, but most everybody else had forgotten all about it. You see, the whole time they were grillin' Nate, they had a crew putting that old lens up in the tower. By nightfall, it was like it never happened." Walter thought back to the days following that awful night, and how broken up Nate had been telling Walter the story.

"And the worst part is, they shut Nate up, too" Walter nearly whispered, staring down at the table. He rubbed his eyes, and when he finally looked up he said, "They transferred Nate out of here shortly thereafter. They told him that if he ever said a word, they'd tell people that Rose was in on it. They'd say she helped steal that Fresnel lens. They said they were sure she was involved, and they'd put out a warrant for her arrest, and it'd be in all the papers. Said they'd make front page news out of her...' and Walter grew silent.

Jake sat there for a minute or two, with his head spinning. In one way, he was sorry he had ever asked about Rose and Nate, but in another he was twisted up inside looking for answers. He didn't know what to say.

Finally, he asked, "Do you think Rose was in on it?"

16
The Stranger

Walter thought about this question, and not for the first time. He'd learned long ago that you never could really tell about people. You thought you knew everything about someone, and then they'd surprise you. Sure, there were the famous folks that crashed and burned over the years like that Jim and Tammy Baker, or any number of politicians, or more recently that Madoff fellow, but that wasn't what he was thinking about. You never really knew those people; only what their handlers wanted you to know.

Walter was thinking about the people you were close to. People like his one-time best friend Gerry Hawkins. Walter thought he and Gerry were just like each other when they were teenagers growing up together in Marshfield. It wasn't until Gerry got arrested that Walter found out that Gerry was an arsonist, and all the fires in town that summer were just Gerry's way of amusing himself. Funny, but Walter remembered there'd been a fire on Western Point the day of the storm when Rose disappeared, and the first thing Walter had thought about was his old friend Gerry.

But Rose was different, Walter thought. He and Sharon and Rose and Nate were closer than friends, they were like family. The four of them had spent hours and hours together, without the distraction of the outside world and the false fronts you were expected to build. Many were the nights they'd sat by the light of a kerosene lamp, cozy with the warmth of the woodstove, playing cards and talking, having a drink or two, or even too many drinks, Walter thought. And it was hard not to know what someone was really like after they'd had too many drinks. No, he thought, Rose wasn't involved. Rose was genuinely happy; they all were. The last thing she'd ever do would be to leave Nate and the beach for something as transient as a pile of money, no matter how big the pile was. All the money in the world couldn't buy what they'd all had together. And Rose had known that.

"No Jake, I don't think Rose was involved" Walter said. "And I don't think Nate was involved. They were happy right here. They had everything they wanted right here on the beach, and neither one of them would do anything to ruin that. But *someone* took that lens. Someone who wasn't happy, or someone who thought they could steal happiness. And when folks get to the point that they think they can steal happiness, why they're liable to do desperate things." And that's what probably happened, Walter thought. Some desperate, miserable thief had taken the lens, gotten rid of Rose while they were doing it, and sentenced Nate to a life of misery.

"Who would pay money for a Fresnel Lens?" Jake asked then. Walter chuckled to himself, and he pictured Jake in a rumpled London Fog trench coat turning at the door on his way out and saying 'Uh, just one more thing..' like Peter Falk used to do on TV, just before he solved the case. God, this boy was sharp, Walter thought.

"Well Jake, funny you should ask" Walter said, but 'incredible you should ask' was what he thought. "The way Nate tells it, there *was* someone willing to pay. You remember I said that Nate had the truck fixed that day?" Jake nodded, and Walter went on. "The week before when Nate was in town on his usual trip, he went to the garage to have the truck looked at so they could order the parts to fix it. While he was at the garage a stranger came in. As it turned out, this character happened to be a wealthy foreigner who'd docked his yacht in Plymouth that very morning. He'd been asking questions about the lighthouse, and someone that he spoke to at the coffee shop had seen Nate pull into the garage. They told the stranger that he ought to go talk to Nate, 'cause he knew everything there was to know about the lighthouse. Well, Nate says that stranger started asking about the Fresnel lens, and what size it was, and all kinds of specific questions. Nate thought he was just one of those lighthouse buffs; he'd met lots of them. But then all of a sudden this stranger says that he and Nate could maybe come to a

71

'business arrangement'. That's what he called it, a 'business arrangement'." Walter shook his head. "I guess that's what rich folks call thievery, 'cause that's what he was proposing." Walter got up from his chair and peeked out the window to where the girls were weeding the garden with Sharon. Then he stepped into the kitchen for a minute, and came back with a drink for himself and a can of Moxie for Jake.

"He offered Nate twenty thousand dollars if he'd help him steal the lens from the lighthouse" Walter said as he sat back down. "Now that's a lot of money, Jake. But it was a whole lot more in 1960. So anyway, Nate figures this guy is just crazy, and he asks him what he wants a lighthouse lens for."

"Well, this fellow says he owns an island with a lighthouse 'down south', and he needs the lens to restore the lighthouse. Nate asks him why he doesn't just get a different type of lens, says he can get it a lot cheaper than twenty grand. Nate says this guy just laughs, and says 'would you buy the love of your life a set of fake pearls?' Well, Nate figures whether or not this guy is serious, he's still crazy, so he tells him that he can't help him. Nate says he never gave it another thought until the lens went missing the following week" Walter said, and took a sip of his drink.

"Did Nate tell them about the guy who was looking for the lens?" Jake asked.

"Oh sure" Walter said. "But remember, nobody besides the Coast Guard knew the lens was missing, not at first at least. So nobody was looking for the lens, and nobody looked for this stranger. Nobody except Nate, that is…" Walter paused, waiting for the next question, but Jake just drank his Moxie and waited. After a minute, Walter figured he might as well finish the story; he'd come this far. And somehow it was good letting it out after all these years. Jake was easy to talk to. And maybe the rumors that tortured his friend Nate would stop with Jake's generation if the real story were out there.

Walter continued, "Nate got transferred to Florida after this all happened. He spent a couple more years in the Coast Guard after that, but then he quit and came back home to fish and live on the island. He's lived there ever since. Nate says he would have quit right away after the way they threatened him. He says the only reason that he didn't was because when they said they were going to transfer him to Florida, he figured he'd be able to track down this stranger who'd talked to him that day about his island down south. See, he'd talked to people in town who'd seen him, and they said this fellow came in on an old eighty foot Chris-Craft yacht named 'Retriever' that was worth a fortune. That's when Nate knew that this fellow was for real and probably knew what had happened to the lens, and more important, what happened to Rose."

"Well a boat that size has to be registered" Walter continued. "Nate knew he'd be able to find it with the help of the records that the Coast Guard kept, and sure enough he did. It turns out that this fellow was from Columbia and he had millions of dollars, but no real record of how he earned it. Anyway, he really had bought a small island in the Bahamas, and the island really did have a lighthouse."

"Nate kept an eye on that lighthouse. He'd make any excuse he could to take one of the Coast Guard boats nearby, or he'd get on a charter boat that fished near the island when he wasn't working. He watched that island for two years, but the lens never showed up there, the lighthouse stayed dark. Finally, Nate couldn't wait any longer and he went and 'talked' to this fellow." Walter stopped here as he thought about the night Nate had returned to the beach and told him what happened. It was one of those nights that he and Nate had had too many drinks, come to think about it.

Walter remembered how Nate had showed up at the door out of the blue, looking ragged and tired. He was unshaven, which wasn't at all like him back then when he was in the Coast Guard. It was raining, so Nate was sopping wet. He carried a duffel bag that was also soaked. That didn't stop Sharon from giving him a big hug when she opened the door and found Nate standing there. Nate had said he'd 'retired' and had just gotten back from Florida.

They'd brought Nate inside and gotten him dried off in a chair next to the wood stove. Nate was clearly despondent, so Sharon had gotten them a drink, and then made herself busy in the kitchen so that he and Walter could talk. Walter had kept the glasses full the rest of the way while Nate told his story.

The part of the story that Walter remembered now was when Nate had 'talked' to this stranger. He'd finally gone to the island in the dead of night in a rented boat with the running lights turned off. He'd anchored on the side away from the house and gone ashore. Nate had watched the house from the bushes. He'd seen the house lights go off room by room, and the servants retire to their quarters which were separate from the main house. After an hour or so, Nate had crept to the house and entered the master bedroom through the unlocked patio doors.

He and the Columbian millionaire had their conversation, Nate had said, with a nine-inch Bowie knife held to the millionaire's throat.

It was no use. The man didn't know where the lens was, and he didn't know where Rose was. Nate had drunk way too much by this part of the story, so Walter knew he wasn't exaggerating when Nate said that he was so upset, he considered slicing the man's throat right there.

Then Nate had said something that still chilled Walter to the bone when he thought about it. Nate had said, "Then that knife started vibrating in my hand. It wasn't me shaking, that knife was shaking itself. I looked at it, and I swear this is true Walter, I swear it…. I saw Rose's face in that knife blade where my reflection shoulda been, I swear I saw her. And her voice, plain as day says *My husband is no murderer.*" Nate had dropped the knife and fled.

No, Walter thought, Jake didn't need those kinds of details. The last thing he wanted to do was to give the kid nightmares. Walter simply said "Well, if the man knew anything, Nate couldn't get it out of him. He gave up, and he came home to the island. He's lived there ever since. He's never hurt a soul, and I wish people would just leave him in peace." Walter sipped his drink and added, "The funny thing about a secret is it never

74

stays that way. Even though the Coast Guard was able to hide the fact that the lens got stolen from the press, the locals found out. Someone found out. And pretty soon the rumors started that Rose was involved. People said she was a thief. They said she ran off on Nate. And that's the part that bothers him most" Walter finished.

They sat there in silence for a minute or so, but it wasn't awkward. They each finished their drinks, and Walter picked up the empties and brought them to the kitchen just as the girls came back in. "You ready Jake?" Jenny asked.

"Don't forget that bluefish frame!" Walter called from the kitchen. He came back with the fish in a plastic bag. It was cold from being in the refrigerator.

"Thanks," Jake said, "and thanks for the drink".

"Anytime Jake, anytime" Walter replied as Jake and the girls went out to the beach.

17

Promises

Later that evening after supper, the kids all met at the tarp by
the fire hole on the front beach. They didn't have to plan it; it
was just what they did at the beach. A week ago, they all had a
different routine that involved homework and early bedtimes,
but that all changed at the beach. Here, they ate supper, went to
the front beach, played or hung out until dusk, and then lit a fire
and talked and told stories until it was time to go home. They
didn't miss the television set or video games, and they didn't
miss the boundaries their parents set when they went out after
supper back home. At the beach they had freedom, and there
weren't many places like that anymore.

They didn't invent this after-supper ritual; they learned it from
their parents, who had learned it from their own parents.
Sometimes the parents would come to the fire too, but mostly
that was when it got warmer. On the cool nights they'd get
together and play cards, and the kids had the fire to themselves.

The five of them fell easily into the summer routine. Jenny and
Michele sat at the fire talking about clothes and movies and
music. Jake and Dragon talked about Lester and Beckett and
agreed that the Red Sox were for real and the Yankees still
sucked. Stevie spent half the time getting wood and feeding the
fire, and the other half pretending he was interested in the Sox
talk while he stared at Jenny across the fire.

They were running low on wood about the time that Jenny's
grandmother called out from the boardwalk at the top of the
dune that it was getting late. Jenny said goodnight, so Stevie
decided he was going home too. Nicky had a long walk to the
point, so he also said goodnight and headed out.

Jake got the shovel and started to bank the fire, but Michele
just sat there, making no move to get up. "Are you staying?"
Jake asked her.

"For a little while" Michele answered. "Can you stay for a
while?"

"Yeah, for a little while" Jake said, and sat back down next to her. They moved in closer to what was left of the fire, and stared into the red coals.

"Jake," Michele said, "can you tell me what happened at the lighthouse?"

Jake was quiet for a while, not knowing what to say to her. He could tell her, he thought, but she'd probably think he was crazy. And part of him was afraid she might be right. He'd been thinking a lot about the things he'd been seeing, the 'daymares'. It would have been a lie to say they were just dreams. And besides, he wasn't sleeping when they happened. And they were more than dreams; they felt real, like he was flipping into a different time and place all without warning. After talking to Walter, Jake was sure they were real. That was even scarier to think about.

What if he got caught up in one of these visions, or trips through time (that possibility compliments of the movie *Back To The Future* that Jake had seen), or whatever they were, and *he couldn't get back*? He'd thought about that a lot, but he told himself that he never really went anywhere. He was still sitting in the boat with Stevie, and he was still at the lighthouse with Michele when he'd zoned out. But it had been worse at the lighthouse, he had passed out.

What if just his *mind* was going and *it* got stuck there? That had been his next thought, and he hadn't figured out why that couldn't happen yet. What if his body ended up in a coma while his mind traveled through an endless horror show? He hadn't figured out why *that* couldn't happen, and he hadn't figured out how to tell Michele about it without making her think he was crazy.

Michele couldn't stand the silence anymore, and she said, "Jake, I told you about what happened to me at school. I didn't want to talk about it, but it just came out. I didn't tell anyone about it before, but I guess I knew I could tell you. And I felt way better after I told you. I don't know why, but it just felt good to talk about it. Whatever it is, you can talk to me. I told you I'd help you figure it out. I'm worried about you, and you promised…"

"I know what happened to Rose," Jake said.

Michele stopped in mid sentence, and she wasn't sure she had heard him right. "What?"

"I know what happened to Rose Withers," he said again. "I saw her at the lighthouse today." Michele felt the hair stand up on the back of her neck. But she didn't call him crazy, and she didn't tell him why he couldn't have seen her. She slid closer to him, took a deep breath and let it out slowly.

"What did you see?" she asked.

Jake told her then. He told her everything; how he picked up the rose and felt it vibrate, how it had gotten dark, the wreck, everything. By the time he told her about seeing Rose getting pulled over the cliff, Michele had her arm around him and she was holding his hand. When she saw the tear roll down his cheek, she pulled his face to her shoulder and she just held him. They sat that way for a long time.

When Jake finally got his composure, he sat up and asked, "Do you think I'm nuts?"

"No, no, no!" she said. "Don't talk like that! You're not nuts, you're just scared. Just hearing it scared me" she said, and shivered as if to prove it.

"Do you believe me?" Jake asked.

"Of course I believe you!" she said without any hesitation. "Things like this happen all the time to some people. I've read lots of stories about it. It's just that they don't talk about it for the same reason you didn't want to talk about it. They're afraid that other people won't believe them."

"Did it ever happen to you?" he asked. "Did you ever see anything like that?"

"No" she said, sounding disappointed. Then she brightened and said "But my aunt did. She saw a ghost when she first moved into her house. It was a lady in an old fashioned dress. She smiled at my aunt, turned and walked away and just disappeared. My aunt told me about it, but she said not to tell. She didn't want anyone to know…"

78

"'Cause they'd think she was crazy" Jake finished for her.

"Yeah" Michele said, and looked back down at the fire.

"Why do you think it happens? Why do you think I saw her?" he asked.

Michele considered the question for a minute, and then said, "I think Rose wanted someone to know what happened. I don't think she can rest until somebody knows."

"Why *me*? Why does she want *me* to know?" Jake asked.

"I don't think Rose wants you to know, I think she probably wants Nate Withers to know. But maybe she can't tell him. Or maybe she tried, but he can't hear her."

"How come I could hear – I mean see her?" Jake asked.

Michele thought she understood this. "I think only a few people can see or hear them – ghosts, or visions or whatever. I'm not sure why, but I think – it's like.." She hesitated, searching for a way to explain. "It's like they come in on a certain radio station, but only powerful radios can get the signal. It's like trying to hear the baseball game on a little portable radio on the beach. The signal comes in and out – it drives my dad crazy. But if he gets in the car, it comes in great on that radio." Michele said, "You're like a car radio, Jake. You can get the signal. That's what I think" she finished.

Jake thought about it, and it made as much sense as anything he could think of. It made as much sense as seeing the stuff he was seeing in the first place. That didn't make a lot of sense, but it was happening, wasn't it? Accepting what was happening wasn't the same as knowing what to do about it though. "Well, I can't exactly go knock on the door and tell Nate Withers I know what happened to his wife" he said.

Michele said, "No, you can't. But maybe you'll see her again. Maybe she'll show you how to tell Nate."

"Great. Just what I need" Jake said, and hung his head. The thought of getting stuck 'there' came back to him.

"Maybe you won't see anything. Maybe she just wanted someone to know.." Michele offered, but not very convincingly. "But you don't have to be afraid. They can't hurt you," she said, and it sounded like she really believed that.

Jake, he wasn't so sure. Suddenly the fire popped and a red ember shot out over their heads, and they both jumped. Then they laughed, embarrassed.

"Maybe it really won't happen again" Michele reasoned. "You said it happened when you touched the rose. Maybe it was like when my dad used to put tin foil on the TV antennae. Maybe it was the rose that brought the vision." Jake was already *sure* it was the rose that brought the vision. "Where do you think the rose came from, anyway?" Michele asked.

"Nate Withers left it there yesterday on Rose's birthday." Jake said it. He said it before he even knew it, if that was possible. Michele was about to ask, but Jake told her, "I don't know how I know that. I just do. I just found out I knew it when I said it..."

Michele felt the goose bumps again, but she tried not to show it. "See" she said, "you'll know why you saw her when the time is right. I'm sure of it now. And you're not alone; you can talk to me about it. I want you to talk to me" she said and held him close again. Jake hugged her back, and he did feel better. He didn't feel lost, alone, anymore. He was still scared, but Michele was right. He did feel better now that he'd told her about it. He didn't know what the answers were, but just knowing that she believed him made him feel better.

18
Seals

When Jake rolled out of bed the next morning, the sky was overcast and the wind was up. The flag on the pole attached to the deck was whipping back and forth. Despite the wind, it was warm that morning.

Jake went into the cottage and found his parents already finishing their coffee and cleaning up the table.

"Good morning" his mother said. "I wasn't sure you were going to get up today!"

"I was tired, I guess" Jake said and rubbed his eyes.

"What's the plan today?" Brian Edison asked.

"I'm not sure," Jake said. "Are you going fishing?"

Brian said, "I was thinking about it, but it looks like it's going to be too rough out there. There's a storm offshore. We may or may not get some rain, but either way, it's going to be too windy. Maybe we can fish tomorrow."

"I'll probably just go see what's going on out front then" Jake said. He got a bowl of cereal and sat down at the table.

"Well, when you go, you can take that bluefish carcass out of my refrigerator and get rid of it" Kelly said and ruffled his hair.

"I know, I was gonna do that this morning" Jake replied. He ate his cereal while he tried to figure out the answer to the riddles that the leprechaun on the back of the cereal box was asking.

After breakfast, Jake took the plastic bag with the bluefish frame from the fridge and started toward the door. Bailey jumped up to follow him out. "No you stay here Bailey" Jake told her. Then he said to his parents "There were seals at the lighthouse yesterday. I'm gonna bring this fish up there and see if they'll eat it. I don't want Bailey to scare them."

"Alright, but be careful. And don't go in the water today unless you check with us. Your father said there might be big waves." Kelly said.

"Okay, I'll see you later "Jake said as he went out. Bailey whimpered at the screen door, not liking it at all.

As he walked along the beach he noticed that there were already decent sized waves, but the tide was pretty low. He shouldn't have any trouble getting out around the base of the cliff at the lighthouse.

Michele came over the dune from her cottage as he approached. "I was just coming to see what you were doing" she said.

Jake held up the bag and said "I was gonna see if you wanted to go feed a seal."

Michele beamed at this. "Yeah. Do you think he's alright?" she asked.

Jake held his hand up to his forehead as if he was trying to pick the answer out of the air. He dropped his hand and said "I don't know – I can't get that station" and he smirked at her.

Michele whacked him on the arm and said "Wiseass."

They started walking toward the lighthouse. After a while, Jake said, "Thanks for believing me last night."

Michele smiled and answered, "Thanks for talking to me. I was worried about you. Do you feel better today?"

"Yeah, I do. You were right" Jake said. "It did feel good to talk about it."

They walked along, mostly in silence. Michele collected some small white rocks and shells, and Jake thought it was good just to have her nearby. The fact that she believed him made him feel much better. Maybe she was right, he thought. Maybe the visions would just stop. He sort of hoped so, but on the other hand he was still curious why it had happened in the first place. He hadn't told Michele about the day in the boat with Stevie, but maybe he wouldn't have to. He didn't know what that was all about, or who the green-eyed sailor was, but maybe he wouldn't have to find out.

"Look at this sea-glass!" Michele gasped, bringing Jake out of his silent debate. "It's blue! You hardly ever find blue sea-glass!"

"Yeah, that's nice" Jake said, not really feeling it. He'd get better at feigning excitement with age, but at twelve years old it was hard to fake it.

"That's nice" she mocked him, and whacked his shoulder again. "You just don't get it" she said and went back to her collecting. Jake didn't argue, he really didn't get it.

As they came up to Gurnet hill, they walked along the beach instead of going up the road to the top. The sand got coarser under their feet, and there were now pea-stones and larger rocks mixed in. Soon they had to slow down to pick their way through the large boulders that were scattered about. The boulders closer to the water were covered with seaweed and kelp, and the marshy smell of low tide filled their nostrils. A few seagulls hovered above them in the wind, occasionally crying their laughing cries before banking and riding the wind off toward the water like they were surfing on invisible waves.

They followed the curve of the cliff, and as they rounded a particularly large boulder they saw the little seal huddled in the same spot he'd found yesterday behind the large rock. They crept slowly closer as Jake worked the fish free from the plastic bag.

The seal poked his head up and turned toward them as they approached. The little seal's face was black except for a whitish-gray patch around one of his eyes. It looked like a negative of Bailey's face, Jake thought. The seal took a tentative hop away, struggling with a sore front flipper. They stopped where they were and Michele whispered, "Well, he's hurt, but he made it through the night."

"Yeah, he looks a little better" Jake replied. That was probably because the blood on his head had been washed away when the tide had come in and forced him to swim, Jake thought. There was a small gash there, but it looked like it had scabbed over.

Suddenly, the mother seal hopped out from behind the rock. She was big, and she looked mad. She started hopping toward them baring her teeth, and then she barked twice and stopped, staring at them.

83

Jake didn't hesitate; he swung the fish around in an arc next to his body and threw it toward the little seal. Momma seal barked again and hopped to where the fish landed. She smelled it, then looked back up at Jake. She didn't bark again, she just looked at him. Then she picked up the fish, hopped over to the little seal, and she dropped the fish in front of him.

Jake and Michele backed away slowly as the mother seal watched them. She didn't look angry now; her eyes were different. They looked rounder, softer, almost grateful. Jake and Michele made it back to the large boulder and then turned and walked away. "Wow, that was awesome!" Michele exclaimed. "I thought she was going to attack us, but she knew. She knew we were only trying to help." Jake nodded. "It's a good thing you had that fish, Jake. Can we come back if you get more?" "Yeah, we can come back. I think we're going fishing tomorrow. I'll keep the perch and skate if we get some" he said.

They walked back, thinking about the little seal, and the mother seal, and the look of gratitude. It was one of those pictures in your head that you'd never forget, Jake thought.

19
Riptide

When Michele and Jake got back, they saw Nicky and Stevie skim boarding at the water's edge. Jenny was sitting on the wooden spool under the tarp, swinging her legs back and forth. "Where'd you guys go?" Jenny asked Michele as they approached.

"We went to the Gurnet" Michele said. "There's a baby seal there who's hurt, and Jake gave him that bluefish to eat."

"What's wrong with it?" Jenny asked.

"He's got a cut on his head, and he hurt his flipper. He probably got hit by a boat" Michele answered. Jake thought again that it was no accident, but he decided not to say anything. No sense getting the girls upset, he thought.

Jake looked down to where Dragon and Stevie were skim boarding. The waves were pretty big now. They'd build and grow tall about thirty feet from shore. Then when they got too tall to hold themselves up, the tops would roll over and turn frothy and white, and then crash down and race onto the hard sand of the beach. As each wave ran out of momentum it would slow, then stop, and then start to slide back down toward the ocean. As the remnants of the wave slid back to the sea, there was a sheet of water less than an inch deep on the hard sand. That was the perfect moment to skim-board.

Jake watched as a wave crashed ashore, reached as far as it could, and then started its backward slide. Stevie threw his skim board then, too far away and too close to the edge of the sheet of water. He ran as fast as he could to catch up to the board and then jumped on with two feet. He skimmed for about five feet and was still waving his arms trying to get his balance when the board ran out of water and stuck to the sand. Stevie went airborne like Superman. He came down on his chest with his arms stretched out before him and slid through the sand and small rocks. Altogether, the ride was about eighteen feet, Jake figured; five on the board, eight in the air, and another five screeching to a stop in the sand on his bare chest. Jake smiled at Jenny and said "Wait for it, wait for it…" and Stevie didn't disappoint him.

"SHIT!" he screamed. "AHH that hurt!" Stevie grumbled as he peeled himself off the beach. He wiped the sand off his chest, and a few tiny scratches were already starting to bleed there.

"Nice wipeout, Stevie!" Nicky yelled.

"Bite me!" Stevie answered.

"Let me show you how it's done!" Nicky bragged as he threw his board. He raced after it, jumped on, and the board immediately shot out from under his feet. He landed on his butt, and sat there looking surprised while his skim board took a long ride along the beach alone. Stevie howled with laughter, pointing at Nicky as he fell to his knees in a fit. Jake, Michele and Jenny joined in, but not with the same gusto as Stevie. Even Nicky cracked a smile as he hoisted himself up off the wet sand.

Jake trotted down toward Nicky's skim-board, taking off his shirt and dropping it on the dry sand as he went. He picked up the board, walked to where the surf of the incoming wave was about a foot deep and dipped the board in to rinse off the sand. Then he walked up out of the surf watching the waves, picked his spot and waited.

When the next wave was running out of gas, Jake started trotting and tossed the board in front of him. He ran about four steps and jumped on. He landed with both knees bent, centered over the board with his arms out low to his sides just as the sheet of water was beginning to slide back toward the ocean. He skimmed along the shore, curving toward the surf as the thin sheet of water slid that way. The next wave broke and the frothy mix rolled toward Jake. Just before it hit him, Jake kicked the board out from under him, arcing it back up the gentle slope of the sand, and he ran after it. As the water started to thin out and slide back, Jake jumped and landed on the board again, sliding down the beach like a puck on an air-hockey table. As he slowed down this time, he squatted down and dragged one hand in the sand, causing the board to spin. He did a three-sixty, then stood up and hopped off just as the next wave rolled over the empty skim board. He picked up the skim board, walked back and handed it to Nicky and said, "That's how you do it, Dragon." Nicky just smiled and gave him a high five. Stevie stood there shaking his head, while Michele and Jenny gave him a round of applause.

Jake said, "I'm going up to get my board, I'll be right back." He bowed to the girls who were still clapping, and walked toward the dune.

When he was halfway up the beach, he heard "Whoa! Look at him go!" and he turned back to see Dragon body surfing in on a large wave. Jake turned and kept walking. When he got to the top of the dune, he heard someone yell "Dragon, are you alright?"

Jake turned, and was shocked to see Nicky out past the breakers – too deep. He was swimming like mad but he wasn't going anywhere. The other three were at the water's edge calling to him and waving their arms in a 'come on' gesture, as if that could help pull him in. "Shit! Riptide!" Jake said out loud. He was about to race back down, but hesitated and looked over the dune toward his cottage. His father was next to the cottage tinkering with the water pump at the well point.

"Dad!" Jake yelled. "Come quick – Nicky's in a riptide!"

Brian didn't hesitate. He took off running after Jake and passed him about twenty feet from the water. "Stay here!" he yelled as he flew by and dove into the water. Brian swam out to where Nicky was, and got there just as he was going under, exhausted. Brian pulled him up, and Nicky coughed and threw his arms around Brian's neck. "Easy, easy!" Brian said. He loosened Nicky's arms and got behind him. Brian put his arm up under Nicky's right arm, across his chest and gripped his left shoulder. Brian treaded water with his other arm as he gently kicked his feet. "We're just going to float for a while. It's alright, just take it easy" Brian said.

Jake and the others watched from the beach as Brian and Nicky floated out a little, and then started to float along parallel to the beach. Jake started to breath a little easier, but the girls were crying, and Stevie stood there stunned.

Déjà vu, Brian thought as he treaded water. He thought back to the time when he was just a boy and he had gotten caught in a riptide. His own father had saved him then, just like this.

His father had said to Brian, *"Don't fight it! You can't beat it. Go with it!"* The words echoed in Brian's mind as he and Nicky drifted along.

When they got about thirty yards down the beach, Brian started swimming toward shore, holding Nicky facing up with one arm. They were making progress, and soon the waves added to their forward momentum. When they got to the breakers, they were flung to the shore, and they washed up in a heap as the rest of the kids ran up and hovered around them.

When Brian caught his breath, and made sure Nicky was all right, he stood up. He wiped the water from his face and said, "Come up to the cottage, all of you." The kids knew it wasn't a request.

Brian began walking, and the others gathered up their shirts and skim boards and followed, but not too closely. "Your old man's pissed!" Stevie whispered. Jake didn't answer him.

20
Wisdom

The walk to the cottage was one of the longest walks in the kid's short lives. They thought they were dead. Jake wasn't quite as scared as the others were, but he had seen his father like that before. It was the way Brian had talked that had them on edge, not what he'd said. He hadn't raised his voice, he hadn't yelled or sworn. He'd just *ordered* them. There was no mistake, it was an order. They were prisoners. They were just getting over being scared to death for Nicky, and now they were scared to death for themselves.

When they got to the cottage, Brian was already inside. They went up to the deck but hesitated outside - none of them wanted to be the first to walk into the lion's den. Suddenly the door flew open and they all jumped. Kelly Edison came flying out and wrapped Nicky up in a bear hug. "Oh Nicky! Are you all right? You must have been scared to death! Come in, come in, you're okay now," she said as she hustled him inside. The others looked at each other with confusion. But suddenly they were hopeful, definitely hopeful. They may live through this yet. They followed Nicky and Jake's mom into the house.

When they got inside, Kelly wrapped a towel around Nicky's shoulders, and she handed towels to Jake and Stevie. "Get dried off now, and I'll make you some lunch. Sit down, sit down" she said as she started taking things out of the cabinets.

Brian was scanning through the books on the shelf attached to the beam of the low ceiling. He found the one he was looking for, and he took it down and started thumbing through it. He glanced at Nicky and said, "Are you okay now?"

Nicky nodded. "Yeah, I'm alright." Then he looked down and added, "I thought I was gonna die, though. Thanks for getting me, Mr. E." Brian smiled then, and the kids let out a collective sigh of relief.

Jenny was wiping the last of the tears out her eyes, and Brian asked, "Are you ladies alright?" Jenny and Michele nodded.

"Good, good. I want you all to settle down so you understand what I'm going to tell you. Eat your lunch and relax" Brian said.

Kelly put peanut butter and jelly sandwiches and potato chips on paper plates and set them in front of each of the kids. Then she poured them each a paper cup of milk.

Brian looked at the book he'd taken down, but he wasn't really reading it. He was thinking back to how scared he had been as a child when he had gotten caught in the riptide. His father had saved him. Brian could almost hear his voice now; *'Don't fight it! You can't beat it. Go with it!'*

Brian thought back to the last time he'd heard those words. No, it wasn't when he'd been saved from the riptide. It was back at the Maritime Academy.

It was the year his father had died. His father had been killed in a car accident near the end of Brian's senior year in high school. Brian was devastated, but his mother had remained strong. She'd helped Brian through it, and told him he had to go on because his father would want him to. She'd said that his father was gone, but not for good. She'd said he'd gone to a better place, but they'd see him again someday.

Brian had heard all of her words, but at first, Brian could only go through the motions. He was beyond the point of having the faith of his childhood, and he hadn't seen enough of life to believe in the everyday miracles that he now knew existed.

He'd gone to the Maritime Academy as planned that summer. Freshmen, or 'youngies' as the upperclassmen called them, had to go through an orientation period during the summer after they graduated from high school. It was partly like boot camp, and the discipline was good for Brian. The other part of orientation consisted of learning some of the basics of life aboard ship, including basic seamanship. Some of the lessons were set up as competitions between the different 'Companies' of youngies. Brian was in Second Company, and there were six Companies in all. At the end of orientation, the Company that had won the most points during the competitions was awarded the 'Admirals Cup', not to mention bragging rights for the next four years.

One of the competitions was a sailboat race. They'd learned the basics, and then the six Companies had to compete against each other. Brian was captaining the boat for Second Company. The course consisted of two buoys about a mile apart. The crews had to start at the first buoy, navigate up and around the other buoy, and then sail back to the first buoy.

On the day of the race, there was a steady fifteen-knot wind blowing directly from the second buoy toward the first buoy. The six boats had set out, tacking back and forth into the wind. It was tedious. Every time the boats would manage to get a little speed, they'd have to change course and tack the other way to stay on the zigzag line toward the far buoy. Every time they changed tack, the boats would come around and stall for a moment until the sails filled with wind again and the boats began to accelerate. The boats would still be accelerating, but then they'd have to change course again to stay on line toward the second buoy.

As Brian battled the wind at the tiller of the little boat, he heard his father's voice say *'Don't fight it! You can't beat it. Go with it!'* It was as if his father was sitting in the boat right there next to him. He *heard* his father's voice.

As the other boats cut to port, Brian kept his starboard tack and went wide. He let the boat run. His heading took him way off course at a forty-five degree angle away from the line between the buoys. He was off course, but still accelerating. Soon the boat was flying along, and they had to lean into the wind to keep the starboard gunwale from going under as the boat flew along on an edge. About halfway down, Brian called for a course change, and they turned ninety degrees toward the second buoy. Again, the boat went faster and faster until they were flying along on the other edge. They came to the buoy and cut around it while the rest of the boats were still fighting their way upwind. Once Brian turned the Second Company boat around the buoy, they sailed back with the wind to an easy victory. In the grand scheme of things, it was a minor victory in an insignificant boat race, but to Brian it was a major step toward getting himself back on course. He'd heard his father's voice.

The kids had finished their sandwiches, and Brian opened the book on the table for them to see. There was a diagram showing the currents involved in a riptide. Brian explained it to them. He showed them how the current runs out at a certain point, and if you try to swim against it you just exhaust yourself. He showed them how the current travels parallel to shore, and then turns toward the shore father down the beach. He explained that to get out of the riptide, you had to go with the current until it turned you back toward shore.

"Don't fight it. You can't beat it. Go with it" Brian said to them. Maybe they'd remember.

The rain started that afternoon and continued into the evening. There would be no beach fire tonight. Since it was a Friday night and most folks would be at the beach for the weekend, Kelly and Brian told the kids to invite their parents to the Edison cottage for a game of cards.

Bill and Terry Malone, Tom and Mary Collins, and Maria Dragoni all showed up carrying snacks and beverages of different sorts. Victor Dragoni wasn't there because Friday and Saturday nights were the busiest nights at his restaurant, so he usually came to the beach for Sundays and Mondays.

Michele, Stevie, Nicky and Jenny were all there. Jenny was going to sleep over with Michele Malone that night, which was fine with Walter and Sharon Guthrie.

The older folks had all greeted each other warmly, and then settled down around the kitchen table to catch up on what the winter months had meant to each of their families. The conversation and laughter flowed as easily as the wine, and it seemed to the kids that there were times that everyone at the table was talking at once and nobody was listening.

Pretty soon the boys were bored with watching their parents carry on, and when they got chased away again from the biscotti on the table that Maria Dragoni had brought, they settled on a different plan. They got a deck of cards, a battery powered lantern, and some chips and cookies and headed for the door.

"Were going under the house to play cards" Jake said to his mother as he opened the door. Kelly barely glanced at him, gave him a little 'okay' wave, and continued to laugh hysterically at the story that Mary Collins was telling. Jake asked Michele and Jenny, "Are you coming?"

The girls weren't nearly as bored; in fact they were hovering around the table trying to hear everything that was said. They even joined the conversation here and there, and Jenny was nibbling on a biscotti she had lifted without being noticed.

"Michele, Jenny – are you coming to play cards?" Jake asked them again. Reluctantly, the girls followed the boys outside.

They made a mad dash across the deck and down and under the house because the rain was really coming down now. Jake lit the lantern and they walked hunched over between the poles that held up the cottage. The shadows of the poles in the lantern light circled around behind them as they made their way to the center of the cottage. They sat down in the sand around a half-sheet of plywood resting on top of four empty plastic milk crates.

Jake set the lantern down in the center of the makeshift table and began shuffling the cards. "Man, I forgot how loud they are when they get together!" he said.

"No shit," Nicky said, "they were giving me a headache!"

"I think it's awesome" Jenny commented.

"Yeah, me too" Michele agreed. "At least they have fun. Back home, they never laugh like that."

"Well, it still gives me a headache" Nicky said. "What's the game, Jake?"

Jake had already started dealing the cards. "Crazy Eights" Jake answered.

Sitting to Jake's left, Stevie said, "I don't like that game. Somehow you always know what I have, and change the suit before I can get rid of my last card."

"Well move to the other side of me, you whine-bag" Jake answered.

Stevie glanced at Jenny, who was sitting to his left, and decided to stay put. "Nah, I'll stay right here, and I'll still kick your ass" Stevie bragged. Jake looked at Nicky, who just rolled his eyes.

The first game lasted a long time. Stevie did get down to one card, but Jake switched the suit to diamonds with an eight, and Stevie had to pick up twelve cards before he got a diamond to play. The rest of them thought this was hilarious, and pretty soon they were making as much noise as their parents were. Nicky ended up going out first. He got up to do a little end zone dance, whacked his head on a support beam and fell back to the sand clutching his skull and swearing. He got zero sympathy, just gales of laughter from the others.

Stevie started dealing the next hand and said, "The game is Knock-out Whist. Dragon can't play – he already got knocked out" Stevie said.

"Funny" Nicky said.

Stevie dealt seven cards to each of them, and then said, "I'll cut for trump." He cut the cards, and turned over the ace of spades. "The death card!" he said. "Someone here is gonna die tonight!" Stevie hissed, and broke into a sinister laugh. He actually did look kind of creepy in the lantern light when he leaned his head back and laughed.

"Stop it Stevie!" Jenny said, and whacked him.

"What? Are you afraid?" Stevie asked.

"Just stop it" Jenny said again.

"Wow, remind me not to tell you any ghost stories" Stevie said.

"No ghost stories tonight" Michele said, and glanced at Jake.

"What's the matter with you?" Stevie asked her. "Are you afraid too?" he persisted.

"I just don't want any ghost stories, and nobody's going to die tonight" Michele answered, a little too forcefully. She looked out at the wind blown rain and shivered.

"Wow, I didn't know you were so touchy…" Stevie replied.

"I'm not 'touchy'! It's just that I'm sick of ghost stories.." Michele trailed off.

"Who's been telling ghost stories?" Nicky said.

"Nobody's been telling ghost stories!" she shouted. "Can you just drop it?"

Jake had been listening to this exchange, and he knew that Michele was trying to protect him, like he was a scared little kid or something. He started to get a little aggravated about this, but when he saw how they were making her squirm, he felt bad for her.

"It's okay, Michele" Jake said. "I've been telling her ghost stories" he said.

"You have?" Nicky asked. "What about? It must be a good one, the way she's acting." Michele gave Nicky a dirty look, and then turned to Jake and shook her head slightly, looking sorry.

"It's okay, Michele. Really. I've been thinking about it, and they gotta know" Jake said to her. "I mean, what if I pass out again? Or what if..what if I don't wake up?"

Jenny, Stevie and Dragon stared at the two of them. Stevie was still holding half of the undealt deck of cards with the ace of spades showing, and Nicky and Jenny just sat with their mouths open. For a time, the only sounds were the howl of the wind and the steady dripping of the rain falling from the shingles onto an old plastic bucket lying in the sand at the edge of cottage. It sounded like a heartbeat.

Finally Nicky broke the silence. "What the hell are you talking about? Pass out? Don't wake up? How do you pass out tellin' a ghost story?" he asked.

Jake looked at Nicky, then at Stevie, and then Jenny. "You guys are my friends, right?"

"Of course we are!" Jenny said.

Stevie nodded, and Nicky just looked at Jake like he was stupid and shook his head. "Are you gonna tell us, or what?" Nicky pressed.

Jake looked down at his cards, not really seeing them, and then looked up directly into Nicky's eyes. "It wasn't a story. I saw a real ghost" he said.

Nicky was about to laugh, but staring back he saw that Jake wasn't kidding. A look of confusion spread over Nicky's face, and he said "What?"

"I saw a real ghost. I saw her fall over the cliff at Gurnet, and I passed out when I saw her" he said.

"Wait a minute" Jenny said holding her hands up, palms out. "Is this a story? 'Cause you're freaking me out."

"No, it's not a story. I was with him when it happened. He passed out at the lighthouse yesterday. It scared the hell out of me" Michele confirmed.

96

The hair on Jenny's neck and arms stood up and she hugged herself instinctively. Stevie just sat there dumbfounded.

"Tell us" Nicky said.

"First you gotta promise me something" Jake began. "You gotta promise not to tell my parents. I don't wanna get locked up in the nut house." They all agreed. "And you gotta promise something else…"

"What?" Jenny asked.

"You gotta promise that if I pass out again, you'll wake me up. Promise you won't let me get stuck there" Jake said. His face told them he was seriously scared of this possibility.

Michele understood now why Jake was doing this. She thought about how terrifying it must be to think you might check out of reality, and not be able to get back. She *felt* his terror. Jake needed all the help he could get. He needed his friends.

"Jake, we promise. I thought you were telling a story, but whatever happened, I can see it scared the hell out of you. We'll watch out for you. And you can trust us, we won't tell anyone, will we?" Nicky said, glancing to the others for agreement. The look in his eyes said it wasn't really a question. They were all nodding.

Jake let out a deep breath, and then he told them what happened at the lighthouse. The rose he picked up, the vibration, the darkness, the shipwreck, the lady slowly being dragged over the cliff, everything. Then he told them what Walter said about Rose later that day, and he told them that he *knew* it was her.

"I know it sounds crazy," he said, "but I'm *not* crazy. I *thought* I was going crazy until Walter told me about Rose. He told me *after* I saw her. I didn't know anything about her, and I saw her *before* I found out about her. There's no way I could dream it, it happened." Jake paused here, and then finally got to what had really terrified him.

"It wasn't like a dream. It was real. I *felt* the rain when it happened. And I never *felt* anything in a dream before. It's like my mind went somewhere. And it was worse this time. I didn't pass out in the boat or at the fire, it's like I'm going farther…"

Jake took a deep breath and said "And I'm scared I won't be able to get back if it happens again. I need you guys to help get me back somehow if it happens again…"

They sat there without saying anything. Jenny, Stevie and Nicky were trying to understand what could be happening to their friend. This was the first time they'd heard of it, and they could see how it was affecting him. Jenny and Stevie were open to the idea that he'd seen the ghost of Rose Withers. Nicky wasn't convinced there were any such things as ghosts, but for the first time he wasn't so sure. Michele was just stunned.

"What do you mean you didn't pass out in the boat or at the fire? Is that what was wrong with you that night? Did you see something at the fire?" she asked.

Jake looked at her sheepishly and said "Yeah. I did. It started in the boat that day after me and Stevie saw Nate Withers, and it happened again later at the fire."

"That's right! You didn't even see the birds diving!" Stevie said. "I shoulda known something was wrong with you."

"And you didn't look so hot at the fire that night" Nicky said.

"What did you see?" Michele asked.

Jake hesitated, and then said, "I saw that fishing boat crash on the rocks at the lighthouse. But Stevie had just told me his bullshit story about Old Man Withers." Stevie grunted. "I figured I was just daydreaming. Then it got weird. The boat turned into an old sailing ship, and it was sinking in a blizzard. I thought I was thinking of something I must have seen in a movie or something" Jake explained. "Later that night at the fire, I saw the old ship again. But this time it was more real. And this time I saw one of the sailors. He looked like a pirate or something – he had a scar on his face, and he had green eyes. He wasn't anyone I ever saw in any movie. He was *real..* and he was staring at me.. 'cause he *knew* I could see him.." Jake couldn't explain it any better.

"When Stevie told you the story in the boat, did he say anything about Rose Withers falling off the cliff?" Nicky asked.

"No, he never said anything happened to her, and he never said her name" Jake answered.

"Did you say anything?" Nicky asked Stevie.

"No! I didn't even know her name, and I don't know what happened to her. I didn't know anything happened to her," Stevie answered. Then he added, "And I might have made up some of the other parts too."

"No shit? I believed every word you told me," Jake said like he didn't mean it. Stevie chuckled and looked down.

"But the shipwreck happened!" Stevie said, trying to redeem himself.

"Yeah, I figured that out when I read the article Walter had from the *Plymouth Sentinel*, wiseass. They don't print stories about stuff that didn't happen. It ain't the *Enquirer*" Jake said. Stevie decided the best response was to keep his mouth shut.

"What does the old ship and the scar-face guy have to do with anything?" Nicky asked.

"I don't know - and I don't know what any of it has to do with me" Jake said.

They heard the door of the cottage squeak open above them, and Brian Edison called out. "Jake? You kids come up now, it's time to go."

"Okay!" Jake called back, and then to his friends he said, "Remember, don't say anything."

"We won't" Nicky reassured him.

"Don't worry, we'll help you figure this out" Michele said as she squeezed his hand.

Jake nodded. He felt better, but he thought he'd sleep inside the cottage tonight. It was too cold and rainy to sleep in the shed, he told himself.

22
Flounder

The next day was bright and clear. The weather front had
blown by in the middle of the night, and the wind had settled
down shortly after dawn. Jake had just finished breakfast when
his father asked, "Are you almost ready? They'll be waiting on
the front beach for us." They'd made plans to fish last night,
and Stevie and his father and Nicky were all coming too.

"Yeah, I'm ready. I just have to grab my fishing rod" Jake
answered.

Jake's mom handed Brian a soft sided cooler. "I put ham
sandwiches and sodas in here. Now don't you forget to feed the
boys" she told him.

Brian took the cooler and gave Kelly a kiss. "You're the best"
he said.

"That's right, and don't you forget it" Kelly answered.

They went out, and Jake ran into the shed and got his boat rod.
He came out and said "Dad, do you have flounder hooks? This
one's pretty rusty."

"Yes, I've got hooks, weights, everything we need in the
tackle box. I stocked up a month ago." Brian had the tackle box,
his fishing rod and the cooler as he started across the marsh.
"Grab a couple of buckets and let's go" he said.

Jake got two white five-gallon buckets from under the deck
and followed Brian through the marsh. Bailey followed Jake at
first, but her excitement got the best of her and she ran ahead of
them. She circled back, cocking her head as if to ask what was
taking them so long, and then ran ahead again.

They got to Jake's little boat, put their gear in and pulled it
into the channel. Bailey jumped in and took up the lookout
position in the bow, panting with excitement. Brian sat on the
forward bench, and Jake pushed off and jumped into the rear of
the boat. He dropped the engine and started it, and headed for
his dad's boat that was moored in the cove. Jake maneuvered
his boat so that he was coming upwind toward his father's boat,

and he cut the engine and drifted right up to the port side of the big boat.

"Nice job!" Brian said. Brian got into the Carolina Skiff and Jake passed the gear onboard. Bailey jumped in and did her customary circle around the skiff, sniffing everything to make sure she was the only dog that'd been there. Jake climbed aboard and tied his boat off to the stern cleat on the skiff. Brian trimmed the engine down, primed it and started it up. When the engine was running, they unhooked the mooring line from the skiff and pulled away.

Tide was on the way out, but it wouldn't be low for almost two hours. There was plenty of water to get Brian's boat out of the cove. They headed back to where Jake had dropped the lobster car.

Jake pulled the pot and started to take quahogs out and put them in one of the five gallon buckets. "How many do you think we need?" he asked.

"Grab a dozen or so" Brian said. Jake counted them out and then closed up the lobster car. He made sure his feet were free of the buoy and rope, and he heaved the pot back over, tossing the buoy out as the rope played out. Brian nodded with satisfaction. He was proud of Jake. Jake was capable and confident on the boat. Brian looked up at the blue sky and said a silent 'thank you' once more.

Brian maneuvered toward the marsh, cut the engine and tilted it back up. The skiff coasted to the water's edge and stopped when it bottomed out in the sand. Jake untied his boat, jumped out and set his anchor in the marsh. He pushed the skiff back into the channel and hopped back in as Brian lowered and started the engine.

They were off. The first flounder trip of the year. Jake was already dreaming of landing a three-pounder and scoring first place in the fishing tournament that ran from Memorial Day until Labor Day. The contest was for everyone who fished at the beach, whether they had a cottage or they were just visiting someone. There were no entry fees, and the prize was just a little plastic trophy for first, second and third place for each type

101

of fish. The trophy wasn't the real prize though, the bragging rights were. Jake already had a half dozen trophies, and he remembered each trophy fish and where he'd gotten it.

He had thought he was going to win for kid's flounder last year, but Jenny Guthrie, of all people, had edged him out in the last week of the summer. Thinking about it still made him shake his head.

Jenny had come down for a surprise visit a couple of days before summer ended. She'd gone fishing with Jake and his dad, mostly because she wanted a boat ride and the other kids were going. Jake had talked her into trying to catch a fish, he let her use his rod, and he even baited the hook for her. He'd shown her how to let the line out until the weight reached the bottom. He was about to tell her what to do if she got a bite when Jenny yelled 'I got one!' She'd reeled up a three and a half pounder, and Jake ended up with second place. The only silver lining to the summer ending was that he only had to hear Jenny tell him 'I'll teach you how to catch the big ones, Jake!' for a couple of days.

Brian navigated the skiff up the back side of the peninsula and around Western Point. When they got to the very end of the point and started to come around it, the water got rough at the 'rip'. The rip was where the sheltered waters of the back bay ran into the ocean. It was always rougher at the rip. Once you got through it, the water usually settled back down, and today was no exception. There was a sandbar at the rip extending out from the tip of the peninsula, and the water was much more shallow there than it was on either side of the bar. Jake was looking down over the bow at the bottom as they crossed the bar. It was shallow enough that he could see seaweed on the bottom waving in the current. His thoughts drifted back to the conversation he'd had with his dad while they were fixing the roof. The sandbar at the rip was squeezing the invisible energy out of the ocean, Jake realized. Tide was bringing all that energy from who knows where back out of the bay, and it was forced to show itself as it raced over the bar, only to go back into hiding when it made it through to the depths of the ocean.

But that energy was still there, and it would show itself again on the way back in. It always showed itself again when the current started, he thought.

They came around the point and went out deeper to avoid the rocks that were scattered under the surface in front of the Head. There were lobster buoys of all different colors scattered through the rocks. Jake hoped that if they caught fish today, he'd get a few of his own pots baited and into the water tomorrow.

They cleared the rocks at the Head and angled toward shore. From here Jake could see how fragile the beach really was. Between the high ground of the Head on his left, and the hill at Gurnet two miles down to his right, the beach was nothing but a long thin sandy strip with low dunes covered with beach grass and bushes, and cottages sitting up on stilts trying to stay dry. It looked like a good storm could wash it all away and leave nothing but two islands sitting there. His dad had told him stories of the 'Blizzard of '78 and the 'No-name' storm of '91 when the beach had been pretty much flattened. They'd lost cottages then, and it was years before the dunes had recovered, he'd told Jake. Jake looked back at the immense ocean, and he hoped it never got angry enough to take away the beach he loved.

As they got closer to shore, three figures walked down from under the tarp carrying fishing rods and a cooler. As the boat coasted in, Jake hopped out and spun the bow out so that the waves wouldn't wash over the transom. Stevie and Tom Connors and Nicky got in the stern with their gear, and Jake pushed them back out and jumped aboard. Brian idled through the waves near shore while Nicky and Stevie put on their life jackets.

"The weather looks like it's going to cooperate" Tom Connors said. "Let's hope the fish do too. Where's the hot spot?" he asked.

"I don't know yet," Brian confessed. "This is my first trip this year."

"You haven't been out yet?" Tom asked.

"No, first time. We'll try straight out by the channel and see how it goes. If that doesn't work, maybe we can try near the Bug" Brian said. The main channel was about a half-mile off shore and ran parallel to the beach. It continued past and eventually the channel split, with the left fork going into Plymouth Harbor and the right curling around behind the beach and Clark's island. 'The Bug' was a small metal lighthouse sitting on top of a rocky shoal next to where the channel split. It was actually named Duxbury Pier Lighthouse, but the locals had always called it Bug light. Walter had explained to Jake that it was because there were plenty of lobsters around the rocks at the little lighthouse, and the old timers used to call lobsters 'bugs', because they looked like big ones. At night the Bug showed just a small red beacon - nothing like the rotating beam from Gurnet.

Brian stopped short of the channel and Jake dropped the anchor. Brian got a couple of quahogs and broke them open on a cleat on the side rail of the boat. He shucked the clams out of the shells, and cut them into strips of bait. Next came a flurry of first time fishing activity, with hooks being changed, weights added, bird's nests in the reels being untangled. Finally, they were all settled in with bait in the water, and they waited. And they waited and waited.

"Good spot" Tom Connors finally said, and grinned at Brian. Brian laughed and shook his head.

"I told you it was the first time out," he said. "Do you want to try over near the Bug?"

"You're asking me?" Tom said. "I'm a plumber – you're supposed to find the fish, captain."

"What do you think, Jake?" Brian said. "Do you want to move?"

Jake hadn't even gotten a nibble yet, and he'd been hoping to move. He didn't want to be the one accused of being impatient, so he hadn't said anything. But he didn't feel like there were any fish here at all. No good way to explain it, but the spot didn't feel good.

"Yeah, I think we should move. I'm not sure about the Bug though. I think we should maybe try closer to Gurnet.'

"Is that okay with the plumber?" Brian asked Tom.

"Fine by me" Tom said, smiling. "The kid's a human fish finder. Go where he tells you" he said, and he meant it. Jake was uncanny, Tom thought. The kid could find the fish. Tom was a huge fan of that show *The Deadliest Catch* about the Alaskan crab boats on the Discovery channel. He recalled watching it last winter and seeing the various boat captains chasing hunches and pulling empty pots for half the season. He thought then that they needed Jake on the boat. The kid had a knack, Tom had thought.

Brian got the motor started and looked toward the bow. Jake said, "I thought the youngest had to pull the anchor?" and he smiled.

Brian laughed and said, "Yeah, I guess you're right. That is the rule.." and they all looked at Stevie.

"Alright, alright" he said, and he moved over to the anchor line. He strained on the line with no luck. Jake moved over to help, and Stevie said, "I got it, I got it!"

Stevie changed his grip and pulled for all he was worth. Finally, the anchor ripped free and Stevie hauled it up. When it got to the surface, it was covered in seaweed. "That's what was holding it" Stevie said.

"I thought you had a lobster trawl for a minute" Jake said. The commercial lobstermen would lay a string of ten pots all on one line. When you caught one of those with the anchor, it was a two-man job to pull it up because you had to drag as many as five pots across the bottom to get any slack in the trawl line.

Brian put the boat in gear and aimed it toward the lighthouse. "Come on Jake, you pick the spot." Jake smiled and took the wheel at the center console. He loved driving the big boat. Jake followed the channel toward Gurnet.

The water was flat calm now, and with the sun shining down Jake could see a distinct difference in the color of the water in the channel. It was a deeper blue, while the shallower water toward shore was greener. When he got closer to the Gurnet, the channel turned to the right and continued out into Cape Cod Bay. Jake continued straight into the greener water of the shallows.

He slowed the boat and looked straight down over the side. He couldn't see the bottom, but he thought he could sense a difference in color as he went along. Maybe he wasn't seeing it, maybe he was imagining it, but he felt like the water was a little greener when he was over a weedy bottom, and it was a little more yellow when he was over sand.

He couldn't see any shapes or weed patches, it was more like a slight change of hue about ten feet down. He wasn't sure exactly why, but soon it felt just right. It seemed that there was more yellow, maybe even a glow in the depths of the water. He wanted to be on a sandy bottom. Jake put the engine in reverse and brought it to a stop. He popped it in neutral and hovered. "Let's try it here" he said.

Jake killed the engine and trotted forward and threw the anchor over the side. He let out some extra line and tied it off in a figure eight on the bow cleat. The anchor caught and the boat swung with the tide, which was coming in now. They settled back into their spots and dropped their lines back down.

"Oh yeah!" Nicky said almost immediately. They could see his rod tip jiggling as he reeled back up. He swung a flounder into the boat and shouted "First fish!" The flounder started flapping and bouncing on the deck, and Bailey flew over to it and pinned it with her paw.

Jake pulled Bailey away, and Nicky began unhooking the fish. Jake felt a tug on his rod, and he let Bailey go to give the rod a yank and set the hook. He had it. He began reeling back up and Bailey hung over the side to greet the fish when it got to the surface. Jake swung the fish up and over Bailey's head, and she snapped around to help as it hit the deck flapping. "Bigger fish!" Jake said.

Stevie was next. "Oh, this one's a monster!" he yelled and reeled as fast as he could.

Tom said, "Slow down, or you'll turn him inside out!" Stevie slowed down, just a little, maybe.

Stevie whipped the fish up and over the side and it hit the deck with a plop and just lay there. "A skate!" Nicky laughed. "First junk fish!" he said.

Stevie caught himself before he cursed, glancing at his dad in the back of the boat. He flipped Nicky the bird behind his back.

"That's alright, it's good lobster bait" Jake said.

Brian and Tom soon hooked up, and joined the action. Before long they had the bucket half full with decent sized flounder. They were all between one and a half and two pounds. There weren't any trophy fish, but they definitely had supper. There was another skate, and half a dozen perch mixed in which they also kept for lobster bait.

After an hour or so, the fish stopped biting. They reeled up and Brian passed the sandwiches out.

"You sure can pick the spots, Jake. We'll have to come back to this one" Tom said.

"It's either the spot, or the incoming tide, I'm not sure, but it felt good" Jake said, as if they could understand. Brian just smiled and took a bite of his sandwich.

"Well, the ladies will be happy" Brian said to the kids. "We'll have a nice fish dinner for them."

They finished eating, and then began stowing the gear. Brian told them to keep the hooks and weights on their rods; he had plenty more. When the rods were back in the holders, Brian started the engine. "Anchor boy!" Nicky yelled.

"Bite me, Dragon!" Stevie shot back, then remembering, he looked back toward his father in the stern. Tom pretended he hadn't heard, and then covered his mouth with his hand to hide his smirk.

"Not in my boat" Brian said, grinning. Tom finally lost it and laughed out loud. The boys looked at each other with relief. Another disaster averted.

Stevie grabbed the anchor and pulled. Nothing. He pulled again with all his strength. He was grimacing, holding his breath, grunting, and squeezing his eyes shut. None of that helped at all. He sagged back down and let out a long sigh. "It's stuck," he said.

107

"Help him out guys" Brian said.

"We probably got a lobster trawl this time" Jake said. He took the line from Stevie, set his feet on the deck and leaned his knees on the side of the boat. He pulled, got nothing, readjusted his grip and pulled as hard as he could. He took all the stretch out of the anchor rope, and it began to feel like a vibrating guitar string about to snap. He kept the pressure on until his arms started to shake, but he kept pulling. Soon he started to see black spots in his vision. Suddenly he saw a 'flash' like a one second commercial on TV. But it wasn't a flash for Mountain Dew, or the newest Toyota truck. It was a flash of the wounded sailing ship in a blizzard being driven backward by a huge frothy wave. Startled, Jake let go of the rope and fell back on the deck. He sat there dazed.

Nicky pushed by Jake and went to the anchor line. "Lemme do it, Mary," he said. Nicky was slightly bigger than Jake, being a year older and all. Whether he was stronger was open to debate. Nicky combined the best of both previous attempts to free the anchor from the bottom. He set his feet, braced his knees, and halfway through the attempt he closed his eyes, grimaced, held his breath...and nothing. "Shit!" he said as he sagged on the rail and took a breath. "Sorry" he said to the back of the boat.

Brian and Tom had enjoyed the show, and they weren't offended by Nicky's commentary. "Alright," Brian said, "tie it off short to the cleat." Jake shook his head and got up off the deck. He reached for the rope, and hesitated. "Go ahead, tie it off" Brian prompted. Jake grasped the rope, expecting to feel it humming like a live wire, but it was just a wet rope again. Jake relaxed a little, and he took a full turn around the cleat with the anchor rope, and then backed it up with two figure eights. He looked back and nodded to his father.

Brian eased the control lever into reverse and started to give it some gas. "We'll pull some slack into the trawl line so we can get the anchor up and untangle it" he said to Tom. The boat's stern started to rise and the bow dipped down as the anchor line tightened up. The boat came to a stop at that bow-down angle, and Brian gave it some more gas. The boat tilted even more, and the wash from the propeller turned white and foamy. He started to give it more gas when the engine roared in protest as the prop cavitated in the air bubbles and lost its pull on the ocean. Brian immediately slid the shifter back into neutral, and the boat drifted forward and settled back to level.

"Wow, stubborn" Brian said. "Hold on, we'll give it a little snap" he told them. The others braced themselves in the boat. Brian eased it into reverse and then gunned it. The skiff shot backwards for a few feet, and the bow came down violently. The boat stopped and leaned forward, engine growling. Just before the cavitation started again, the bow eased back up and the boat started to edge backward through the water. It didn't get any easier, and after they had plowed in reverse for twenty feet or so at near full throttle, Brian slowed the engine and dropped it back into neutral. "That doesn't feel like a lobster trawl. It feels like we caught an old mooring," he said.

Brian shut the engine down and walked forward to the bow. The boys moved over to the opposite side of the boat from the anchor line to make room for Brian. Jake leaned on the side of the boat and looked around. The silence seemed complete with the engine off. The ocean was flat calm again like a sheet of glass. It could have been made of ice. There were no other boats around them. The closest one that Jake could see was a small tanker on the horizon heading north toward Boston. There wasn't a cloud in the sky and the sun was beating down as if it was mid-summer. The air had the stillness and heaviness that usually settled in on only the hottest of July days. There were heat shimmers dancing on the water, making the tanker in the distance look like a mirage. Jake started to lose focus, and his eyes got that far-away look.

Brian tested the weight of the anchor line, and then turned to Tom and said, "I'll need some help here." His voice sounded far away and muffled to Jake, as if the heavy air was too thick to let the sound through. It was like hearing the radio in a car that was parked with all of the windows rolled up.

Brian and Tom each got hold of the anchor rope and pulled. The rope came up two feet. "Hold on" Brian said, and quickly repositioned his grip father down. When he took the strain back, Tom slid his hands down farther and re-gripped the rope. "Ready? Pull!" They straightened up again and got two more feet of the rope into the boat. Brian slid down and gripped again, and Tom quickly followed. "Pull!" Brian groaned. Their breathing grew heavier each time they stopped between two-foot pulls. Jake could barely hear them now.

A single sharp cry caused Jake to look up. It sounded like it was right in Jake's ear, but he could still barely hear the two men straining just a few feet from him. A lone seagull was hovering high overhead, flapping his wings lazily every few seconds, riding a thermal updraft. Jake stared at the bird, and despite its altitude, it had a clarity that was missing from the rest of his surroundings. He could see every feather, and even the texture of its sharp curved beak. The gull cocked his head to the side, and stared down at the boat with one ghostly eye.

As Jake stared at the eye of the seagull, his vision seemed to waver and then the scene changed completely. It was as if he'd fallen into the pages of *The Sword In The Stone* and come under Merlin's spell. All at once he was seeing what the seagull saw. He had a bird's eye view of the action playing out around him.

He saw the yellow-green water dotted here and there with shadows of small kelp beds below. For the most part, the surface of the water was as still as death. The only disruption was a series of expanding circular ripples emanating out from the center, directly below. In the center, Jake could see their boat, which looked very small from this vantage point. He heard "Pull!" as plain as day now, and the two men heaved up. Each time they pulled, the front of the boat dropped and then bobbed back up, causing another series of ripples to be born and race away from the boat. Below the boat, Jake could see a large shadow slowly working its way up from the depths. The circular ripples looked like the rings of a target, and the boat

110

was in the bull's-eye of the target, with the shadow growing below.

Then the view tilted and the boat slid behind, and Jake felt himself gliding along on the warm air, keeping pace with the expanding ripples below. He could feel the air below his outstretched arms/ wings, but it wasn't *pushing* him upward. Instead he felt as if he was being *pulled* upward, like a giant vacuum cleaner was sucking the air from the top of his wings, holding him aloft. His stomach was fluttering, like he'd just gone over an unexpected bump in the road, but the feeling didn't stop like it usually did. It was like someone was tickling him from the inside out, and he felt like giggling. He felt exhilarated! He was *flying*! He could see almost all the way around his head at once, somehow. He tilted his head first one way, then the other marveling at the view as he kept pace with the expanding circles of energy on the surface below.

The gull cried once more and Jake shivered and blinked his eyes. When he opened them, he was back in the boat. He felt dazed and heavy, and it took a few moments to focus his eyes. He glanced up to see the seagull gliding slowly away from the boat. He was still leaning against the side of the boat, he'd never left. But his mind had. His mind had gone airborne. He was about to tell himself that he'd imagined it, but he knew right away that it would be like trying to fool himself with a card trick. It would be like telling both sides of a knock-knock joke and still trying to laugh at the punch line.

His father was tying off the anchor line to the cleat on the bow. Tom was leaning over the side saying, "What the hell is it?"

"I don't know" Brian said. "There's too much weed on it. Let's get it to shore and find out." Brian finished securing the anchor line and moved back to the console. Nicky and Stevie went to the anchor line and looked over the edge.

"Holy crap!" Stevie exclaimed. "It's huge!"

Slowly, almost hesitantly, Jake moved to the anchor line. He leaned over and looked down. He saw the huge dark shape straining at the end of the anchor rope, struggling to get free. Jake started to recoil, but saw that his eyes had deceived him. It wasn't alive, trying to break free. It was a massive blob of seaweed with the shaft of their anchor sticking out of it. It was hard to make out the actual shape because the seaweed and kelp were waving every which way in the water. It looked like it could be a headless man with his arms outstretched and hanging down slightly, totally covered with seaweed and kelp. Jake stepped away, not wanting to see anymore, not wanting to see a severed head with green eyes nearby, slowly sinking to the bottom, grinning up at Jake.

Jake knew that was just his imagination, and he shook off the image. But he couldn't shake off what he'd seen from the seagull's eyes - that was real and he knew it. He didn't understand it, but he knew he hadn't imagined it. He didn't think he was crazy, but if he was, then crazy was *real*.

The sound of the engine starting brought Jake back to the present. He looked up and Nicky was staring at him. "Are you alright? You don't look so good" Nicky said quietly. Bailey had noticed too. She sat on her haunches whimpering up at Jake, licking his hand occasionally and offering her paw to him.

"I'm not sure..." Jake whispered back.

"It happened again –I knew it!" Nicky hissed.

"Shhh! Quiet, I'll talk to you later" Jake said. He reached down absently and started scratching his dog behind the ears. "It's okay girl," he said.

Brian eased the boat into gear and pointed the bow toward the far end of the beach. They cruised at barely headway speed with the starboard corner of the bow sagging down with the strain of their catch.

Jake kept picturing the bird's eye view he'd gotten as they made their way slowly back to the beach. And he thought about the *feeling* of having his wings pulled upward, floating in the air. He *had* felt it. His shoulders felt strained and sore. They felt like someone had bent his arms back behind him in a wrestling match. It wasn't the kind of soreness in his biceps he'd expect from pulling on an anchor rope. The anchor rope hadn't caused it. He wiggled his shoulders a little, and he knew he hadn't imagined it. Daydreams don't give you sore shoulders.

Nicky watched Jake on the way back, and he knew something had happened to him. Jake hadn't passed out, but he had definitely *zoned* out back there. Nicky decided to keep an eye on his friend until he got a chance to talk to him alone. Nicky had been a little excited at first, thinking it would be cool to hear about Jake's latest vision, or whatever it was. But looking at him now, Nicky was feeling a little uneasy. Whatever was going on, it wasn't happening in some TV show. It wasn't some crazy story on the Internet. It was happening to his best friend, and Jake wasn't the kind of guy that made stuff up. He wasn't a kid looking for attention, or some bullshit artist that lied to you. Jake was solid. Nicky trusted Jake more than anyone, and even though he was younger than Nicky, Jake was the kind of guy that he could admire, a guy he wanted to be like. And just knowing that Jake was scared made Nicky a little less sure of himself, even a little scared too.

Bailey paced nervously the whole way back, doing slow laps around the boat as if she was on patrol. Every time she went by the anchor rope weighing down the starboard corner of the bow, she whimpered and looked sideways at it. Then she'd look back at Jake as if to make sure he was still okay. Then she'd do another slow lap, not looking happy. "Don't worry Bailey, we won't sink" Brian said to her. Nicky didn't think the dog was worried about sinking...

24
The Catch

When they finally got close to shore, the mystery catch started to drag on the bottom. Brian eased the boat into neutral and they hovered there idling.

"Now what?" Tom asked. The boys looked at Brian for the answer.

"We'll have to drag it" Brian said. "We'll put a buoy on it and come back with a tow rope" he decided.

Tom looked over the side and said, "We're still pretty deep, I'd say ten feet or so." Brian looked over and nodded.

"We'll get a little closer," Brian said. He eased the boat into reverse and spun the wheel all the way to one side. He gave it a little more gas and the boat pivoted around until the stern was facing the shore, and then he gunned it. The boat dragged backwards toward shore and the object fell over flat and followed the boat, tearing up the sandy bottom as they went. When the boat was in about three feet of water Brian put it back in neutral, went forward and dug under the raised bow deck for a buoy. He tied the buoy to the bitter end of the anchor rope. They were close enough to shore that the waves were forming despite the calmness of the ocean, getting squeezed out to go breaking up on shore. The waves were pushing them toward shore, keeping the anchor line tight and keeping the boat from coming too close to the object that held them there.

"You boys hop out and get the dingy down here. I'll put the boat on the mooring" Brian instructed. "Tom, hold on for a minute, and then you can hop out too" Brian said. The boys got the fishing rods, the coolers and the bucket of fish and climbed off the stern of the boat. Bailey jumped out and followed them onto the beach. They dropped all the gear on the dry sand and walked up toward the tarp where the little dinghy was sitting near the dune. Bailey kept on walking up and over the dune. She'd had enough of this adventure, and wasn't at all eager to see what they'd pulled up from the ocean floor.

"Alright Tom, untie that anchor and hop out the back. I'll idle offshore until they get the dingy down here, and then you can throw me the rope from the dinghy" Brian said.

"Aye aye, captain!" Tom said and gave him his best Benny Hill salute. He untied the anchor rope and threw it overboard with the buoy, then quickly walked back and hopped out. Brian eased the boat into gear and worked his way to deeper water, giving the submerged object a wide berth.

When he got the dingy rope from Tom, Brian tied it off to the stern cleat and pulled the boat out to the mooring that he had out beyond the low tide mark. He secured the boat and rowed back to shore. The others were waiting there for him, waiting for instructions. "I'll get the truck and be right back" Brian said walking by them toward the dune.

"What do you think it is, Dad?" Stevie asked Tom.

"I don't know, it could be pirates' treasure" Tom said, with a gleam in his eye. "It could be a dead-man's chest!" he said. "It could be a dead pirate! Arrrrg!" Tom growled gleefully.

Stevie looked at him skeptically, Jake looked pale, and Nicky looked pissed. "A dead body don't weigh that much" Nicky said, a little too forcefully. He looked at Jake, and then out toward the buoy. "It's probably an old piece of junk, that's all" he mumbled.

Brian came down the cutoff over the dune in the truck, and turned around and backed it down to the water's edge. He got out and dug in the storage box in the bed of the truck, and pulled out a fifty-foot towrope he had. He put a loop and a slipknot in the end of the rope. "I don't want to snap the anchor line. I need a volunteer to go slip this on, Jake" Brian said, smiling at his son.

Jake didn't move immediately and Nicky stepped up and grabbed the rope. "I'll go with him," he said.

Nicky and Jake walked out into the waves. They walked past the buoy in the surf and followed the anchor rope out. As they got closer they could see the dark shape of their mystery catch lurking below the surface. When they got closer still, they could see the seaweed on it waving back and forth, back and forth as

115

the small swells formed on the surface and rolled past. To Jake, the seaweed looked like a million little arms beckoning for him to come closer, come closer. He hesitated and tried to focus. "Are you okay?" Nicky asked.

"Yeah Dragon, I'm okay" Jake said, willing himself to be 'okay'. He took the rope from Nicky and took two more steps. The object was still a mystery with all the weed on it, but some of the weed had been lost on the trip back to the beach. It vaguely resembled a capital 'T' lying on the bottom. Jake knew it was going to be too heavy too lift. "I'll dig a little sand out from under the end so we can slip the rope around it" he said. Jake moved up and extended his foot like he was going to dig up a quahog. He dug into the sand near the end, and his foot touched the object. He immediately shivered and went slack, slowly sinking into the water.

Nicky grabbed him and pulled him upright "Jake! What's the matter? Jake?"

The whites of Jake's eyes were showing, and then his pupils rolled back down and stared unfocused. "Jake!" Nicky said again, almost frantic now.

Jake's eyes slowly came back into focus. "The ship...the ship..." he mumbled.

"What frigging ship? Jake are you alright?" Nicky said again.

"I saw the ship again..."

"Shit, you're scaring me now" Nicky said.

"Are you two okay?" Brian yelled from shore.

"Yeah we're fine!" Nicky yelled back. "I got the line tangled around Jake's foot. My bad! One minute!" he said. Nicky took the rope from Jake and said, "I'll do it. Are you okay?"

"Yeah, I'm okay now. Just tie it and let's get outta here," Jake pleaded.

Nicky reached his foot forward then stopped. "Screw it" he said and touched the end of the blob. Nothing. No shock, no visions, no problem. Quickly he worked the sand out from under the end of the object, and then took a breath and ducked under. He slipped the loop around the end and then cinched up the slipknot. He stood up and shook his wet hair back out of his face. He wiped his eyes and looked at Jake. "You okay?"

"Yeah, let's go" he said and turned toward shore. Nicky fell in step next to him and they walked back through the waves.

They walked a little off to the side when they made shore, and Nicky whispered to Jake, "We gotta talk." Jake just nodded.

Tom and Stevie walked off to the other side as Brian got into the truck and eased it forward. He took the slack out of the rope, and then gave it some gas. The big engine revved, and slowly the rope slid out of the ocean, like a scarf coming out of a magician's sleeve. Finally, the foam of the waves at the shore darkened, and then the blob of seaweed broke through and slid onto the shore. Brian pulled it about twenty feet more and then stopped the truck and got out. They all walked up for a closer look.

Brian reached down to where his anchor was lodged and shook it loose. When he did, a big chunk of seaweed fell off, and it was swarming with all kinds of miniature marine life. There were sea worms and baby eels, starfish and moon snails, sea urchins and baby horseshoe crabs. You name it, it was in there.

Nicky thought about that stupid spaghetti sauce commercial he'd seen a gazillion times, where every ingredient you could think of was 'in there'. He looked at the blob and thought, 'Barnacles? It's in there! Hermit crabs? It's in there! Baby lobsters? It's in there! But what the hell is it?' he thought.

Brian reached into the bed of the truck and pulled out a shovel. He scraped one end of the top of the 'T' and the seaweed and everything else came off in big chunks. The eels and fish went squirming and flapping in the sand all around where Brian worked the shovel. Soon, the shape started to emerge.

The seaweed on the very end had hidden a triangular shaped metal plate that almost looked like the spade on a deck of cards. The plate was attached to a thick metal shaft, and the shaft was curved like a smile once the seaweed was removed. "It's an anchor fluke!" Brian said. "It's a big frigging anchor!"

"Holy shit!" Tom said. "That thing's got to be ancient! They don't make them like that anymore, do they?" he asked.

"Nope, no way. This has got to be a hundred years old – older probably," Brian said.

"Unbelievable," Tom said. The boys were awestruck, especially Jake. The anchor shaft was almost seven feet long. None of the little boats around here had dropped this. This was from a ship, and Jake was pretty sure he'd seen it.

"Let's get it up above the high tide line" Brian said. He got back into the truck and put it in gear. He pulled the anchor slowly up the beach and turned near the dune, stopping when the anchor was next to the tarp. He got out and unhooked his towrope, and threw it into the bed of the truck. The others had followed him up, careful not to step on the trail of weed and sea creatures the anchor had left in its wake.

They gathered around it and stared, each wondering where it had come from, and where it had been. It was old, that was plain to see. The curve of the spade shaped fluke showed a craftsmanship that was missing from the machine made anchors of this century. They wondered what story it had to tell. That basic human need to know was at work in each of their imaginations, and they all wanted to know the story behind this huge anchor...all except Jake of course.

Jake was more worried that he might actually find out the story. And he wasn't sure that he wanted to know. He wasn't at all sure that he wanted to know.

25
Acceptance

Brian untied the towrope from the truck and was stowing it in the storage box when Michele and Jenny came over the dune from the Guthrie cottage. "Where did that come from?" Jenny asked, pointing at the huge old anchor.

"Jake caught it with our anchor when he picked our fishing spot!" Tom Connors announced. "He sure knows how to pick 'em too, because we got plenty of flounder for supper" he said, holding up the bucket of fish.

Jenny leaned over and looked into the bucket. "Wow, that's awesome! You got a ton!" she exclaimed. "But now you gotta clean 'em all.." she said with a mischievous smile.

Nicky was next to Michele whispering something to her. She started to look worried and glanced at Jake.

"She's right, Tom. We've got some work to do. There's a fair amount of filleting to do" Brian said.

"Wait a minute," Tom said, "you know I can't fillet. I'll just butcher them," he pleaded.

"That's okay, you can skin the fillets. I'll show you how again. Come to think of it, I show you every year and you seem to forget" Brian responded.

"Alright, alright, you win. I suppose if I don't help they'll go bad before you get it done" Tom said to Brian. Brian just smiled at him.

Michele spoke up then. "Do you guys want to take a walk? I wanted to see how that baby seal is doing," she said, looking at Jake.

"What seal?" Brian asked her.

"There's a baby seal at the rocks near the lighthouse. He's hurt. We saw him when we walked up there yesterday, and Jake gave him the bluefish to eat" Michele answered.

"We can take the perch we caught to him," Nicky prompted, looking at Jake hoping he'd get the hint.

"Yeah, we can do that" Jake said finally.

Brian looked them over, sensing that something was up. He thought it couldn't be anything too sinister, so he decided not to ask. "Well, take the perch then, but make sure you're out of there before high tide. I don't feel like going swimming today" he said and stared at Nicky. Nicky looked down at his feet, and Brian showed just the hint of a smile.

Jake found a crumpled up plastic grocery bag in the truck and put the perch in it. "We'll cook the fish for supper at our cottage. Tell your folks they're welcome to come over" Brian said to the kids.

"Are you coming Stevie?" Michele asked. Stevie was still staring at the anchor, thinking about pirates.

"What? Oh, yeah I'm coming" he said.

"How about you?" Michele asked Jenny.

"Yeah, let me just tell my grandmother" she said and ran up over the dune. A minute later she came running back down. "My grandparents will come for supper. Gram said she's got plenty of potatoes she'll bring to make french-fries," she told Brian.

"Sounds good. You guys be careful now," he said to them. He and Tom got in the truck and headed up to the cottage to start cleaning the fish.

Jake was looking at the anchor, and Michele grabbed his arm and pulled him. "Come on, it's not going anywhere. Tell us what happened," she said.

"What happened?" Stevie asked, not sure what he missed.

Nicky rolled his eyes and said "You're friggin' dense. You were standin' right there went Jake zoned out, and you never even noticed. Remember not to get a job as a detective when you grow up."

"Bite me" Stevie said, not for the last time that summer. They started down the beach toward the lighthouse with Jake in the middle of their little group.

"What happened?" Jenny said. "I wasn't there."

"Yeah Jake, what happened this time?" Michele asked, putting her hand on his arm.

Jake hesitated as he walked along, thinking about how much he could tell them, wondering again if they'd think he was nuts. Jenny and Michele watched him with concerned expressions on their faces. Nicky wasn't so patient.

"Listen Jake, we told you we'd help you. I caught you in the water out there, didn't I? How the hell are we supposed to help if you don't tell us, huh? Now talk" he ordered.

That snapped Jake out of it and he laughed a little. "Yeah, you're right. Thanks Dragon, and thanks for covering for me with my dad" Jake said.

"Told you I would, didn't I?" Nicky answered.

"Yeah, you did. But thanks" Jake said again.

"So?" Nicky asked.

Jake looked at the girls and started talking. "We weren't catching any fish so my dad told me to pick a new spot. I'm not sure why I felt like trying down near the bend in the channel, I just did. I can't explain it. It's not like it's one of my favorite spots or anything – I haven't had much luck there before. But today, it just seemed like a good spot. I can't explain it any better. Anyway, we caught a bunch of fish pretty quick. When we went to leave, Stevie tried pulling the anchor and it was stuck.." he said. Jake hesitated, trying to recall exactly what happened. He'd gotten a little blurry back there. "Well then I tried to help, and it was okay at first. But all of a sudden it was like I got a shock, and I saw the old ship in the blizzard again. It was just for a second – like a flash almost. It was the same ship I saw the other day in the boat with Stevie – the one I told you about last night" he said.

"The sail boat?" Nicky asked.

"Yeah, but it's big – a ship, not a boat. And it's old, like one of them tall ships, but not so fancy" Jake said. Nicky thought of the tall ships he'd seen come into Boston Harbor with all the sailors dressed in white standing on the deck and hanging onto the rigging.

"Like I said, it was just a flash, like if you flicked a flashlight on and off in the dark, you can see the picture in your eyes for a minute" Jake went on. "But that wasn't so bad, and I've been

121

thinking about that ship a lot anyway. I thought maybe that's why I saw it – 'cause I was thinking about it." Jake paused and rubbed his eyes as if trying to erase the picture.

"But then I saw something else" he said, pausing again, struggling for words.

"Go on Jake, just tell us," Michele said, sensing his hesitation. "Just tell us."

Jake nodded and resumed the story. "Then I saw us. I saw all of us in my dad's boat, but I saw it from the air. I saw it from above." The words came in a rush now. "I heard a seagull and looked up at it, and then *I was* the seagull and I was looking down at us. I could feel myself gliding, I could feel the wind. And I could see us all in the boat, and my dad and Stevie's dad trying to pull up the anchor, and every time they pulled it made a ring of ripples that went out from the boat, and I could see the shadow of the anchor under the boat, and we were in the middle of the rings of ripples and it looked like a target and we were in the bull's eye.."

"Holy shit" Nicky said, feeling his friend's desperation and fear.

"And it wasn't a dream. It wasn't a vision, or my imagination. I don't know if you believe me or not, or if I'm crazy, but it was *real*. It was *real*. For a little while, I was really *looking* through the seagull's eyes, and I was really *flying*. And then the seagull took off, and I was back in the boat. And my shoulders were sore from flying. They're still sore.." he finished. He walked along looking down, afraid to look at them. He didn't want to see their faces, the skeptical looks, or the looks of pity. He knew he'd said too much, and there was no way they could believe him. No way. If he'd heard one of them tell the story, *he* wouldn't believe *them*. He pushed up the sleeve of his shirt and rubbed his shoulder, and it was still sore.

"Oh my God!" Michele exclaimed. They all stopped and looked at her. She looked shocked.

"What?" Nicky said.

"Jake, take your shirt off" she ordered.

"Huh?" Jake asked, bewildered.

122

"Just take your frigging shirt off!" she yelled.

Jake dropped the bag of perch in the sand and, still confused, he pulled the tee shirt over his head. When he got his head out of the shirt, he saw the stunned look on his friends' faces.

"What?" he said, looking down at the shirt in his hands.

"Look at your shoulders!" Stevie nearly whispered.

Jake looked at his shoulders and understood their shocked expressions. Both shoulders were bruised and starting to turn black and blue. It looked like someone had tried to pull his arms off, but gave up when they wouldn't tear loose. Jake rubbed his shoulder again, and it was much more painful now that he'd seen it, for some reason.

"Holy shit" Nicky said again. No one knew what else to say.

"Well, I guess I'm not imagining it" Jake said, sounding relieved. Somehow, as bizarre as it was to be injured by whatever had happened to him in the boat, it was still better than going crazy and only *thinking* it was real.

They continued to stare, and feeling self-conscious, Jake pulled his shirt back on. "Do you believe me now?" he asked.

"We believed you," Nicky lied.

"Bullshit" Jake said, smiling at his friend.

"Well, they believed you" Nicky stammered. "And I believed that you believed" he said. Then after a few seconds he continued, "So maybe I thought you were sick. Whatever. I was still worried. I was still watching out for you. I caught you when you started to pass out, didn't I?"

"When was that?" Jenny asked.

Jake answered her. "When we went out to tie the rope to the anchor and I touched it, I flashed again and saw the ship. I started to pass out, and Dragon caught me." He looked at Nicky and said, "Yeah, you were watching out for me - thanks."

"And I believe you now" Nicky said. "I don't friggin' understand it, but I believe it" he said. "I'm sorry I didn't believe you earlier, but it was..it was.."

"Unbelievable?" Jake said, smiling.

Nicky laughed. "Yeah, it was friggin' unbelievable!" he said.

The laughter helped relieve the tension, but it was short lived. Stevie put an end to the laughter when he yelled, "It's not funny! What's the matter with you?" His voice cracked a little when he asked, "Jeez Jake, what's happening to you? You're seeing ghosts! You're passing out!" He sniffed and wiped his nose with his arm and said "And now you're gettin' hurt 'cause it's not your imagination – it's real! And that means the ghosts are real too – it's not funny!" He wiped away the tears that came. "It's not funny.."

They were almost to Gurnet now. Jake was touched by the concern that Stevie showed, but he still felt a little relieved. He didn't feel the fear that Stevie had suddenly felt. He was a little past that, because despite his rationalizing, Jake had thought it was real all along. And he'd already stared to deal with it. He'd begun to get over his fear when he decided to tell his friends the truth last night. And talking to them now, he felt a little stronger still.

"It's okay Stevie" Jake said. "It's okay. Think about it for a minute. Yeah, the ghost's are real. But they didn't hurt me. I just – I just think they're trying to show me something. I don't know what it is yet – but I think that's what they want. They're not trying to hurt me -I got hurt *flying*. I was *flying*! It was awesome…"

Stevie was unconvinced. "Well what if something else happens? What if you get hurt bad?"

Jake thought about this. "I don't know," he said. "But maybe if I can figure out what they're trying to show me, they'll leave me alone. Maybe it will stop" he said hopefully.

"You better figure it out then," Stevie said.

"He's right" Nicky said. "We better figure it out."

They started walking along again in silence, with Jake in the middle of the little group, as if the other four could keep him sheltered from the things that were happening to him. There were no more doubts – it was easier to believe when you were twelve or thirteen. The protective blanket of adult skepticism wasn't there to tell them not to believe what they'd all seen with their own eyes.

They reached the spot where they could take the cutoff to follow the road up the hill, or continue on the beach to the rocks at the base of the cliff below the lighthouse. It was still an hour and a half before high tide, and the tide wasn't going to be especially high today. It was only supposed to be a nine-foot tide, meaning the high tide would be nine feet above the mean low tide mark. The real high tides on the beach ran twelve or even thirteen feet above low mean tide. Jake knew it was only a nine-footer because he had checked the tide table this morning. So much of his day depended on whether the tide was high or low, it had become second nature for him to check when he got up in the morning.

"Tide won't be high until after four, and it's a wimpy tide today. We should be able to walk out to the rocks," Jake told them. They continued along the beach past the cutoff without discussion. They had all gotten used to Jake being tuned in to the tides, or when the moon was going to be full or new, or whatever else affected the fishing or clamming around here. They trusted him on such matters.

They had to stay higher in the rocks than when Michele and Jake had come yesterday morning, and they were on the big boulders next to the base of the cliff that had been left there by the melting glacier back when the beach first came to be. The boulders didn't slow them down, because they'd been all over the rocks both here and down at the Head their whole lives. They fell into a rhythm, their eyes picking out safe footing two steps ahead of where their feet were landing. They had to hop across the larger gaps between boulders, and they just naturally sped up into a trot.

Stevie was the first to go into a full run. Jake and Nicky quickly took up the challenge and soon passed him, practically flying from rock to rock in their bare feet that had already started to toughen from being shoeless for four days. Rock running was one of those games that was second nature to the kids on the beach, but it horrified any of the city kids that visited only once or twice a summer.

The trick to rock running was confidence, and pure childhood reckless abandon was the fuel for that confidence. Aside from Jake's experience earlier that day, it was the closest thing to flying that any of them had ever felt. You had to react in three dimensions, going from side to side while hopping from high rounded boulders to low flat rocks half buried in the sand, all the while flying forward at break-neck speed. In your mind you saw your feet landing two rocks ahead of where they were in real time. It was like your spirit was soaring along and your body was trying to catch up, always two steps behind. Your subconscious mind sent the signals – left foot high on the boulder, right foot low on the flat rock, left on the side, right on the jutting shelf, and all these silent signals came without the benefit of words ever forming in your mind. There wasn't time for words – you were totally in the moment and even words couldn't keep pace with your soaring spirit. The silent stream of signals was filled with warnings that were lessons learned from past failures. They were guideposts like the flags on a slalom course on a snowy mountainside. These guideposts included seaweed patches, sharp spots and sandy patches among the rocks, all of which would cause a tremendous crash and burn when you hit them. Only the childhood confidence of immortality allowed you to reach a full run in spite of these hazards, and only at a full run could you feel the absolute freedom of full flight, the complete and total now-ness of your existence.

Standing high above them up at the lighthouse, Nathaniel Withers looked down at the kids running along the rocks. It was obvious to him that they were locals by the pace they kept. As he watched, he recognized the one in the lead as the Edison boy that Walter was so fond of, the one he'd given that old boat to.

Nate recognized the others also. He knew Walter's granddaughter Jenny of course, he'd watched her grow up. She was with her dark haired girlfriend – Michele, that was her name. And while he didn't know their names, he'd seen the other two boys plenty of times. One was from the beach and that older one was from out on Western Point. Nate had long ago stopped socializing with most of the folks on the peninsula; it was too awkward for him to see the furtive glances, or hear the whispers when he passed by. But despite his isolation, he still recognized most of the residents because it was such a small community.

And it still was a community, one where everyone knew their neighbors and watched out for them. Nate sometimes missed that sense of community, that sense of belonging, but that was water under the bridge. He knew he'd always be the boogieman to the little ones, and something worse to those alleged adults prone to bad-mouthing others just to try to feel better about themselves in contrast. Nate had long ago accepted his place in the village consciousness, and he was okay with that. Truth to tell, he liked his privacy anyway, and it was easier this way. He still had a few good friends around like Walter and Sharon whom he visited discreetly, and he didn't mind keeping his distance from the others.

Nate had long ago accepted his place, but what he couldn't accept was not knowing what had happened to Rose. The not knowing gnawed at him, it was chronic. He knew he'd never find peace, and with each passing year he knew the chance of finding out the truth became more remote. The fact was, he'd just about given up hope of finding out the truth. It was too long ago, he thought. He glanced down at the kids below him on the

127

rocks, and he realized that to them, all those terrible events of that night would be like ancient history. And as each year passed, there were fewer and fewer people that were even alive back then. Soon he'd be gone too, he thought, and that might be just as well. If his death would finally bring relief from the restlessness that constantly drove him to visit this empty lighthouse, then that would be just fine, he thought. The problem was, he wasn't sure if even death would bring relief, and that thought haunted him the most.

*

Jake came to a halt behind a big boulder and Nicky and Stevie came huffing up to stop beside him. Soon Michele and Jenny caught up to them, and they peered around the boulder to see if the seals were there. They saw the little seal curled up at the base of the cliff in the little hollow behind the rock, and he appeared to be sleeping. At least they hoped he was asleep.

"Do you think he's okay?" Michele asked.

"I dunno" Jake whispered. "I think so, but I'd like to know where the mother seal is before we go find out."

As they waited there scanning the rocks and water for the mother seal, Jake started to get that feeling. It was like a tingling on his neck and behind his ears. He never knew where that feeling came from, and in fact he never worried about knowing. He didn't need to know where it came from to understand what it meant. Someone was watching them, and Jake knew it. As Jake tuned in to the feeling to sense from which direction he was being spied on, the others started to feel it too. Apparently, this was one of those unexplained signals that just about any old radio could pick up.

Jake looked up suddenly to the top of the cliff, and the others followed his gaze. They saw Old Man Withers standing there looking down on them. Jake and Nate Withers locked eyes, and immediately Jake felt a deep sadness, an emptiness like he'd never experienced before. It was like a physical pain that almost made Jake cry out.

Nate Withers looked startled for a moment, and then perplexed as he felt Jake's steady gaze. There was something about it that was unsettling, unnerving. Nate felt as if he was exposed, he felt vulnerable, like a man connected to a lie detector must feel. He turned his eyes away quickly and the connection was broken. He stepped back and disappeared from view. Jake sucked in a deep breath and let it out slowly, only now realizing that he'd stopped breathing.

"It's Old Man Withers!" Stevie hissed. "What's he doing spyin' on us?"

"He ain't spyin' on us, numbnuts" Nicky spat. "He didn't know we'd be here. You think he spends his time following you around? You ain't that interesting" Nicky finished what he thought was a reasonably good slam.

"Bite me Dragon" Stevie answered half-heartedly, still looking up as if he expected some evil to come hurtling down the cliff toward them.

"He's just taking a walk, Stevie. He's not spying" Jenny said. Nate had visited her grandfather enough times; she knew he was just a sad old man and not mean like most of the kids thought he was. She wished she recognized him sooner so she could have waved to him. The truth was, she kind of liked him, but she didn't feel like telling her friends that. She knew how most people felt about Nate Withers, and it wasn't worth arguing.

In a strange way, she thought she understood Nate Withers now. He missed his wife deeply, even after all these years, and Jenny knew how *that* felt.

Quite often in her young life, she had sorely missed her father, even though she had never even met him. In a way, that might have been worse, she thought. At least Mr. Withers had his memories, while Jenny just had a big hole in her heart where the memories should have been. So many times she wished she could fill that hole.

Jenny had asked her mother about her father of course, but it was painful for her to dredge up that sad chapter in her life. Besides, there wasn't a lot of history there. It had been a whirlwind romance, her mother had told her. Neither of them was young by any stretch, they were old enough to know better. But the fact was that they'd fallen deeply in love, even though their time together had been brief. They had made plans for the future, but the future never came. Her father had been killed before they could even get married, but Jenny had come along just the same, and her mother told her that Jenny was the only reason she'd been able to go on. She called Jenny her silver lining, her reason for being. Inevitably the conversation would turn to the two of them, building their lives together, while her father's life remained largely a mystery to Jenny.

"There's the mother seal!" Michele exclaimed, pointing into the water. Jenny looked and saw the big seal's head poking out of the water, watching them.

Jake stood up and pulled a perch out of the bag he'd been carrying. He held the fish up for the mother seal to see, and then he started walking slowly toward the little seal curled up behind the rock. The mother seal pulled her head down and disappeared below the surface. Jake walked slowly until he was about fifteen feet from the little seal. Suddenly the mother seal burst out of the water and lunged up onto dry ground barely ten feet off to Jake's right. "Jake – look out!" Nicky yelled.

Jake just stood still and looked at her, and he held up the fish again. The big seal watched him warily, but she didn't come closer. The little seal raised his head and looked at Jake. He wiggled and rolled and stood up on all fours. He looked much better now. There was just a thin line of a scar above the gray patch around his eye now.

Jake tossed the perch toward the mother seal, and pulled out another fish and tossed it toward the baby. Then he dumped the rest of the fish in the sand and slowly walked backwards until he was near the big boulder. He slipped behind the rock with the others.

They watched as the mother seal smelled the fish, and then lifted it gently in her teeth and hopped over and dropped it in front of the little seal. The baby seal snapped up the fish and threw its head back, swallowing it whole. He picked up the second perch and made that disappear just as quickly. Then the little seal started hopping forward toward the pile of perch Jake had dumped in the sand. He moved awkwardly on his wounded flipper, but to Jake it looked like even that was getting better.

The kids slowly backed away as the little seal approached the pile of fish, and the mother seal hopped behind, watching them. They watched as the baby hungrily dug into the pile of perch. The mother seal's eyes never left the kids, but she didn't bare her teeth or bark. When the baby had finished eating, the kids turned and started picking their way back through the rocks again. "He looks way better" Michele commented as they made their retreat.

"I thought the big one was gonna attack you" Nicky said to Jake.

"Nah, we gave the baby the bluefish yesterday. She knew we weren't gonna hurt it" Jake said. Nicky looked at his friend and saw the certainty there. Nicky wasn't sure if the big seal had sensed the same confidence in Jake and decided not to attack, or if it really had come to understand Jake's intentions. Either way, it was still pretty amazing to Nicky. But nothing about his friend seemed to surprise him anymore.

They made their way back along the rocks slowly. There was no rock-running this time. They were thinking about the scene they had just witnessed. It was the closest any of them had come to the seals - ever, and it was pretty cool. They watched the scene in their mind's eye over and over again, while their feet navigated them through the rocks as if on autopilot.

The kids made their way back down the beach talking about
the seals, and how cool it had been to get so close to them.
There was a debate about how the little one had gotten injured.
The theories were that he got caught in a storm and had been
battered against the rocks by waves, that a boat hit him, that he
was attacked by a shark, and Jake's theory that commercial
fishermen had intentionally injured him. As far as Jake was
concerned, this wasn't a theory. While he didn't argue the point,
he knew that this was what had happened. He knew it just as he
had known that Nate Withers had been looking down on them
from the lighthouse cliff. He could feel it, and he didn't
question the feeling. He didn't tell the others this because it
didn't matter what they believed, and it wasn't important to
convince them that he knew the truth. They believed him about
the important things that were happening to him, and that was
enough. Choose your battles, his father had always told him,
and this one wasn't worth the energy.

He also didn't want to explain the feeling that surrounded the
little seal's encounter with the fishermen. It was an angry
feeling, laced with vengeance and plain meanness, driven by
greed. It wasn't a feeling Jake wanted to describe to his friends,
and it wasn't something he could describe. It would be like
trying to explain what a banana tasted like to someone who had
never eaten one, Jake thought. It was harder than it sounded,
and words only went so far.

The conversation turned back to Jake's visions from earlier,
and the bruises on his shoulders. They were hesitant to bring it
up at first, but their curiosity about what it really felt like to fly
was overwhelming. Jake understood their enthusiasm, and tried
to explain it to them, but again, all he had were words.

"It was like balancing on a fence" Jake said. "I mean at first,
you see that you're up high and it's a little scary. But then you
realize you're not falling yet, and you stop being scared and
start looking at why you're not falling." He searched for the

words, and then continued. "You know how when you're standing on a fence and you get afraid of falling, you fall? But if you forget about falling, and concentrated on *not* falling, you can balance? And then, when you stop *thinking* about balancing, and just do it, you can walk on the fence?" The others were nodding; they'd all walked along the wood rail fence surrounding the field at the lighthouse.

"Flying is like that. At first you see how high you are, but you're not falling. Then you feel why. It's like you're balancing. You're being pulled toward the ground by gravity, but your wings are being pulled up by the wind. If you slow down, or the wind stops, you start to sink, but if you flap your wings and push forward, or the wind starts, you get sucked up again. So you balance between falling and rising, like leaning back and forth on a fence. I was just getting the hang of it too, it was like I was just ready to stop thinking about it and just do it – but then it stopped. It was over.." he trailed off.

They were back to their end of the beach now, and one by one the kids left the little group as each arrived at their own cottage, promising to see the others at supper. When Jenny went up to her house, only Jake and Nicky were left to walk past the anchor lying near the tarp. Jake looked sideways at the old anchor and shivered.

Nicky noticed and said, "It really bothers you, huh?"

Jake nodded. "Yeah, it...it makes me cold when I look at it. It scares me a little."

"Yeah, I can see that" Nicky said. "We gotta find out why."

"I know" Jake said.

They walked by the anchor and paused at the path that led over the dune to Jake's cottage. "I think I know how we can find out," Nicky said. Jake just looked at him, waiting. Nicky looked down at his feet and shuffled a little. "I think if you touch it long enough, you'll see what it's trying to tell you" he said finally.

Jake knew that Nicky was right. He had already thought of this himself, but not with much enthusiasm. "Yeah, I think you're right" he said, "but I'm kind of scared to..."

"I don't blame you" Nicky agreed, "I'm kind of scared to see you do it."

They stood in silence for a few moments until Nicky said, "Well, let's think about it. I'll see you at supper, okay?"

"Yeah, I'll see you at supper" Jake replied, and he started up over the dune. He didn't glance back at the old anchor lying near the tarp. He knew it was still there.

*

An hour later the crowd was building at the Edison cottage. The Malones, Collins and Dragonis had all arrived; all except Victor Dragoni who was still up in Boston for the busy Saturday night at his restaurant. He'd be down in the morning. Brian Edison had already set aside a bag of flounder for Maria to take home for Victor.

"Maria, here's some fillets for Victor – I'll leave them in the fridge but make sure you take them home tonight" Brian said.

"Oh, he'll be thrilled! Thank you so much!" Maria replied.

"You're welcome. I wish he were here so he could cook the fish. He'd do a much better job of it" Brian said. "So it's not going to be fancy, I'll just fry them up" he said.

"That's perfect" Bill Malone interjected. "My cholesterol was getting a little low anyway." Bill didn't look like his cholesterol was getting too low. Since he'd started his own construction company ten years ago, he spent more time entertaining clients than he spent actually doing any physical labor, and he was losing the battle of the bulge.

Jenny arrived then, followed by Walter and Sharon Guthrie. Kelly Edison saw them first and said "Why, if it isn't the Guthries. Welcome, we're glad you could make it!"

"Fresh fish is about the only thing that could get him out of the house at night these days" Sharon commented.

"Well, my darlin', with a lass like you at home, what sane man would want to go out" Walter countered, his eyes smiling their eternal smile.

Walter and Sharon sat down at the table on the deck with the other guests and Kelly offered them a drink. "It is a special occasion, so it would be kind of rude not to join you" Walter reasoned.

"I guess every day is special then," Sharon said.

"At my age, you're right" Walter replied.

Kelly went into the cottage to get the drinks, and Jenny followed her. The other kids were sprawled out on the furniture and the bottom bunks. "Hi Jen" Michele said. Nicky waved, and Stevie smiled at her and sat up a little taller on the couch. Jake didn't notice; he was lying in one of the bunks with his nose buried in a hardcover coffee table book with a picture of a schooner on the front.

"Hi Jake!" Jenny called loudly.

"Oh, hi Jenny" Jake answered. "I didn't see you come in."

"Obviously" Jenny said.

Kelly went back out with the drinks, and Jenny asked, "Whatcha lookin' at?"

"I was looking at different types of sail boats" Jake replied.

"Well, did you find it?" Jenny asked. They all knew what *it* was.

"I think so – not the exact one, but the same kind of ship" he said.

"What kind is it?" Nicky asked.

Jake looked back at the book. "It's called a brigantine" he said, and he turned the book around to show them a picture. The ship had two masts, with square sails on the front mast, and triangular sails on the rear mast. The ship in the picture was cruising along on calm water on a bright sunny day. It wasn't at all like the setting in Jake's vision, but the ship looked to be right to him.

"Lemme see it" Nicky said, and he grabbed the book from Jake. He looked at it for a while, and then read the description printed under the picture in the bottom corner of the page. "Huh" he grunted.

"Huh, what?" Michele asked.

Nicky looked up from the page. "It says here they were used by pirates," he said. Nicky looked at Jake for a reaction, but Jake just sat there.

"That's a pirate anchor? Holy crap!" Stevie said.

"Pirates weren't the only ones that used them," Jake said, maybe a little too hopefully.

"Well, we'll find out" Nicky said as he closed the book and laid it aside.

"What do you mean 'we'll find out'? What are you talking about?" Michele asked.

"We'll find out at the fire tonight" Nicky said. "You still up for it?" he asked Jake. Jake didn't say anything, he just nodded.

"What are you talking about?" Jenny asked. Stevie watched the conversation go back and forth, and he looked as confused as ever.

Kelly Edison came back in to get a plate of cheese and crackers that she'd forgotten on the counter. She looked at the silent group of kids all staring back at her. "Did I interrupt something?" she asked.

"No. When's supper gonna be ready?" Jake asked, despite the fact that he wasn't that hungry.

"In about twenty minutes" Kelly replied. "Can you last that long?" she asked.

"Yeah, just about" Jake lied.

Kelly went back outside, and Michele immediately pounced on Nicky. "What the hell are you talking about?" she demanded. "How are we going to find out at the fire?"

Nicky said "Whoa, whoa, not me! Ask him!" They all looked at Jake.

"I'm gonna grab the anchor and see what it's trying to tell me" Jake said.

They sat silently for a few moments, and then Jenny asked him, "Do you think it will work? Do you think you'll see something?"

Jake nodded, "I'm almost sure of it. I felt it through our anchor rope today, and it was way stronger when I actually touched it out in the water with Dragon." He paused for a moment before

136

continuing. "I'm pretty sure I'll see something – that's not what I'm worried about. I'm worried about being able to *stop* seeing it" he finished.

"Then why are you going to do it?" Michele pleaded. "Why not just leave it alone?"

"Because it won't leave me alone!" Jake replied forcefully. "Sorry, I don't mean to yell at you." He let out a long breath. "I mean, I think it's the only way to get done with it. I can't explain it, but I can *feel* it lying out there on the beach. It's like it's pullin' me or something. It's like it won't leave me alone until it tells me" he said.

Michele got up and walked over to Jake. She sat down on the edge of the bunk and asked, "Are you sure you want to do this?"

Jake breathed a short laugh. "I'm sure I *don't* want to do it," he said, "but I'm more sure I want it to be *over* with. I mean, I've been down the beach for a week, and I feel like I'm going crazy already. If you guys didn't believe me, I think I would have gone crazy. You said they want to tell me something, and I think you're right. I just want to find out what it is, that's all. I just want to find out and be done with it. I can't take a whole summer of this." Jake closed his eyes and rubbed his temples. "I just want to get it over with, and I want you guys to be there. I want to do it with you all there. Then if something happens, you can pull me away from it, maybe. I mean, if Dragon wasn't out in the water with me, I might have drowned today when I passed out." He opened his eyes and looked at them. "I want you guys there with me" he finished.

Michele took his hand and squeezed it. "Okay Jake, okay you're right. We'll be there with you," she said.

"Dinner's ready!" Kelly called from the deck. Michele bent over and gave Jake a quick hug, and then got up and wiped her eyes. They all got up and went out to the deck for supper, but already they were past that. Already they were thinking about the fire they'd have later, and the anchor lying on the beach.

Dinner was awesome, if fried flounder was your thing. There were french-fries and onion rings to go with it, and a salad for those who wanted to be a little more sensible, but Bill Malone wasn't on that list. By the time it was over, his cholesterol meter was reading full once again.

The great dessert contest came next, and by the time each of the ladies had put their contributions onto the table, there wasn't room to eat there. Brian exerted his power as host, and persuaded the other adults that thirst indeed was a dangerous thing, and he convinced them to have another drink with dessert.

Soon there seemed to be more conversations going than there were people present. The sun was getting low over the back bay, and the high clouds there were turning brilliant orange and purple. The bay was flat calm, and presented a mirror image of the painted sky, dissected by the thin dark line of the mainland in the distance. It looked as if a parallel world existed just below the surface of the serene waters of the bay.

The setting sun was the silent signal that it was time to get the fire ready. The kids told their parents they were going down to the front beach for a fire, and the parents barely acknowledged them, they were so immersed in laughter and conversation. It's not that they didn't care; it's just that they didn't worry. The kids were safe on the beach, they were safe at the fire. It had always been that way.

28

Shivers

The kids left their parents with Jenny's grandparents talking and laughing on the deck of the Edison cottage. They made their way down the path to the front beach, stooping to pick up stray bits of firewood as they went. There was a decent pile of scrap wood growing down near the fire-pit already, made up of contributions from whoever was working on their cottage, but picking up driftwood and scraps was just a habit for them. When they got to the beach they turned left and headed toward the tarp, giving the anchor laying near the dune a wide berth as they passed. Jake still shivered as he went by, and it wasn't because the night was cold.

Nicky got the shovel and cleaned out the hole for the fire. The wind-driven sand constantly worked to fill the hole, and each night throughout the summer the kids would work to un-fill it. It was customary to scrape the bits of coal and wood to the center at the end of each night and let the fire burn out. Some of the newer people who'd bought cottages on the beach would bury the fires, but they'd learn their mistake the following morning when they walked barefoot through the hot sand and discovered that the embers were still burning. Better to leave the hole open so all could see it, and mark it with a log or shovel or an old beach chair so that nobody stepped into it.

Nicky had the hole dug to his satisfaction and went about flicking the larger pieces of charcoal back into the pit with the tip of the shovel. Jake busied himself by building a little tee-pee of kindling and old newspaper, supporting a few larger pieces of wood. He didn't glance toward the anchor lying over by the dune; he decided to ignore it until the fire was blazing.

Stevie lit the little pile with a wooden stick match from the box they'd brought from the cottage. He added scraps of cardboard and blew on the embers until the tee-pee was blazing. They settled in a circle close to the edge of the fire-pit. With the sun fully set, there was a chill in the air down here on the beach that none of them had noticed up at the cottage, and Jake wasn't the only one that felt it.

Nicky laid a couple of pieces of pine trim on the fire to get some good flames going. Nobody said anything yet; they just stared into the hypnotic flames and let their minds wander. Usually they would all drift off on separate subconscious journeys, but tonight they were all thinking about the anchor lying just beyond the reach of the firelight. Jake continued to stare at the fire, but the others grew restless and began to glance at him and then at the spot where the anchor lay in the gathering darkness.

Nicky was the first to break the silence. "So, what do you want to do tonight?" he said, and then stared at Jake. Jake looked back at him and chuckled.

"Funny guy" Jake said to him.

Nicky looked back to the flames and asked, "What's the plan? How do you want to do this? And what do you want me to do?"

"I'm not sure this is a good idea" Michele worried.

"Yeah, I'm not sure it is either" Jenny agreed. Stevie just watched, turning his head like he was a judge at a tennis match.

"You got a better idea?" Nicky asked. "I didn't think so."

Jake threw a few more scraps on the fire and finally looked toward the anchor. The others followed his gaze. "I think this is the best way," he said. "I mean, I think I gotta get it over with." He looked away, and slid a little closer to the fire holding his hands out to feel the warmth. "I think the best thing is to just go do it. And Dragon, you can stay next to me."

"And do what?" Nicky asked again.

"Just watch me, I guess. Just make sure I'm okay, you know? If something happens, I mean if it looks like something bad is happening, then pull me away from it, okay?"

"That's it? That's your plan?" Michele asked angrily.

"That's all I got so far," Jake said, and he and Nicky began to laugh.

"It's not funny!" Jenny shouted. "Jeez, you act like it's a joke! Did you forget about the bruises on your arms? Did you.."

"No I didn't forget!" Jake cut her off. "How could I forget? That's why I gotta get it over with, see? I don't want to wait around for something else to happen. I don't want something to happen when I'm alone. I want to find out what this is about, and get it over with while you're all here with me" he said. "Now if you don't wanna be here, fine. But I'm gonna get this over with!"

"We want to be here," Michele said. "Of course we want to be here. And you're right, I think. I think you do have to find out what it's trying to tell you," she said. "It's just, it's just that it.."

"It's just that it sucks" Jenny finished for her. "It sucks, and we're worried, but Michele's right. We want to be here."

Jake nodded. "I know, I'm sorry. I don't mean to yell at you." He took a deep breath and let it out slowly. "I'll just go touch it and see what happens. Maybe nothing will, but if it does, just stay beside me" Jake said to Nicky. "And pull me away if it doesn't look okay. But don't pull me away for nothing. I want to have a chance to see. Only if it gets bad, okay?"

"No problem" Nicky said. "Whenever you're ready."

"And you guys keep the fire going good" he said to Stevie and the girls. They nodded, and Stevie threw on some more wood.

Jake got up, and Nicky rose with him. They walked slowly over to the anchor, and it grew colder with each step. When they were next to it, Jake sat down in the sand, and Nicky squatted down next to him.

The weak firelight showed that the seaweed had already started to dry on the rusting hulk. There were shells and dried mud stuck to it here and there, but the hermit crabs and eels and sea worms had abandoned it. The only movement they saw was just a trick of the flickering firelight. There was an odor growing on it now, though. It smelled like low tide, but even worse. It smelled more like that time when the blues were running hard, and they had driven all the baitfish right up onto the beach. The beach had been covered with porgies all along the waters edge, wrapped up in the seaweed that collected there. After a couple of days in the sun, the whole beach smelled like rotting fish. The anchor had started to smell like that. It smelled like death.

Jake reached out hesitantly, then drew his hand back and looked at his friend. "Watch me, but let me finish, okay?"

"I'm with you Jake" Nicky said.

Jake reached out again, and then grabbed the shaft of the anchor. It felt rough and slimy at the same time, and it was cold. Nothing happened. Jake looked toward Nicky, confused.

"Nothing hap.." Jake started, but he didn't finish.

Nicky watched as Jake's eyes rolled back in his head so that just the whites were showing. The firelight caught his face just right, and his eyes seemed to glow for a split second. Nicky started to lean back at first, but he caught himself and reached in and put his arm around Jake's shoulders as he started to sag toward the sand. Nicky was about to call out his friend's name, but Jake's eyes slid closed and he began breathing rhythmically as if he was in a deep sleep. Nicky held him there feeling slightly relieved, but still he felt himself begin to shake, a result of how shocked he'd been to see the glowing whites of his friend's eyes.

*

It was cold. Jake was disoriented, and the cold was the first sensation that helped to bring his senses back. He could feel the sting of sleet on his face as the scene around him began to take shape. He was on the deck of the brigantine. There was an eerie half-light, and he saw that the dome of the sky was a deep gray-white, and sleet was pummeling him from the direction of the lighthouse. Or the lighthouses, he thought. The outline of the land was as familiar to him as his own face, but the buildings silhouetted there were all wrong. He was looking at Gurnet point, that was for sure, but it was a place that didn't exist anymore. The 'lighthouses' were really just two large lanterns mounted on each end of a single building. Most of the other buildings Jake was used to were gone, and the land was a mix of wooded sections and what looked like pasture or farmland.

142

The ship was heaving up and down in the howling wind. Each time it would rear back, he could feel the whole deck shudder as the ship strained against the anchor line. Each time the anchor reined the vessel in and pulled the bow back down, the masts groaned like old rocking chairs as they bent against the change in momentum. Each time the bow came back down, there was a horrendous crash as the heaving seas drove the hull to a stop and forced it back upward.

There were just a few sailors on deck; one at the helm and a small group huddled at the bow, working to keep the anchor line secure. They were oblivious to Jake's presence. One sailor came limping down the ship's rail from the bow, checking each line of rigging as he went. He shuffled toward Jake, who stepped out of the sailor's path. The man looked right through him as if he wasn't there, and continued down the rail. The wind was growing, the light was fading, the temperature was dropping, and the sleet was turning to snow.

Suddenly there was a tremendous crash, and the bow was driven up and sideways violently. Jake desperately gripped the rail to keep his footing. The ship lurched sideways and accelerated, and Jake was nearly heaved over the side into the angry froth below.

"She's part'd!" a sailor called from the bow. "The anchor cable's let go!" The helmsman sounded a bosun's whistle as he wrestled with the wheel trying to get control of the floundering ship. Another huge crash, and the ship shuddered and rolled dangerously to starboard, the yardarm of the foremast dipping into the frothy brine. Jake slid across the pitched deck and grabbed onto a rope that held a dory tied to the deck. Slowly the ship stopped rolling, and began to lean back upright. Jake felt like a mouse riding a giant clock's pendulum.

Seconds later a throng of sailors flooded out of a hatch and onto the deck, like ants abandoning a flooded anthill. There was a flurry of activity as orders were shouted, and sails were unfurled and made fast. The roaring wind caught the sails and turned the ship violently again, so that the vessel was headed away from the lighthouse and toward Plymouth Harbor. It

143

began to race along, despite the limited amount of canvas the crew had set.

"Come about!" a panicked voice shouted. "Come about or we'll be grounded, sure!" The helmsman fought the wheel and the ship tried to turn into the wind, but the force of it prevented the full maneuver. A quarter of the way through, the force of the wind coupled with the crash of another angry wave rolled the ship again, threatening to capsize it. The only choice was to turn back, trying to counter the roll. The ship pulled itself erect once more, and with seawater raining down from the sails, it began to race toward the harbor once again.

The ship raced past the end of the beach now, and entered the gap between the head of the northern peninsula and the end of the long beach that reached up from the south, the two peninsulas forming the sheltered harbor. Unfortunately, the channel didn't run straight into the harbor. At a point just past the gap (where Bug light now sat, Jake thought) the channel split and turned behind the two peninsulas. The helmsman tried to make the turn at the split, but once again the wind and waves contrived to force the ship to roll and continue straight ahead. The ship was driven onto the flat with a tremendous jarring groan, and it ground to a halt floundering on its starboard side.

One again, there was chaos on deck. Orders were shouted, frightened men were running every which way. Jake was suddenly shocked to see that some of the 'men' were really boys, some as young as he was.

The ship was being pounded, and it was lying on its side on the submerged shoal, the starboard side underwater. A number of the crew had already fallen or been washed overboard, and the others were working frantically, sawing at the bases of the masts. With a splintering snap, one mast finally let go and was torn away from the vessel by the angry waves. The second mast also broke free, and as it was swallowed by the sea, lines of rigging wrapped a terrified seaman like the tentacles of a giant octopus, and he was dragged to his death in the foamy sea.

The ship partially righted itself now, but the pounding of the waves continued. The crew scrambled back to the hatch, and the

first few of them went below decks. The others that tried to
follow were pushed back out of the hatchway, as the men who
had just gone below came scrambling back out to the deck.
"She's stove in!" one of them shouted. "We're aground and
stove in! God help us!"

Another huge wave crashed into the crippled ship, and Jake
closed his eyes as the foam washed over the rail, soaking him.
The slushy brine rolled across the deck of the crippled ship,
carrying men and boys over the starboard side rail, screaming
and calling out for help as they went to their sudden deaths.
They never knew that they were the lucky ones.

Jake squeezed his eyes shut and braced himself for the impact
of the next wave. He was colder than he ever thought possible.
His wet clothes were already beginning to stiffen as they froze.
His fingers and toes were so cold they felt like they were on
fire, and that made no sense to Jake. He stiffened every muscle
in his body for the impact of the wave, and his ears were filled
with the sounds of the storm, the angry surf, and the anguished
cries and sobs of men and boys.

*

Suddenly there was silence. Silence and utter, desolate cold.
Jake opened his eyes, and looked at the ghastly scene that
surrounded him. The ship was covered in snow, and it was full
daylight again. The ocean had reverted to a pacified state, the
energy of the storm absorbed once again. There were ice floes
and a slushy mix covering the ocean, rising and falling on the
undulating swells that rolled under the surface in a rhythm like
the breathing of a sleeping giant.

Jake was still clutching the rope. He tried to let go, but he
couldn't move his hands. They were frozen in place. He tried to
move his arms, his legs, anything. His whole body was as rigid
as a cement statue. His eyes were all that remained to take the
frantic orders that his brain was still trying to issue. His eyes
and his brain, and nothing else left. An internal mutiny. A
consciousness trapped in a statue perpetually frozen, never to
run the rocks again, never to cast a fishing line or glide on the
waters edge on his skim board on a warm summer day. The

wave of despair slammed into his soul like a physical thing. He moved his eyes back and forth frantically, searching for redemption, looking for the way out that had never eluded him so completely before. The next stop would be madness, he knew. He fought off the panic, he willed himself to close his eyes and focus.

When he opened his eyes again he was able to look at his surroundings. The deck was a giant ice sculpture. As he stared, familiar forms began to take shape, human forms. They were frozen in place, frozen as they had died. They were huddled and sprawled everywhere, some holding to the ropes and structures, others with hands folded in eternal conversation with their maker.

There were others here now, from a different world. They weren't covered in ice and they were moving about the deck in dry clothes, their breaths visible in the icy sunlight. They were from the land of the living. They were walking among the frozen forms, and they were prying them free from their places on deck. They were shaking them and prodding them, looking for signs of life. When the signs weren't there, they would drag the statues to the rail, and then heave them overboard.

Others from the land of the living waited below in small boats. They worked methodically with oars and long poles, pushing the frozen souls through the slushy ocean like logs in a river. Others waited on a larger vessel at the edge of the channel. They used boat hooks to catch the grotesque statues and haul them onboard.

Jake noticed a glint of color in the white sculpture closest to him. He looked toward it and saw the green eyes. They were barely two feet away, and they were staring at Jake. It was him, the green-eyed sailor, frozen two feet away, staring into Jake's trapped blue eyes.

The green eyes seemed to bore into Jake's soul. There was no way Jake could look away, and the peripheral scene faded until only the green eyes remained in a glare of white. Then Jake felt the man speak. He *felt* it in his mind, he didn't hear it. The green-eyed sailor spoke inside Jake's head. "I thought the Arnold was to be our redemption, and it may yet be," he said. Then the green eyes went white. They turned into icy orbs in the man's frozen face. Jake's eyes focused on the larger scene again as two men from the land of the living lumbered up to the frozen sailor whose eyes were once green, but now were ice. They grabbed him by the arms, and with a mighty heave tossed him over the rail into the ocean below.

Then they turned toward Jake. As they took a step toward him, he closed his eyes and began to cry in his mind, because that's all that he could do now. He felt them grab his arms. He tried to cry out, but the scream only echoed in his head. He felt them pull, yet he didn't move. He screamed again silently. He felt them claw at his hands, still frozen on the rope, and his fingers started to loosen. He cried again, and the next pull tore him free from the rope. Then he heard his own voice screaming "Noooooooo!" as they pulled him toward the rail to toss him into the frozen sea...

*

Jake landed in the sand. His tormentors still had his arms, and he lashed out at them, trying to free himself from their clutches. And this time his body responded. He'd broken free from the icy prison, and he was flailing at his captors screaming "Noooo! Get away from me!" He opened his eyes and it was dark again, and the shadowed forms around him were still holding him. They were silhouetted by the firelight, and they were talking to him.

"Jake! Jake, it's okay!" Nicky's voice broke through to Jake's mind. "You're okay! We got you!" he said.

"We're right here Jake, you're okay!" Michele pleaded.

Jake's vision cleared and he saw his friends gathered there, holding him. The flames from the fire danced in the background. He was back. He was on the beach, and he was back with his friends. He relaxed then, and slumped back against Michele and began to shake uncontrollably.

147

"It's okay Jake, it's okay" she said, and there were tears in her eyes. Nicky, Stevie and Jenny looked on with shock and concern etched on their faces.

"He's freezing" Michele told them, and she pulled her sweatshirt closer around him. "He's freezing, Nicky. You almost killed him!" she spat.

Nicky shrugged his shoulders and held his palms out. "Hey, he told me to let him finish" he said.

Stevie reasoned, "Well, at least you can't see his breath anymore." Michele answered this little consolation with a sharp whack to Stevie's shoulder. "Jeez! I didn't do it! Hit Dragon!" he whined. Nicky shrugged again, but leaned back out of her reach as he did so.

Michele glared at Nicky, then looked down at Jake. "Are you okay?" she asked.

Jake nodded a little between shivers. "I'm so cold" he said.

"Get closer to the fire," she said, and she started to pull him up. Nicky reached in to help, and Michele smacked him hard.

"Jesus!" Nicky yelped as he pulled back out of range.

Michele helped Jake over to the edge of the fire hole and sat him down. She wrapped her sweatshirt around his shoulders again and put her arm around him. Jake sat for a long time, shivering. Jenny sat on the other side of Jake and started rubbing his back to warm him. Nicky and Stevie took up safe positions across the fire, even though they were sitting in the smoke from the little blaze.

After a long time, Jake's shaking began to subside. Finally Michele asked him, "What happened? What did you see?"

Jake stared into the dancing flames, grateful for the warmth. He thought of what he'd seen, and shivered violently again. Michele held him closer. Jenny rubbed his back and said "Tell us when you're ready, Jake."

Jake stretched his palms out toward the flames. He looked toward the lighthouse just as the beam flashed by, just as it had every night since the night that Rose had disappeared a half-century ago. He looked up toward the Big Dipper hovering in the night sky over the tarp, and from there his gaze drifted up to

148

the North Star. Jake let his eyes relax and look beyond, out into space, and then finally back inward, into the nightmare from which he'd just escaped.

"I saw the shipwreck" he began. "It got wrecked in a blizzard, and everyone froze." He looked back down, and the flames reflected in his eyes as he said, "I froze too", and he shivered.

Michele and Jenny leaned closer, trying to give him warmth. "I saw the green-eyed sailor. He froze too. He froze like a statue in the blizzard right there on the deck of the ship next to me," Jake said.

The fire popped and crackled as they waited for Jake to continue. Jenny spoke first. "Did he say anything? I mean, did he tell you what he wants?" she asked.

"I'm not sure," Jake answered hesitantly. "He said something, but he didn't really *say* it. It was more like I heard him in my head, but he was already frozen and his lips didn't move.." Jake tried to explain, and then he glanced at their faces to see if they were ready to lock him in the loony bin yet. They weren't. They were believers, all of them. They'd seen him start shivering as he held the anchor. They'd seen him squirm and whimper after that, while the screams were ringing inside of Jake's trapped mind, but they didn't know why. And the clincher was, they'd seen his breath. They'd seen the icy clouds of his breath as he exhaled, and that was something a crazy person couldn't fake. No sir, you couldn't fake that on a summer night. If Jake was crazy, then they were too.

When they'd seen his breath, that was when Michele and Jenny told Nicky to pull him free from the anchor. Nicky said no, just a little while longer. Nicky reminded them that they all heard Jake say to let him finish. Nicky said that if Jake didn't finish, then he either wouldn't find out what he needed to, or that he would have to do it again. They didn't want that did they? Did they? While Michele and Jenny struggled to find the answer to Nicky's question, that was when Jake had felt what the green eyed sailor had to say.

"What did he say?" Nicky asked from the smoky side of the fire.

149

"He said 'I thought the Arnold was to be our redemption, and it may yet be.' That's what he said" Jake answered through the smoke.

"Ahhh, I see" Nicky said with a knowing look. Then he assumed an expression of deadpan confusion. "What the hell does that mean?" he asked, and he laughed.

Jake returned Nicky's perplexed look. "How the hell do I know?" he said, and he began to laugh too. Nicky laughed even harder, and it was infectious. Jake began to laugh harder with him, letting out all the emotion that was still bottled up inside him, whistling past the graveyard, as his dad probably would have said.

"What the hell is wrong with you?" Michele screamed at Nicky. He couldn't answer her, he was laughing too hard. Oh, he wanted to stop laughing, he really did. The look on Michele's face should have been enough to scare him into silence. But he felt like he had farted in church and had gotten the giggles, the kind that wouldn't stop no matter how much you wanted them to, no matter how much you didn't want to draw attention to yourself. It was hopeless. Nicky and Jake were laughing so hard they could hardly breathe, Jake from sheer emotional release, and Nicky just because he shouldn't.

Michele and Jenny glared at Nicky, and Stevie moved a little farther away from him and kept his head down just in case. Stevie didn't get it, but he had a feeling Dragon was going to.

Finally, they got it under control, and Nicky and Jake managed to stifle their giggles. Then Nicky asked, "And what the hell is an Arnold?" and it started all over again. Nicky rolled on his back laughing and pounding his hand in the sand, and Jake cackled until his eyes started to water.

The darts from Michele's eyes had no effect. She had to wait them out. She looked at Jenny, and they both shook their heads, as grown women will do when they know that they're surrounded by the hopeless.

The laughter finally died down, but it took a good while. Stevie just watched, waiting for the next shoe, but it never did

150

fall. Soon the only sound was the crackling of the fire and the never-ending sound of the waves on the shore.

Jake grew somber again. It had felt really good to let it out like that, but the time to laugh had past. Jake knew they wanted answers, but so did he, and he didn't have them. He owed them something, though. He owed them because they had pulled him back, before he could get thrown into the icy waters of that other world. He tried to pay as best he could.

"I don't know what it means," he said. "All I know is what I told you. I guess I still gotta figure it out" he said. He glanced at the anchor lying in the sand. He didn't feel it anymore. It didn't pull him like it had before. Whatever he still had to figure out, he didn't think the anchor was going to help him with it anymore. He thought it looked like just an old anchor now, and that was something of a relief.

29
Traps

Sunday morning dawned bright and clear. Bailey stood up on the bunk in the shed and stretched her front paws all the way out while she let out a yawn, and then she stood up straight and sneezed. She looked down at Jake who was still all tangled up in the covers. She cocked one ear and started her wiggler going, staring down at him, waiting.

Jake had slept fitfully last night. He couldn't recall his dreams, which was probably a good thing. He opened one eye just a crack against the sunlight that was streaming in through the window of the shed. He saw Bailey's face hovering over his, and he shut his eye and mumbled "You're breath stinks." Whether it was the remark, or the fact that Jake looked to be ignoring her, Bailey took offense and gave Jake a poke in the ribs with her paw. "Ow!" Jake groaned, and he sat up in the bunk. Bailey started licking his face, apparently pleased that he'd gotten the message.

Jake checked the tide table and saw that it was low at 10:30 that morning. That was good. He knew they had to get rid of the flounder frames from the fish they'd caught yesterday, and they'd be putting in the lobster pots this morning. With a low tide, Jake would be able to see the bottom well enough to drop the pots in the sandy spots, but near the big rocks where he knew the lobsters hid. The anticipation of getting the lobster pots set pushed the events of the night before out of Jake's mind for now.

Jake stumbled out of the shed and stretched, while Bailey walked a little off to the side and relieved herself. "Feel better now?" Jake asked. Bailey came out of the squat and wiggled her stub of a tail so hard that her whole back end fishtailed as she came back to Jake for a scratch behind the ears. "I guess so" he said, and the two of them shuffled up to the deck.

Brian and Kelly Edison were sitting at the table having coffee when Jake came into the cottage. "Good morning" they said in unison.

"Mornin'" Jake responded. He went to the cabinet and got the cereal. He filled his bowl, splashed in some milk, sat down and dug in. Bailey went to her food dish and started her breakfast.

"How'd you sleep?" Kelly asked.

"Good" Jake lied. "We doin' pots today?" he asked his father around a mouthful of cereal.

"That's my plan, if you can give me a hand" Brian said.

Jake swallowed and said, "Yeah, I can help. I planned on it. Besides, Stevie went with his parents to pick up his sister – she was up in New Hampshire with her friend this week and she's coming back today. Nicky's dad is coming down today, and he figures he'll have chores to do all day. It'll be boring on the beach, so it's a good day for it."

"Good," Brian said, "we'll load the truck when you're done eating." He paused, and then added, "Then you can help me put up the screen house when we get back. The midges are going to get bad soon." The midges were sand fleas, and they could be pretty annoying at sunset when the weather turned humid.

"No problem" Jake replied. He ate his breakfast in silence while staring at the cereal box trying to find the path that the leprechaun needed to follow to get to the pot of gold. When he finished, he put his bowl in the sink and said, "All set."

Brian got up, kissed Kelly and said "We'll see you in a couple of hours."

"Okay, you boys have fun. Get me some lobsters" Kelly instructed as they went out the door. Bailey raced out behind them, not sure where they were going, but positive that she wanted to go too.

Brian and Jake went out behind the cottage to the pile of lobster pots that were stacked there. "How many do you want to bring?" Jake asked.

"A half dozen, I guess. We have enough fish for six pots." They loaded the wire mesh pots into the bed of the pickup truck. Jake got the bucket of flounder frames from the foot of the stairs and looked into the bucket. Brian had covered the bait with sand to keep it fresh, but the flies were still gathering around the fish tails that poked out of the sand. They buzzed angrily as Jake set the bucket into the back of the truck. Brian cut a handful of fresh bait bags from the spool of yellow plastic mesh stored under the deck. He tied a knot in the end of each bag and threw them in the bait bucket. "I guess we're good" Brian said, and the three of them got into the truck.

They drove down the cutoff and onto the beach. Brian pulled down to the water's edge and they unloaded their gear. Then he pulled the truck up to the tide pool and tied the anchor line of the dingy to the trailer hitch, and dragged the little boat down to the receding water.

Jake helped Brian get the dingy the last few feet into the water, and Brian said "Pull the truck up to the dune while I go get the boat."

"Okay" Jake replied, masking his enthusiasm. Jake loved to drive. It was one of the benefits of coming to the beach with his father in the off-season when nobody was around. Jake had been a competent driver (on the beach, at least) for over a year.

Jake drove the truck up to the dune and parked next to the anchor lying there. He got out and looked at it. The anchor didn't seem to have any pull now, but Jake remembered the mojo that it had last night. It seemed like a dream now with the sun beating down on him, but he knew it wasn't. Then Jake heard the engine start on the big boat, and he turned back toward the water and the day ahead.

Brian beached the boat and Bailey immediately jumped in and took up her position as hood ornament, panting in anticipation. Jake and Brian loaded the gear, turned the bow out and pushed off through the gentle waves. Brian hopped in first and trimmed the engine back down when they had enough water. Jake climbed in and put on his life jacket as Brian started the engine and pointed the boat toward the rocks down near the Head.

"Might as well get 'em baited" Brian said with his 'I'm-talking-to-you-baitboy' smile. Jake smiled back, and then trudged forward to the bait bucket with his arms hanging and his jaw drooping, trying to look like life was so unfair. He reached into the bucket and pulled out a bait bag, then reached in for a handful of fish guts. "Hold on! Bring it to the stern,

154

boy! I don't want to smell that crap!" Brian called, the grin on his face even bigger.

Jake dragged the bucket to the back of the boat and began filling the bags with fish guts. This was the only part of lobstering that he didn't like, but the rest of the experience was worth it. The ideal situation was when Stevie came with them, because the rule was that the youngest guy in the boat was the baitboy. Still, this wasn't bad because the bait wasn't even a full day old, and it had been cool overnight. It didn't smell at all. There had been times when other fishermen from the beach had given bait to Brian for his pots that had sat in the sun for a couple of days. It had been a week before Jake could get the smell off his hands.

Jake had six bags loaded to the top with flounder frames and skate, and he was sifting for the last of the skins when he found two more small fish in the sand at the bottom of the bucket. "There's still a couple of perch here," he said.

"They were hiding under the flounder in the bucket yesterday. You can put them in the bags" Brian said.

"Can I keep them for the seal?" Jake asked.

"Yeah, that's fine, we have plenty of bait" Brian responded.

Jake dumped the sand out of the bucket and rinsed it over the side, careful not to catch too much water and lose the bucket behind the slow moving boat. He kept a few inches of fresh seawater in the bucket and threw the perch back in. Then he proceeded to hang one bait bag in each of the lobster pots, and close and secure the tops with the bungee cords.

As they neared the rocks, Brian slowed even further while Jake got the first buoy line coiled and the pot ready to drop. Jake looked over the side and saw large boulders covered with seaweed and kelp gently waving in the current. There were sandy patches between the boulders, and Jake saw a few crabs scurrying sideways along the bottom as they cruised past.

"Whenever you're ready" Brian called.

Jake lifted the first pot and picked his spot. He tossed the pot out from the boat level, so that it landed flat on the surface and sank slowly, bottom side down, through the ten feet of water to the ocean floor. Jake played the line out and tossed the buoy away from the boat so it wouldn't get caught in the propeller as they past. He picked up the next pot and repeated the procedure. After the third pot, he asked "Do you want to do them all in a row, or do you want to put the others a little deeper?"

"Let's try a little deeper" Brian agreed, bringing the boat around to port. He'd learned to pay attention to Jake's hunches. They made another line of three pots parallel to the first, but about forty feet farther out. As Brian headed back toward the beach, Jake sat down on the bow and looked back at the rows of buoys bobbing in the water in two neat little lines, brimming with potential. Then he looked past them, toward the Bug where the channel split, and the flat beyond in the harbor where he'd almost frozen to death the night before. He shivered and pushed the thought away.

Jake turned around and sat on the cooler that was mounted like a bench just in front of the center console, behind which his father stood at the wheel. Bailey was still on the bow, wagging away and turning her head from side to side, the constant lookout. Beyond her, at the other end of the sandy strip, Jake could see the Gurnet with its familiar outline, and the lighthouse sitting on top. He thought of how different it had looked yesterday.

"Dad, was there ever a farm at the Gurnet?" he asked.

"That's how it started out" Brian replied. "Way back, there were cattle and farms on the Gurnet, and up on the Head, too. In fact, the first lighthouse keeper was a farmer who the government bought the land from. That was back in the seventeen hundreds. After that, during the Revolutionary War and the War of Eighteen Twelve, there were soldiers there and up at Fort Standish on the Head, and they raised cattle and crops to eat" he explained. Brian didn't wonder why Jake was asking; he knew his son was curious about everything pertaining to the beach.

They were in front of the tarp now, and Brian pointed the boat toward shore. "I'll just drop you off and put it on the mooring" he said. Jake took off his life jacket, grabbed the bucket with the

156

perch, and kneeled on the bow next to Bailey. He knew she preferred to be let off on shore and wasn't fond of swimming, like most boxers. Their chests were too big, and they tended to flip up backwards in the deeper water.

When they were in three feet of water and Brian put the boat in reverse, Jake gave Bailey an unceremonious shove and jumped off next to her. They waded to shore as Brian backed out and turned toward the mooring. When they got to the sand, Bailey stood next to Jake and shook, making sure he got good and wet. Then she snorted and walked up toward the dunes without a backward glance.

"That's the thanks I get? You didn't have to come!" he called after her. He followed her up toward the tarp. He saw Jenny and Michele sitting on the wooden spool there as he approached.

"Whatcha got in the bucket?" Michele called out.

"A couple of perch. I thought I might feed the seal later" he said.

"Later when?" Jenny asked.

"I was thinking this afternoon. It's gonna be warm, and I thought I'd take the boat to the creek. You wanna go?" he asked.

"Yes" they both answered, in that tone of voice that said the question couldn't be dumber.

"Well, if you start being nice to me, maybe I'll take you" Jake parried.

"We're always nice to you!" Michele protested.

"Yeah, and you shouldn't be so picky. We're all the friends you got today!" Jenny said.

"Yeah, that's true, I guess you can come. But we gotta wait 'til there's enough water in the bay. We'll go later – besides, I have to help my dad first" Jake told them.

"Sounds good" Jenny said.

Brian walked up behind Jake. "Good morning ladies" he said.

"Good morning" Michele replied.

"Hi Mister E." Jenny said.

"Is this smelly lobsterman bothering you?" Brian asked, ruffling Jake's hair.

157

"Just a little" Michele responded, and stuck her tongue out at Jake.

"Well, I'll take care of that. You ready to tackle the screen house?" Brian asked.

"Yeah, I'm ready. See you later" Jake said to the girls.

"See ya" Michele said.

Jake and Brian got into the truck and drove up to the house. Bailey was already up on the deck, lying in the sun. She started wiggling when Jake walked up, unable to hold a grudge.

30
The Creek

Jake and Brian were just finishing putting up the screen house on the deck of the cottage. There was a side door to the cottage that led to the deck that overlooked the back bay, and that door now led directly into the screen house. It was like adding an extra room to the cottage for the warm weather. You could sit in there and have supper while watching the sunset over the bay, and the midges couldn't get at you.

Jenny and Michele showed up as Jake and his father were picking up the tools. "Are you almost ready to go, Jake?" Michele asked.

"Yeah, we just finished" Jake said turning to face them. "We're only going for a couple of hours you know," he said, looking at all the gear that the girls were carrying. They each had beach bags and towels, and they were carrying plastic shopping bags. "What did you do – stop at the grocery store on the way over?" he asked.

"No, we brought sandwiches, snacks and drinks. But you don't have to have any if you don't want" Michele replied with what she hoped was complete indifference.

Brian chuckled and offered, "A lady is always prepared, Jake. Better get used to it."

Jake shook his head in resignation. "We're gonna need a bigger boat" he mumbled, like Chief Brody in *Jaws* when *he* first saw the beast.

They started down the stairs, and Brian told them out of habit to wear their life jackets. He knew he didn't really have to remind Jake.

Jake grabbed the bait bag he'd put the two perch into, and started across the marsh followed by the two Sherpas, with Bailey bringing up the rear. Brian watched them go, a little wistfully.

They got to the point in the marsh where the little boat nestled in the high grass. Jake put the plug in, picked up the anchor and placed it in the bow, and grabbed hold ready to pull it to the channel. He looked up at the two well-prepared ladies, who were just standing there like they were waiting for their limo to arrive. "It ain't gonna carry itself!" he barked.

That startled them into action. They put their gear into the little boat and grabbed the handles on either side of the transom. By the time they got to the channel, Jake felt like he had dragged the boat as well as both of them. He was about to comment, but Bailey ran up and jumped into the boat. She took up her position in the bow and looked expectantly at Jake, panting and ready to go. Jake just shook his head.

"You two might as well get in too," he said to the girls, handing them their life jackets and putting his on. The girls got in and sat on the forward bench facing the rear of the boat. Jake pushed the little boat into deeper water and it was immediately swept up in the current of the incoming tide. He hopped over the transom and dropped and primed the engine in one practiced motion. It started on the first pull. Jake pointed the bow down the middle of the channel and gave it some gas. The boat seemed to move right along with the extra help of the current.

The girls had been worried about Jake since last night's events at the fire. They had been talking about it as they sat under the tarp that morning while Jake was out in the boat with his father. Now that they finally had him alone, Michele couldn't wait any longer.

"How did you sleep last night?" she asked him.

"Good" he said, automatically. Michele was looking at him hard, trying to read his face, and Jake considered her question again. It wasn't just small talk, he realized. "Well, maybe not so good. But not bad.."

"Did you have any dreams?" she asked, getting right to the point.

Jake thought before answering this time. "I don't know, but if I did, I don't remember them. I remember thinking about it this morning, but I couldn't remember any dreams" he said, satisfied it was the truth.

Michele's face relaxed and she sat back on the seat a little. "That's good, I guess," she said. "I was worried about you" she added, and looked down at the bottom of the boat.

Jake felt a little ripple in his stomach as he sat there considering what she'd said. It wasn't so much what she said, but more the way she said it. In a weird way, it made him feel really good that she was so worried about him. Really good. The best he felt all day, actually. They cruised along in silence, feeling the warm sun and listening to the sounds of the water splashing and the gulls calling, and everything seemed just right.

Suddenly Bailey stiffened in the front of the boat, and Jake felt it. He saw that the hair was standing up on her back and she was staring at the island on the port side. Jake turned that way, and the girls followed his gaze.

"Is that a coyote?" Jenny exclaimed.

Jake nodded. The coyote sat at the edge of the bushes just as it had the first time Jake had seen it. And like the first time, it seemed to be staring right into Jake's eyes. Jake stared back, and he let off on the throttle unconsciously. The boat slowed and cruised along at headway speed as they stared at each other. Jake felt a strange calm come over him. He didn't feel any malice in the coyote's stare. His eyes weren't wild looking, he wasn't panting, or glancing back and forth furtively like the coyotes that Jake was used to seeing in the wintertime. If anything, the animal seemed placid and serene. He just sat there stoically, looking at Jake as if he'd been expecting him as much as the rising moon. The way he sat there regally, it reminded Jake of King Moonraker on the Island of Misfit Toys.

Bailey began to growl, and the coyote shifted his gaze to her, then stood up slowly and turned and walked back into the bushes.

"Wow, that was cool!" Michele exclaimed. "I never saw a coyote before, did you?"

"I've seen them in the winter, and I saw *him* a couple of days ago with Stevie" Jake answered.

"You didn't tell us!" Jenny complained.

161

"You weren't down yet," Jake answered. Bailey settled back down as they cleared the end of the island, and Jake sped the boat back up to cruising speed.

"What do you think he eats?" Jenny wondered.

"Girls" Jake replied without missing a beat.

"Jerk" Jenny shot back, and they all laughed. The girls shifted their attention to the beach sliding past them on the starboard side, while Jake began scanning the surface for signs of fish or diving birds. A lot of good it would do him with no rod in the boat, he thought.

A few minutes later they reached the mouth of the creek. The creek followed a winding route into the salt marsh nestled in the corner of the backward 'L' shape of the peninsula. It started out about twenty feet wide, but got narrower as it got closer to the back side of the hill that the lighthouse sat upon. The creek eventually turned into nothing more than a muddy ditch that disappeared in the marsh at the base of the hill.

There was enough water in the creek now so that Jake could maneuver the boat halfway across the marsh. When the water got too shallow Jake killed the engine and pulled it up, letting the boat glide until in ran aground in the mud. The sides of the inlet were roughly four feet high, and they were made of black mud topped with tall green marsh grass. From where they now sat in the boat, all they could see was the blue dome of the sky separated from the black mud by a line of green.

Jake took off his life jacket and stepped out of the boat. He sank down into the mud up to his ankles. Jenny looked at his feet, and summed up her feelings on the situation quite succinctly. "Ewww" she said and grimaced.

Jake smiled and said, "You can sit in the boat until tide comes all the way in if you want, but I'm going to feed the seal. He reached into the bow for the anchor, then trudged over to the side and stuck the anchor into the grass. Bailey jumped out of the boat and walked uncertainly over to Jake. He hoisted her up from the mud and set her onto the marsh grass. Bailey stood there for a moment, looking like she was wearing boots with the mud half way up her white legs. Then something caught her eye and she shot off across the marsh in hot pursuit.

Jake slogged back and grabbed the bait bag. His feet made sucking sounds with every step. "You comin'?" he asked. Reluctantly, Michele got up and stepped tentatively out of the boat, holding Jake's hand for balance.

"This is so gross" she complained as she started toward the bank. Jake steadied her as she trudged to the muddy grass-topped wall.

Jake cradled his hands together and said, "Come on, I'll give you ten-fingers. Michele grabbed hold of the marsh grass, put one foot into Jake's cupped hands and he lifted her up so she could step onto the top of the bank. He boosted Jenny up, and then climbed up beside them. They walked across the stiff marsh grass without too much discomfort – they'd been shoeless for a few days now. Bailey was nowhere to be seen, most likely having gone up toward the lighthouse looking for rabbits.

They left the marsh and walked over the dune to the front beach. They turned left and started across the rocks at the base of Gurnet Point. When they got to the point, the little seal saw them and sat up expectantly. He hopped toward them with hardly a limp. Jake took the two perch out of the bait bag and tossed them to the little seal, who gobbled them hungrily. The seal barked once, looking for more.

"That's all we have" Michele said to him. Jake pointed toward the water, where momma seal was poking her head up watching them. He motioned with his head that they should go. They turned and walked back the way they'd come. "He looks way better," Michele said.

"Yeah, he's gonna be fine" Jake agreed. "As soon as he's ready, they'll probably leave. It's getting pretty late for them to be here."

"I'm gonna miss them" Jenny said. "They're so cool."

"Do you want to go up to the lighthouse?" Michele asked.

"Sure" Jake said, "We'll see what Bailey's up to."

They walked back to where the Gurnet sloped down to meet the beach, crossed over the small dune and followed the road up to the lighthouse. When they got to the top, they saw Bailey race out of the bushes, trot along for a few steps with her ears at attention, and then crash back into the brush at the edge of the field. They walked across the grass and up the steps to the base of the lighthouse. They walked around the octagonal foundation, looking up at the structure, and then turned to take in the panoramic view of the beach. The sandy strip looked so fragile from up here, like a good wave could wash it all away and leave the Gurnet and the Head as two little islands looking across the bay at each other.

Jake knew the stories of how that very thing had come close to happening in the Blizzard of '78, and again during the No-name storm of '91. He'd heard his dad and Walter talk about those storms hundreds of times, and he'd seen 'The Perfect Storm', which was what the movie people named what the locals remembered as the No-name storm.

He hoped that it never happened. He didn't know what he'd do without the beach, and even worse, without his beach friends.

They sat down on the top step in the sunshine, and Jake let his thoughts turn inward. He looked toward the old foundation on the opposite hill, but there was no rose, no clue. There was no feeling at all. He had hoped he might see or feel something when he was up here. He hoped maybe he'd find out something about the anchor and the shipwreck in the blizzard, and old green eyes, as Jake had come to think of the frozen sailor. But if the lighthouse knew anything, it was keeping its secrets. It had already told Jake what had happened to Rose, and a lot of good that did. It wasn't like he could walk up to Nate Withers and say 'Excuse me, but I thought you might like to know what happened to your wife.' Nope, he couldn't do that, and so knowing what happened was a burden, not a relief. He wished he could just force another vision, but he didn't think that was possible. It seemed like the old anchor had run out of power too. He didn't feel anything from it anymore. Thinking about these dead ends just made him frustrated. He tried to push the images out of his head, and the more he pushed, the more he thought of them. The scenes started coming rapid fire, like glimpses of the kings and queens when you flicked the end of a deck of cards. He saw Rose, the wreck of the fishing boat, the brigantine, green eyes, Rose, the fishing boat, faster and faster. Then another scene burst into his mind. It was Nicky flailing in the riptide, and then he heard his father's voice saying, 'Don't fight it. You can't beat it. Go with it.'

His anguish must have been showing on his face, because just then Michele touched his arm and asked, "Jake, what's wrong?"

He looked at her, sitting there in the sunshine on the lighthouse steps, her long dark hair waving in the gentle breeze, and his mind cleared. "I was just thinking" he said. "I was wishing I could figure things out, and I was kind of hoping that coming back up here might help me find some answers."

He paused, and Michele waited for him to go on. "I just want to get some answers," he continued. "I mean, what good is it to see this stuff if I can only talk to you guys about it. If I said anything to Nate Withers, he'd think I'm crazy. And I don't even know what the shipwreck in the blizzard is all about. And if I figure that out, what good will it do. I mean, whatever the answers are, I can't say anything. The answers don't do any good." He fell silent. Michele didn't respond, but she took his hand in hers.

Jenny spoke up then. "Well I got some answers" she said.

Jake looked at her, startled. "Did you see something? Do you know about the shipwreck?" he asked, excitement rising in his voice.

"No," Jenny said, "and I don't care about the shipwreck. That's not my question" she said, and looked down at her feet. Jake and Michele exchanged a bewildered look. Then Jenny looked up and there were tears showing in the corners of her eyes. "Don't you see, Jake? It's *real*! What you're seeing is real. Other people might think you're crazy, but we *know* it's real. We saw the bruises on your arms after you flew. We saw your breath when you were in the blizzard. It's real!"

Jenny wiped her tears, and then looked at Jake. "All my life I've wondered if anything happens after...you know...after you die. I've wondered if you go on. My dad died before I was even born! I never even met him. I always wondered what he'd be like, what his voice sounded like, what he smelled like." Jenny sniffed, then took a deep breath and let it out slowly. "I always wondered if I'd ever find out. And sometimes, when I didn't think I would, when I didn't think there was anything...you know, after.." and she began to cry.

Michele slid next to her and wrapped her in a hug. "It's okay, Jenny" she said.

Jenny got herself together and continued. "But don't you see? It's real! You saw a woman that died years ago! You saw sailors that died who knows how long ago. And one of them talked to you! You heard him. He was real! That means we *do* go on, that means *my dad* went on, don't you *see*? Someday I'll get to *meet* him!"

And they did see. They hadn't thought of this aspect, because they'd never felt the pain that Jenny had lived with. They'd never asked the questions. Jenny had always asked the questions, and now she had her answers. "It's real!" Jenny shouted, and laughed.

"Jeez, Jen, I never thought of that" Jake said.

"I know!" Jenny said, and laughed again, tears leaking at the corners of her eyes, but happy tears now. "I know, Jake, but I did, and I got my answer. So even if you don't get yours, I got mine. And thanks" she said and leaned over to hug him.

Jake felt relief, he felt some of Jenny's joy, and he felt a calmness. He wasn't so frustrated anymore. He could wait. He thought he could never find out about the shipwreck, and still be okay now. They'd had an answer the whole time, he realized, but only Jenny had agonized over the question. "You're welcome," he said, "glad I could help" and they all laughed.

"Well, nothing's going on up here, you wanna go to the creek?" Jake asked. "Bailey!" he shouted, and then whistled. There was a rustling in the bushes and Bailey came running out, ears perked up, and stood still with one front paw raised and a question on her face. "Let's go swimming" Jake said, and started down the steps of the lighthouse.

*

They arrived back at the creek to find the little boat floating serenely next to the bank. The tide had finished filling the little river in the marsh. Jake didn't stop when he got to the edge, he just dove right in. The girls stood on the bank and dipped a foot in to test the water. "It's nice!" Michele pronounced, taking off the shirt she wore over her bathing suit. She dived in and Jenny soon joined them. They swam a little way and then floated on their backs looking up at the puffy clouds that were breezing across the blue sky. The tide was still coming in a little, and the slight current carried them slowly upstream.

The water was perfect. When the tide was high in the afternoon, the sun would heat the black mud in the empty creek all morning. When the little river filled, it was the temperature of bath water. The three of them floated along enjoying the warm water with the sun caressing their upturned faces.

Jenny was the one that turned the peaceful flotilla into a full-scale naval battle. As she drifted up next to Jake, she couldn't suppress the urge to splash water onto his face. He retaliated with gusto, and the over spray from the miniature tsunami he sent back at Jenny swamped Michele. She quickly abandoned any inclination toward neutrality, and Jake found himself fighting a war on two fronts. Bailey sat on the bank watching the splash fest until she became collateral damage. She snorted and shook the water from her face, then walked off into the marsh looking for something drier to do.

Jake was being overrun by the two-pronged attack, and he decided to go nuclear. He took a breath and ducked under the murky water. The girls waited for him to resurface, looking around nervously, ready to pounce. When he popped up behind Jenny, she turned just in time to see Jake drop the double handful of black creek mud on the top of her head. She

167

shrieked, and then promised Jake that this was to be his last day among the living. She ducked under to wash the mud out of her hair, and when she resurfaced, Jake was already standing on the bank smiling down at her.

"You're gonna get it, you son of a.."

"Hey! Don't say nothin' bad about my mother!" he cut her off, pointing his finger for effect. A mud ball hit him on the side of his face just then. He glanced to his right to see Michele already shaking with fits of laughter. Another handful of mud stuck to his chest, as Jenny took advantage of his moment of distraction. He stood there smiling at them. As they reloaded and fired the second salvo, he didn't run or retaliate, but just stood smiling while the mud stuck to him. As they continued to pummel him with mud, he appeared to grow bored and rested one hand on his hip, while inspecting the fingernails of his other hand. "I was thinking we should do a mudslide since I'm already dirty" he finally said with a yawn.

"Yeah! Mudslide!" Jenny agreed. They began throwing mud up onto the marsh grass. Jake dove into the creek and joined them. He began heaving great big armloads of mud up to the grass.

"You two get up and squish it" he told them. The girls climbed up and started stomping around like they were at the vineyard crushing the grapes for this season's wine. Jake splashed water, added mud, a little more water, a little more mud, while the girls trampled it down to an even black brown paste.

"Let's see if it's ready" Jake said, climbing up to join them. He stretched his arms out to the side and let himself slowly topple face forward into the slop. He landed with the sound of a pumpkin smashing on a Halloween night. Then he pushed himself up and stood there, covered in dark goo from head to toe. "It's ready" he said and started trotting out into the marsh. The girls giggled and pointed at him, as he made a wide turn and picked up speed, now running full tilt back at the slimy stripe of black in the marsh grass. They realized they were too close just as Jake dove headfirst, arms outstretched, and slid through the mess. He shot off the bank and finished his dive

168

into the water. When he came back up, he was totally clean. He turned back to see the girls standing there, splattered up and down with black splotches, looking mortified.

"Well, you might as well go now, since you're all dirty anyway" Jake laughed.

Jenny shot him a quick finger, but smiled while she did. They walked a little way into the marsh. Jenny went first, trotting tentatively along and then going into a baseball slide. She didn't have enough momentum, and ended up sliding up close to the edge of the bank before coming to a stop, sitting in the mud. "Ewww" she whined, and then hop-slid the rest of the way into the water.

Michele went next, running faster, and then trying to slide on her feet, like skim boarding without a board. She did pretty well too, until one foot caught and she lurched forward face-first into the mud. Luckily she had enough momentum to carry her the rest of the way in.

They each took a few more turns, with Jake covering all the possibilities – head first, side slide, the luge, two feet, and one foot. When they finally tired of mud sliding, they took a long swim and washed the mud and grass out of their bathing suits and hair.

Jake helped the girls get back onto the bank without getting muddy again, and they sat in the little boat. The girls dried off with their towels, and then Michele offered hers to Jake. He thanked her, and then dried his face and hands. Michele took the sandwiches and chips out of the bags they'd brought, while Jenny passed out bottles of Gatorade. Bailey's sixth sense kicked in, and she came trotting back up to the boat, sat down in the marsh grass with one paw up, and put on her best I'm-really-hungry face. Michele reached into the shopping bag and pulled out a little baggie with just a few pieces of sliced turkey in it.

"I made you lunch too" she said, and fed Bailey a slice at a time. Jake smiled at this, and Michele returned the smile then looked away.

169

They finished their lunch, and Michele said she'd like to pick some heather from the marsh before they went back. Jenny told Michele she'd join her in a minute. Michele walked off into the marsh toward a large cluster of the miniature purple flowers, while Jenny began gathering up the empty bottles and wrappers.

As soon as Michele was out of earshot, Jenny stopped packing and looked at Jake. Her serious look scared him for a second.

"She likes you, you know" Jenny said.

Jake glanced at Michele walking through the marsh. "I like her too" he said, automatically.

"No, dufus. She *likes* you" Jenny emphasized.

"I..." Jake started, but then forgot how to talk. His stomach did little back flips, and he felt dizzy. He sat there gazing off toward Michele. She was kneeling down in the midst of the heather, her long dark hair waving gently in the breeze, arranging a lavender bouquet in her hands. Jake felt a rush of warmth, and he could feel the color coming into his face.

"Well?" Jenny pressed. "Do you like her?"

"I..." Jake stammered, "I...well, yeah, I like her."

Jenny's grin screamed I-knew-it! "Why don't you ask her out?"

"Ask her out where?" Jake said, voicing an argument he'd already had with himself while fantasizing about this very thing. "We're at the beach, remember? Did they put in a movie theater I don't know about or something?" he asked defensively.

"No, you dope. You don't have to ask her to go out" Jenny said, as if this made perfect sense. When she saw his confused look, she rolled her eyes knowing he didn't get it. "Look, you don't have to say 'do you want to go to the movies' or even 'do you want to go out'. Just ask her to go for a walk or something. But go just with her, that's all. Get away from Stevie and Dragon. Just go for a walk and see what happens. Nothing's gonna happen hanging around with four or five people all the time, see?"

Jake thought about the other day when Jenny had asked him to go for a walk to the lighthouse, and how nice she looked, and how good she smelled, and how stupid he was. Damn. Jake hung his head and sighed.

"Just ask her" Jenny said, and got up to go join Michele. Jake watched her go. He watched them gather bunches of heather, and his stomach continued to dance. He tried to see if Jenny was saying anything to Michele, but she wasn't. She glanced at Jake occasionally, but that was all. She was all about picking flowers now. Jake figured they may talk later, but he'd never know. Oh, he was in it now, he thought.

When the girls came back to the boat, Jake stood up and called for Bailey, put his life jacket on, collected the anchor, fiddled with the engine, and generally did whatever he could to keep from making eye contact with either of them. The ride back was calm and uneventful, except for the tempest Jake felt in his gut. Feelings of warmth, infatuation, and terror alternately washed over him, but he tried to look calm on the surface. He made small talk on the way, always concentrating on some distant object. When they got back to the point, he said he'd take care of the boat, and yes, it was fun, and yes, he'd see them at the fire. When they finally walked off through the marsh, only Bailey was left to see his slack-jawed, round-eyed stare as he watched them go.

31
The Arnold

As the sun set over the back bay that Sunday night, Jake made his way over the dune to the front beach. He could see that the fire was already lit, and Nicky, Michele and Jenny were gathered there in front of the tarp. Jake felt anxious, nervous, apprehensive and excited all at the same time. Nicky sat on one side staring into the flickering flames, while Michele and Jenny looked to be having a private conversation on the other side. To Jake they looked like co-conspirators, plotting some scheme that would lead to his ultimate humiliation. Jake walked toward them, glancing at the old anchor as he passed. The anchor was now half buried in the sand, and was starting to look like yesterday's news. As Jake approached, rehearsing in his mind the nonchalant greeting he'd use, Jenny looked up and said "Hi Gramps."

Jake stopped and stared at her blankly. He turned to look behind him when he heard Walter's voice answer her. "Hello little miss." Walter was walking up the beach barely twenty feet away.

"Oh, hi Walter, I didn't see you coming" Jake said.

Walter looked a little surprised at this. "I guess not, doin' a little wool-gathering, are ya?" Jake didn't have a ready answer. He thought he understood the question, but he didn't really know what the hell Walter had just said. He stood there slack-jawed with his brow furrowed in frozen bewilderment.

"Where ya comin' from?" Jenny asked, leaving Jake in the wake of the conversation.

"I was down to Molly Tilton's" he said. Walter had become the designated husband to most of the old widows on the beach strictly by virtue of his longevity. "She was havin' trouble with her water, so I went to get her pumpin' again" Walter continued, with that little glint in his eye. Nicky stifled a laugh, and Walter shot him a hard look, but the merriment in his eyes gave him away.

"Is she pumping again?" Jenny asked with a smirk.

"Well now, I don't believe she's pumped that hard in years."

That was it for Nicky. He started laughing so hard he cried. He rolled over in the sand and buried his face in the crook of his elbow, trying in vain to control himself. Walter glanced at him and said, "The boy's got the giggles." Jenny shook her head slowly and gave her grandfather a reproachful look.

Jake had caught up now, and Walter shifted his gaze to him. "And where've you been? I waved to you when you came over the dune, but you walked along like a zombie. Something on your mind?" he asked.

Jake looked back at Walter's bushy eyebrows, their shadows long in the firelight, punctuating a question mark. "Yeah, kind of. I guess I was just thinking about some stuff" Jake half mumbled, and he sat down in the sand near the fire.

Walter bent down and turned a short fat log up on end for a seat, and settled down on it. "What kind of stuff?" he asked. "Anything I can help you with?"

Jake's mind raced in silent reply; 'Sure, your granddaughter is playing matchmaker over there, and I'm scared shitless. Can you do something about that? Send her back home for the rest of the summer, maybe?' Jake got hold of himself, and he settled on a diversionary tack.

"I was wondering if there were any shipwrecks around here" he said.

"Hundreds of 'em" Walter replied immediately. He looked toward the anchor lying in the sand, confident he knew now what had gotten to Jake.

"Hundreds?" Jenny asked, a note of skepticism in her tone.

"Hundreds" Walter said with certainty. He looked at their young faces gathered in the firelight, and saw that they still weren't sure he was serious. They were going to take some convincing, he thought, and that was thirsty work. Walter reached into his back pocket and slipped out a hip flask. He glanced up at the dune in front of his cottage, took a sip, and slid the flask back to its hiding spot. He looked around at them, and settled his gaze on Jake.

173

"There's an old ship tied up to the wharf over in Plymouth Harbor. Do you know it?" Walter prompted.

"Sure, the Mayflower II" Jake answered.

"That's right. It's a replica of the original Mayflower" Walter said. "The one the Pilgrims came on.." he paused, "In 1620.. Almost four hundred years ago now." He saw by their looks that he'd have to be more direct. "Look, this little harbor was the busiest port in the New World at one time. And it stayed one of the busiest ports for over two hundred years. It all started here. Why, there's been thousands of ships in and out of Plymouth over the years. And all types of ships, too. Why, there were the Pilgrims of course, and all the other settlers who followed them. But there's also been plenty of others too. There's been warships during the Revolution, and again in the War of 1812. Why, one of 'em even shot the lighthouse back then!" Now he had their attention.

"Were there pirates?" Nicky asked.

"Sure, pirates, and privateers, and later on there were rum-runners, you name it" Walter said, warming up now. He took another swig from the flask, and went on. "Now those ships weren't like the ships today. They didn't have any navigation systems, or radar, or even any radios – nothin' at all like that. They were sailed by men who figured out where they were by using the stars and the sun. And sometimes they didn't figure too good, either, so lots of them ran into trouble. They also didn't have good charts that showed them where all the shoals and flats were, so plenty ran aground. And there was always the weather. They didn't have weather reports every ten minutes on the radio to tell 'em when a storm was coming. They watched the sky and the waves and wind, and they had to try and guess how bad it was going to be when the storm hit. Sometimes they guessed wrong. Hell, even with all the computers and such, sometimes we still guess wrong today." He paused here and his eyes seemed to look into the distance, the shadows of the storms of '91' and '78' and others dancing in his eyes. After a moment he refocused and said, "There's been hundreds of shipwrecks along this coast. A few were famous, but most of 'em you never heard of."

The sky had darkened enough to show the first stars in the east. Walter sat quietly for a time, watching the flames, with the sound of the waves gently washing the beach halfway down to low tide. "That old anchor you found means someone ran into trouble there. And judging by the looks of it, it was quite a while ago, too. I'll bet it has a story to tell" Walter said.

Jake glanced at his old friend and thought, 'you got that right'.

Nicky spoke up then. "Was there ever any shipwrecks right out front here?"

"Oh sure, there's been a few. Shipwrecks, boats sinking, drownings. It's all happened. Why, I'm sure even a few Indians lost their canoes and drowned out front. They were on the beach before even the Pilgrims showed up you know."

The kids knew the stories of the natives who came to gather clams and hunt deer and rabbit here long before the settlers arrived. As night fell, they had probably sat around a fire, just like this one, listening to the endless rhythm of the waves and looking at the same stars.

"Any big ones? Big enough to have an anchor like Jake found?" Nicky persisted.

Walter furrowed his brow and thought for a minute. "That'd be a decent size boat, like a schooner or a brig," he said. "There's been a few, I guess. The most famous would've been the Arnold," he said absently, gazing at the fire.

Jake nearly jumped when he heard the name. The hair on his neck and arms stood straight up. He looked at Nicky and the girls, and saw the shock that he himself felt written on their faces. They looked at each other, like scared rabbits. Nicky was the first to recover. He made an expression that told the others to stay cool, and then he put on a mask of pure indifference. "The Arnold?" he asked, hoping to get Walter going again.

Walter looked up from the fire, and his gaze came back into focus. He looked at Nicky. "Say what?"

"You said the Arnold. It was famous?" Nicky pressed.

175

"Oh, The General Arnold" Walter said, nodding. "It was famous around here, anyway. It was the worst shipwreck ever in Plymouth Harbor," he said.

"What happened?" Jake asked, finally regaining his voice.

"You don't know the story? Why I thought everybody.." Walter started, and then looked at the curious faces gathered around the fire, faces two long generations removed from his own. He shook his head and chuckled, thinking about how many times he'd said Jenny sounded like a broken record when she was younger and being 'persistent', only to be finally told by his darlin' bride that he sounded like an old man, and that Jenny had never even heard a record, broken or otherwise. Then he recalled when she was a little older, he'd heard one of Jenny's compact disks skip, and he realized that progress had come full circle.

Jenny read his face, and tried to put him back on track. "Gramps, what happened to the Arnold?" she asked.

Walter leaned back and let out a slow breath. He absently took another swig from the flask, and Jenny knew it was going to be a long story. That was fine, they had all night. Nicky threw a couple of pieces of wood on the fire, and they all slid in a little closer to its warmth, settling in.

"The General Arnold" Walter began, "was a privateer during the Revolutionary War." He noticed the question on Jenny's face, and realized he could lose them all at the get-go if he talked about broken records and such, like they heard them every day. He took a mental step back.

"A privateer was like it sounds, it was a ship that was privately owned, but it was used to fight the English during the Revolution." He looked around, and saw that he still had them for the moment. "See, the colonies had declared their independence in 1776. Well, old King George didn't take kindly to that, and he sent the Royal Navy over here to argue the point. Now the colonies didn't have much of a navy, or an army for that matter, so it was up to regular folks to fight the war. Well, the Continental Congress, which was our government at the time, decided they needed ships to fight the Royal Navy if we

176

were to have any chance. They decided to use privateers. The way it worked was, they gave private ship owners permission to sink, or better yet capture the British ships. For payment, the ship owners and crew got to divide up and keep anything they captured that couldn't be used in the war effort, including the ships they managed to get."

"Like pirates!" Jake said.

"Just like pirates, Jake, just like 'em. In fact it was the pirates that originally came up with the idea. The difference between a pirate and a privateer depended on who was writin' the laws at the time, that's all." Walter was pleased to see Jake was getting back to being himself. It wasn't like him to be so oblivious, and Walter had been a little concerned.

"Now The General Arnold was a privateer. The ship left Boston on Christmas Eve in 1778, two years into the War for Independence. They were carrying supplies for General George Washington's army, such as it was. It was stormy, but the army needed the supplies so they left the harbor and headed south. Once they got clear of Boston Harbor they saw how bad it really was. As I said, the army was waiting, so the captain decided to press on. Well, the winds picked up, they waves grew even bigger, the snow got worse, and the captain realized it was cookin' up to be a real nor'easter. He decided to put in here and ride out the storm on the lee side of the Gurnet. Well, things only went from bad to worse. It turned into a full scale blizzard, the original 'Blizzard of '78' you might say." Walter took another swig and sat quietly for a moment, scenes of the Blizzard of '78 that he'd lived through flashing through his mind.

"On the first night, the anchor line snapped" he said. "There was no chance of getting the boat underway with the wind and the waves as high as they were. No chance at all. The ship was driven aground over there on White Flat" Walter said, pointing vaguely in the direction of Bug Light.

"Well, it was three days of hell from there. The weather got worse, the temperature plummeted, the bay plugged up with ice floes, and the snow kept coming. The bottom of the ship got stove in, so they had to ride out the storm on deck, trying to use sails and anything they could find for cover. It was hopeless. Those that weren't washed overboard with the waves froze to death in place. Out of a hundred or so men on board, only about thirty survived. And all the while, the folks in Plymouth could see the ship and crew dying out there, but there was nothing they could do about it. They tried launching boats but the waves were too big and clogged with ice. The ice was everywhere, but it wasn't solid enough to walk across. They say a few of the Arnold's crew tried it, but they didn't get far." Walter looked off toward White Flat. The beam of the lighthouse swept across his face once, twice, three times before he went on.

"It was three days before the storm blew itself out and the townsfolk could reach the ship. It was the worst thing any of 'em had ever seen. Men frozen in place, holding onto ropes, holding onto each other, or holding their hands folded in prayer." He thought about stopping the story there, but he'd come this far, so he might as well bring her home.

"They say that when they got them back to Plymouth, they had to thaw them out in the town brook so they could straighten 'em out for a proper burial. And even then, it wasn't as proper as they would've liked. See, a lot of the crew had just boarded in Boston that Christmas Eve. I imagine they were quite a mix. Oh, I'm sure there were some with nothin' holding 'em back, and probably some who were anxious to get away from one thing or another, but there were family men, too. Patriots. Men who believed in what we were fighting for. Men who believed strong enough to leave their families on a Christmas Eve, and sail off to war to fight for freedom. But the thing is, we'll never know." He looked around at his young audience, and mixed with the awe, he thought he read a hint of appreciation on their faces. That was good, he thought. The old stories shouldn't be forgotten.

"No sir, we'll never know. There's a marker on a mass grave in the cemetery over in Plymouth. It was put there in honor of the men who died on that ship. But their names aren't on it. The thing is, we don't know their names. The ship ran into the storm that Christmas Eve as soon as they left port. The captain never even got the chance to put the names of the crew into the ship's logbook. We'll never know their names, but we should never forget what they did." Walter paused then, and the kids thought the story was over. But there was a little more to it.

"The strange thing about it," Walter continued, "is that there's those who say it wasn't the storm that doomed the General Arnold."

"What do they say?" Jake asked, fascinated.

"They say it was the name that doomed the ship." Walter replied. "See, the ship was named after General *Benedict* Arnold. Benedict Arnold was the biggest traitor of the Revolutionary War, but people didn't know it 'til later on. Some say that the ship went down while Benedict Arnold was plotting his treason. They say his treason caused it" he finished.

The kids had all heard of Benedict Arnold, of course. They'd learned about him in their American History classes, but they'd never known a ship had been named after him. And they'd never dreamed that the ship had met such a horrible fate so close to where they now sat.

And unlike the jaded adults who might deny what rings true by pushing it off to a safe distance and labeling it as a 'coincidence', the kids weren't inclined to scoff at the idea that Benedict Arnold's treachery had caused the disaster. They believed it could happen that way. They still had that peculiar and fleeting wisdom of youth. Especially Jake. Having experienced first-hand the events of 'the past' in just the last few days, the idea that a man's actions could have such far reaching consequences felt true. And Jake was still wise enough to trust his feelings. And now Jake *knew* that the anchor lying a few feet away had come from the General Benedict Arnold. He just didn't know why.

Monday morning dawned bright and clear. Jake was awoken
by the slobbery rough feel of Bailey's tongue on his face. He
opened one eye and pushed her away. She dodged around his
arm and gave another wet lick, her tail shifting into overdrive.
Jake pulled the pillow over his head for protection. Bailey
pawed at the pillow until Jake relented. He sat up, swung the
door to the shed open to let Bailey out, and then flopped back
down on the bed as the door swung back closed.

He lay there and thought back to the night before. He'd been
all twisted up inside worrying about what Jenny had told
Michele about their little talk at the creek, but he hadn't had to
face that music because Walter had diverted them all with his
story.

And what a story that was. Jake was still amazed that Walter
had told the story of the wreck of the General Arnold, the very
ship that Jake had been aboard 'over there'. The word
coincidence never even entered his mind. He was years away
from that. He knew that the answers were closer now, and he
was sure they'd come in time. He just had to relax and go with
the flow.

He thought about the day ahead. Last night as they left the fire,
Nicky had told him that his father Victor had talked to Jake's
dad yesterday, and Brian had agreed to take them out to get a
few sea clams today. Victor wanted to make a clam chowder.

Stevie wouldn't be back with his mother and sister until later
in the day, and Jenny and Michele weren't much for sea
clamming. It would be just the four of them, Jake thought, and
he wouldn't have to worry about facing the girls until this
afternoon. He felt relief at that, but wasn't sure why. Part of him
was aching to talk to Michele, and another part was terrified of
the possibility. He pushed the thought away.

Jake sat up and pulled the tide table off the nail on the wall.
Low tide was a little after eleven o'clock, and it wasn't a real
low tide. Still, they only needed a few of the big sea clams to

make a chowder, and if they got a dozen of them, they could bait the lobster pots too. That shouldn't be too hard, Jake thought. It would be easier to get clams if the tide was lower, but they'd just have to walk in the water about waist deep. No problem.

He changed into his bathing suit and went up to the cottage for breakfast. When he went inside, he was shocked to find out it was already ten o'clock in the morning. No wonder Bailey wanted him to get up. Jake remembered thinking about the General Arnold as he lay in bed last night, and then realizing that the answers were coming. He'd relaxed then, and had the best sleep he'd had in days.

Twenty minutes later, Jake loaded the clamming forks into the boat on the front beach, and he and Bailey jumped into the skiff as Brian backed it out through the waves. They cruised around the Head, and Jake spotted his buoys on the way by. He counted all six, and that was good. They usually lost a pot or two during the course of the season, and Jake always counted the buoys when he went past without really thinking about it.

As they went through the rip, the boat rocked on the ever present waves there, and then the water went flat calm as they turned around the point and glided up to the shore in front of Dragoni's cottage. Nicky and Victor were walking down to meet them.

"Gooda mornin' Brian! Howa you doon' Jake?" Victor called.

"Hi Victor. You all set?" Brian asked.

"Ya, ya. Let's go getta the clams!" he said. Victor had grown up in Italy, and that had a lot to do with the success his restaurant had enjoyed in Boston's North End. While he was a great cook, he wasn't much of a sailor. He almost fell climbing aboard, and Nicky just rolled his eyes. They managed to get Victor safely on board, and they were off.

Nicky sat up forward with Jake on the raised front deck, with Bailey standing between them pointing the way. Victor stood next to Brian at the center console, holding the grab bar in a death grip, but smiling like a kid at Christmas. Nicky leaned over and whispered in Jake's ear. "Thank God for your dad. My old man had me working like a dog yesterday."

Jake looked back at Victor Dragoni. He couldn't imagine the stocky, balding, affable restaurateur being the merciless taskmaster that Nicky always made him out to be. He reminded Jake of McHale on that old TV show about the navy patrol boat, except Victor didn't look like he had any sea legs at all. He bobbed and staggered with every wave, but his face was the picture of pure joy. As they approached the rip, Jake slid one of the buoyant boat cushions out from under the front deck just in case he had to toss it at Victor if he lost his grip and went overboard. Brian noticed this and smiled with a slight nod at Jake.

They made it through the rip without incident, and Brian angled the boat toward starboard in the direction of Bug Light. They cruised out to the lighthouse, and Brian slowed a little. A lobster boat was heading out the channel just past the lighthouse, and Brian crossed the channel once it had passed. Jake could see Long Beach stretching up from the mainland towards them, the other barrier that protected the harbor along with their beach. Jake looked into the gap between the beaches toward the mainland. The water looked uniform in the harbor, but Jake knew that White Flat lurked there under the surface right in the middle, and a picture of the floundering Arnold flashed through his mind. He pushed it away.

As they approached the tip of Long Beach, they could see the sandy stretch of Brown's Bank rising out of the water about a hundred yards off shore. The bank was a sand bar that ran perpendicular to the tip of Long Beach, along the outer edge of the channel leaving the harbor. This end of the sand bar was higher than the rest, and it was exposed at low tide. Father out, it wasn't uncommon to see sailboats get caught up on it if they drifted out of the channel and got their keels stuck in the submerged sandy bank. Many times Jake had watched from the beach as an errant sailboat grounded as tide ran out. The boat would slowly tip sideways as the water receded, and then slowly tip back as the tide came back in. It usually took about

182

four hours of cruising time away from the amateur sailor's day when he had the misfortune of finding the underwater shoal.

Brian guided the boat toward the gap between the end of Long Beach and the start of Brown's Bank. The sea clams were easier to find on the far side of the bank, and the water was calmer there, sheltered from the channel as it was. He tilted the engine up slightly as they glided through the shallow water in the gap. When they were through, Brian tilted back down and headed up the back side of the sand bar. "What do you think, Jake?" Brian called to the front of the boat.

"I'd try in there" Jake said, pointing toward a little cove scooped out of the back side of the bar. They angled into the cove, and Brian killed the engine and raised the prop out of the water. They glided toward shore, and finally grounded in the soft sand about thirty feet from the sandbar.

Jake tossed the anchor, and he and Nicky took off their life jackets. Brian passed out buckets and the clamming forks, which looked like pitchforks on long shovel handles. They climbed out of the boat almost without incident. Victor took a tumble on the way out of the boat and fell into the water. As he got up and wiped the water from his eyes, Jake and Nicky were stifling their laughter, and Brian just said dryly, "You can get the ones that are out deep since you're already wet." Victor let out a hearty laugh and they all joined in. Then Victor turned and splashed water at Nicky and Jake, yelling, "You thinka dat's funny?" still laughing.

Bailey stood on the bow, head cocked, ears up, still not getting what was so funny about getting soaked. She started whimpering as she leaned over to jump, and then backed off, afraid of how deep the water may be. Jake walked over and lifted her off the bow and set her down. Once she realized she could stand, she headed right for the sandbar without a backward glance.

They spread out and started searching for clams. One way to find them when you were in the water was to just walk along poking the fork into the sand as you walked. When you felt the fork tines hit something hard, you'd dig it up. The sea clams

183

were only a few inches below the surface, but half of what you dug up wasn't clams. There were rocks and rock crabs, and even the occasional chunk of coal left over from an old coal barge that had grounded on the bank about a hundred years ago. There were moon snails the size of baseballs, and spider crabs that looked like miniature king crabs, and yes, there were sea clams.

Sea clams grew as big as eight inches long, and they were delicious. When they were shucked, cleaned and ground up, you could use them for chowder, or baked stuffed clams, or white clam sauce over pasta, or whatever. They were the most versatile clams around, as far as recipes went.

The other way to find them was the method that Jake favored – the way his father had showed him. He would walk very slowly through the water, placing his feet as lightly as he could so he wouldn't send vibrations into the sand. He'd keep the sun at his back so he could look deep into the water without the glare blinding him. If you walked slowly and lightly enough, and if you could look far enough away through the water, you could actually see just the tip of the clam neck outlined in the sand about twelve feet away. The twin holes in the neck looked like a miniature figure eight drawn in the sand. The problem was, as soon as you started to get close, the clam would sense you and pull its neck back down, and the sand would cover the spot so quickly, it would look like nothing was ever there.

Jake was an expert at stealthily moving along, spotting the clam necks, and remembering the spot before he got close enough to make them close up. He had tried to show his friends how to do it, but until they were able to finally do it once and see what to look for, they couldn't do it at all. It was like trying to learn how to whistle. You didn't really get it until you got it.

While Victor and Nicky slogged along poking over and over, digging and digging, and then cursing when they came up with a horseshoe crab or something, Jake crept quietly along digging selectively, efficiently collecting clams. He had half a dozen in a few minutes time, and he finally heard Victor call out "I got one! Over here dey are!" Jake looked to see him holding a small sea clam up to the sky, triumphantly staring up and grinning like it was the Olympic torch he was wielding. Jake saw that his dad was chuckling, while Nicky just scowled and shook his head.

Brian asked Jake how he was doing. "Pretty good, I got half a dozen" Jake called back. "I'm gonna walk over and check the other side of the bar." Brian nodded. He knew that between the two of them they already had enough clams, and Jake wanted to scout around for spots to try later in the summer when this spot got a little light.

This side of the bar was covered in ripples, just like the tide pool on the front beach. Jake walked across and the sand grew higher and smoother as he went. When he got to the other side, the sand bar was about three feet high and perfectly smooth, the only blemishes being the paw prints that Bailey had left as she'd run down this side of the bank. At the edge, there was a steep drop off as the sand dove down toward the channel.

Jake stood on the edge of the drop looking down where the waves from the channel ate at the edge of the bar, looking for bubbles or clams spitting as they tried to dig deeper in the sand. He saw a sea clam that was partially exposed, futilely trying to dig faster than the waves could uncover it, a slow motion race for survival.

Jake hopped over the edge and bent to pick up the clam. As he straightened up, he sensed something down to his right. He looked that way and saw Bailey trotting along at the extreme end of the exposed sand bar. He was about to turn and climb back up, but he felt a tickling sensation as his neck hair stood up. He looked intently down the bar, shielding his eyes from the glare off the water. When his eyes adjusted, he saw a small dark spot on the edge of the sand bar about halfway down. Curious, Jake began walking that way. As he approached, a sense of unease came over him.

His feeling of foreboding grew with every step, but his curiosity kept him moving. Something felt *wrong*. Something felt *bad*, like the feeling you got when you saw maggots on a hot summer's day, with the sound of flies buzzing in your ears.

As he got closer, he saw there was a seagull there, working at the shadow.

He stopped when he was within spitting distance of the shadow and put his fork and bucket down. The dark mass was buried in the side of the bank, like the pictures of dinosaur bones he'd seen hanging out of canyon walls. It was covered in seaweed, and the gull yanked a ribbon worm from the depths of it, stretching it out to about two feet before it finally snapped free. The seagull sucked it down greedily, then cawed once at Jake and flew off.

Jake took a hesitant step forward. He stared at the rotten pile of seaweed and barnacles, and there were sea worms and tiny crabs skittering through the mess. As he looked, he noticed a clean edge, a straight line in the mass of chaos. He leaned forward and bent down to look more closely. There was definitely something there. Slowly, he reached out and pushed the hanging strands of weed and kelp to the side. There was a flat surface underneath, and then Jake saw there were letters there. He saw an A, and an N and a D, and suddenly the word ARNOLD flashed into his mind. He felt dizzy, and then fell back in the wet sand at the channel's edge. A large wave hit him in the back, as if trying to throw him back into the weedy shadow. Jake jumped to his feet, ashen and shaking. Bailey was there, standing up on the sand bar looking down. Her head was down, and the hair on her back was up, and she breathed a low growl as she peered over the edge at the buried hulk.

Jake waited until he stopped shaking, forcing himself to breath regularly, willing himself to calm down. Then he reached down and pushed the weed to the side once more. He relaxed some when he looked this time. It wasn't ARNOLD; that had been his mind playing tricks. It was ANDE. And it wasn't the timbers of an old brigantine that he was looking at. It was the transom of a much smaller boat. Jake could tell it was smooth beneath the barnacles and weed, and it was painted wood.

Jake thought about Walter saying there were hundreds of wrecks along this coast. Well, he'd just found one of them. As he stood there looking at it, the waves seemed to grow just a little more urgent. He noticed that the water was now up to the edge of the buried wreck. Tide had turned, and it was now coming back in. The ANDE would sink again in an hour or two.

Jake grabbed the bucket and fork and climbed back up onto the top of the bank, and Bailey licked his face before he could straighten up. Her hair was still up, but she was wagging and sniffing, apparently happy that Jake had decided to put some distance between himself and the wreck. They walked back across the bar together, and when they got to the other side Jake saw that the others were climbing into the boat. He waded out and put his gear in the boat, then lifted Bailey aboard. He pulled the anchor and pushed the boat out until there was enough water for the engine, and then he hopped in.

"I found an old wreck" he told his father.

"A wreck?" Brian asked, starting the engine.

"Yeah, it's buried in the other side of the bank. If you go around, you can probably see it before tide comes in" Jake said.

"Show me" Brian said as he put the boat in gear.

A few minutes later, they were idling just off of the channel side of Brown's Bank. The waves in the channel had grown with the incoming tide, and even though the water level was higher, Jake had no trouble pinpointing the location of the wreck. The current was scooping the sand out and exposing more of the hulk. It reminded Jake of the coffins that resurfaced after Hurricane Katrina had swamped New Orleans a couple of years ago.

"We better let the Harbormaster know" Brian said. He took out his cell phone and called it in to Plymouth.

"Plymouth Harbormaster's Office, Corbett speaking."

Brian was surprised at first that Harry Corbett had answered, but then he remembered that it was Monday morning – regular business hours. Harry Corbett was *the* Plymouth Harbormaster and had been for over thirty years. He had been Assistant Harbormaster even before that. Nobody knew the waters around here better than him. All the locals knew Harry.

"Hi Harry, it's Brian Edison."

"Brian, how are you?"

"Fine, Harry, I'm good."

"What can I do for you? Everything okay?" Harry asked.

"Yeah, we're okay. But we're out on Brown's Bank doing a little clamming, and my son came across an old wreck buried in the sand."

"A wreck you say?"

"Yeah, it looks pretty old, so it's no emergency or anything. But it looks like it's washing free, and you might want to take a look before it turns into a hazard."

"Whereabouts?"

"It's on the channel side in the edge of the bar, and I'd say we're about a quarter mile from the Bug."

"Okay, I'll send a man" Harry said.

"Don't bother now," Brian said. As they watched, the water was already covering up the bar, and the old boat with it. "Tide's coming, and it's just about under. It's still pretty much buried, so I don't think it'll be a problem right now. Better come next time the tide's out, or tomorrow maybe?" Brian offered.

"Sure thing, we'll take a look. Thanks for the call, Brian, and give my regards to the family" Harry said.

"Will do. Take care Harry."

Brian turned to Jake and said, "They'll check it out, Jake. Harry Corbett says hi." Jake smiled at that. Then Brian said, "Jeez, Jake, you're on a roll. First the anchor, now this boat. Think maybe you can find some buried treasure before the summer's over?"

"I'll try" Jake said.

"Well, let's see if your luck continues when we pull the pots. I'll settle for a couple of lobsters" Brian joked.

They pulled the lobster pots on the way back in, and Jake's luck held. They got four keepers and a short, which they threw back, all of them in the three pots that Jake had set out in deeper water. Brian admitted defeat and moved the other three pots out deeper. They now had a line of six pots in a row, all freshly baited with sea clams.

When they got back to shore, they still had a dozen clams in the bucket. Victor said he didn't need that many, and Nicky asked Jake if he wanted to take a couple down to feed them to the seal.

"There's plenty of time before tide comes in, and I'd like to see how he's doing" Nicky said to Jake.

Jake had been thinking the same thing, sort of. Actually, he had been thinking it might be a way to ask Michele to go for a walk alone, but he wrestled with the idea, and hadn't quite convinced himself that he was ready yet. He realized now that since it was Nicky's idea, he could put that battle out of his head for now. "Yeah, that's what I was thinking too" Jake told him.

Michele and Jenny were sitting in the shade under the tarp when the boys walked up. "Did you get any clams?" Jenny asked as they approached.

Jake held up the mesh bait bag with two sea clams inside. "Two clams – that's all you got?" Jenny chided.

"No, we got enough to bait the pots, make a chowder, *and* feed the seal, smartass" Nicky parried. "Me and Jake are gonna walk down now. You wanna come?"

Jenny shot Jake a disapproving look. Apparently, a group walk wasn't in the script she'd imagined for the afternoon. Jake felt the anxiety creeping back, but quickly pushed it away. Almost imperceptibly, he tilted his head and glanced toward Nicky, and gave a tiny shrug of his shoulders. The gesture said 'not my fault, girl'.

"Sure, we'll go with you" Michele answered for them. Jenny shot another visual dart at Jake as she got up from the sand and brushed off the back of her shorts. Jake just chuckled to himself. He'd seen her use that look behind her grandparents' backs many times when she didn't get her way. It didn't help then, and it wasn't going to help now, Jake figured.

They set off toward the lighthouse walking down along the hard sand at the water's edge. Jenny kept trying to arrange the little formation so that Michele and Jake were next to each other, but Michele kept wandering out of line to pick up shells or the occasional bit of sea glass, and a frustrated Jenny soon gave up on the idea.

Jake seemed to be the only one that noticed her futile efforts. Nicky kept sliding back in step next to Jake every time Michele wandered off, and Jake noticed Jenny's anger build every time he did it. Nicky reminded Jake of a shiner swimming lazily through the weeds, unaware that a hungry striper was lurking, watching every move. That image made him smile. Nicky was walking along, talking, telling jokes, and generally just being Nicky, but on this particular day those actions were enough to make Jenny seethe. It's a good thing Nicky didn't notice, or he would have really put some effort into sending her over the edge, Jake thought.

Just as they got to the far end of the beach, the Connors' Blazer came rolling over the cutoff toward them. Stevie's sister Sam was driving, and his mom was sitting in the front seat next to her. His father had stayed home to go to work, so Stevie was alone in the back seat. Stevie was already climbing out of the back door as Sam brought the truck to a stop. "Hi guys! How are you?" Sam greeted them.

"Hi Sam!" Jenny and Michele said in unison.

"Sorry, but you get my little brother now. I've had enough of him already!" Sam teased.

"How was New Hampshire?" Michele asked her.

"It was awesome. I'll tell you about it later, but we have to go unpack the groceries and get them in the fridge now" Sam said.

"Okay, see you later."

Sam pulled away and Stevie said, "Thank God you guys showed up. If I had to listen to them yak about haircuts and Uggs anymore, I was gonna slit my throat." The girls gave him a sour sideways look, while Nicky and Jake nodded with empathy. "What's up?" Stevie asked.

"We're goin' to feed the seal," Jake said.

"Cool. He still up there?"

"Dunno. We'll find out" Jake replied.

They set off toward the rocks, and Jenny seemed to back off just a little now, resigned to the fact that her plan would have to wait. Nicky never even realized the trouble he'd avoided. Stevie took off across the rocks, with Nicky and Jake in hot pursuit a moment later. When the girls caught up to them, the three of them were standing there scanning the surface of the water. The seals were nowhere to be seen.

"Are they gone?" Jenny asked.

"They ain't here" Nicky said sarcastically. Jenny whacked him, a little harder than the offense warranted, but she figured she owed him one.

Stevie laughed, Nicky protested, Jenny and Nicky started to squabble about the glaring character defects the other possessed, while Jake began walking slowly toward the rock that the little seal had sheltered behind for the last few days. As he got closer, he felt a tingling on his neck and arms. An image came to him then of the little seal flying through the water, following his mother, moving like a bullet through the underwater world with shafts of sunlight hanging down like party streamers. Jake felt the joy, the serenity, and the plain *rightness* of being in your natural element, doing what you were supposed to do. His perspective changed so that he was looking through the eyes of the little seal. He saw the mother dart left into a school of shiners, and Jake immediately darted right, into a smaller group of fish that had broken from the school, snagging the wriggling fish in his jaws as he flew through. Movement caught his eye, and Jake flew toward it and snagged a rock crab in a seaweed patch in the sand. The mother seal flew up next to him to dig out another crab, and a swirl of sand flew up in her wake obscuring Jake's view.

"Do you think he's gone for good?" Michele asked. She was standing next to him now, and Jake's vision cleared. He was standing in the little hollow in the sand that the seal had burrowed behind the shelter of the rock, staring absently toward the water.

"Yeah, he's gone" Jake said, a little remorsefully.

"Do you think he's okay?" she worried.

Jake looked at Michele's concerned face, smiled and said, "I'm sure he's okay."

Michele saw that he meant it, that he wasn't just saying it, and she smiled back at him. Jake thought her smile was the most beautiful thing he'd ever seen, and he felt a wave of warmth in his stomach. The image of Michele smiling there at the base of the lighthouse cliff, with the sunlight dancing on the water behind her, and the breeze playing in her hair seared itself into Jake's memory. Standing there with her felt *right*, he felt complete, he felt only *now*, and the future and past didn't exist anymore, as if they ever had.

192

A shriek broke his reverie, and they turned to see Nicky chasing Jenny through the rocks holding a horseshoe crab, threatening to tangle it in her hair.

"We better go before they kill each other" Michele sighed. Jake nodded and they turned to leave.

Just then something caught Jake's eye. It was just a flash in his peripheral vision. Jake turned back and looked around. Then he spotted a glint of silver poking out of the sand where the little seal had burrowed behind the rock. Jake bent down and grasped it. When he pulled, a tarnished silver chain snaked out of the sand. There was a gnarly blob of dried mud and weed on the end. Jake rubbed it in his hands until most of the weed and mud had come off, but he still couldn't make out what he'd found. He imagined a pendant like the one in that movie 'The Pirates of the Caribbean'.

"I found a necklace" he said, and held it out for Michele to see.

"Wow, what is it?" she asked, leaning in closer.

"I dunno, I'll have to clean it," he said. Another shriek pierced the air. Jake shoved the chain into his pocket and followed Michele to rescue Jenny. Nicky was sitting on top of her now, dangling the horseshoe crab inches above her face.

Before they reached her, Stevie launched himself at Nicky and knocked him over into the sand. Jenny got up and fled, leaving Stevie to face certain death when Nicky recovered. Jake and Michele stepped in just in time to save Stevie's life, and calm was restored, except for a little verbal sniping on the long walk back down to their end of the beach. Jenny was the principal instigator, still seething over her belief that Nicky had kept Jake and Michele from making a connection.

Later on that night, Stevie, Nicky, Jake and Jenny sat clustered together next to the fire. The wind was swirling, and there was just one narrow spot to sit upwind where they were safe from getting the stinging smoke in their eyes.

Michele walked into the circle of firelight, and Jenny quickly slid over to make room for her to sit between herself and Jake. "Squeeze in here, the smoke's bad" Jenny told her, and coughed as the smoke attacked her new position to prove the point. Smooth, Jake thought.

Michele sat down in the gap, and dropped a rag with something inside into Jake's lap as she did so. "What's this?" he asked.

"It's silver polish," she answered. "I thought you might like to clean up that medal you found today."

"What medal?" Jenny asked.

"Jake found an old medal up at the Gurnet today."

"Why didn't you tell us?" Jenny protested.

"Because you and Dragon were busy killin' each other," Jake answered dryly. Jenny shot Nicky an evil look as she remembered how he'd screwed things up. Nicky was still oblivious about that, but he smiled as he thought that terrorizing Jenny with the horseshoe crab had been a pretty pleasant way to spend a Monday afternoon.

Jake pulled the chain out of his pocket and passed it to Jenny. After she examined it, she reached out to give it back and Nicky made a grab for it. Jenny pulled it back out of his reach and stuck her tongue out. "Piss off Dragon" she said, and handed it quickly to Jake.

Nicky rolled his eyes and sighed. "Can I see it?" he said to Jake. Jake smiled and put the medal in Nicky's out-stretched hand. Nicky looked at the medal, and seemed unimpressed.

"Lemme see" Stevie said, conducted his own examination, and then passed it back to Jake.

Jake put some of the silver polish on the rag and started cleaning the chain as they sat watching the flames dance in the busy wind. He slid the chain through the moist rag, and as it started to shine, the firelight reflected off the links in tiny sparks. Jake put some more polish on the rag, and then held the medal between his thumb and forefinger and began to grind them back and forth. "Did your father make the chowder?" Jake asked Nicky.

"No, he shucked and ground up the clams and put 'em in the freezer. He says he's gonna make it next weekend when everyone's around."

"That's good" Michele said. "I love his chowder."

"Yeah, he can cook alright. He ain't much of a sailor though" Nicky said, smiling at Jake. Jake chuckled, remembering Victor's not-so-graceful dismount out on Brown's Bank earlier.

Jake took the medal out of the rag and held it up to the firelight. The side that had been under his thumb had come pretty clean. "Whoa, check it out! It's Saint Elmo!" he said.

"Cool. Who's Saint Elmo?" Nicky said.

"He's the patron saint of sailors" Jake replied.

"Maybe you outta give it to my old man" Nicky said dryly.

"Maybe I will" said Jake, and flipped the medal over and began working on the other side with his thumb.

A shooting star blazed across the sky, and it lasted so long that they all got a good look at it.

"That was cool!" Stevie exclaimed.

"Yeah, that was a good one" Jenny agreed.

"I wish one would land here. They're worth thousands of dollars" Stevie said with authority.

"How do you know?" Nicky challenged him.

"I seen it on TV!" Stevie said defensively. "Some kid found one, and sold it to the Smithsonian for like five thousand dollars!"

"For a rock?" Nicky asked incredulously.

"It's true. I saw the same show" Michele interjected.

Nicky looked at Michele and was about to say something, couldn't think of anything good, then closed his mouth and shook his head. Stevie grunted, crossed his arms and nodded once smugly. "I wish one would hit you in the head" Nicky mumbled at Stevie.

Jake examined the medal again. "I think it says something," he said, holding it close to his eye and tilting it toward the firelight.

"What's it say?" Jenny asked.

"I don't know, I can't read it yet," Jake said, returning it to the rag. He dumped a little more polish on it and started kneading again with his fingers.

A gust of wind spun into the fire. The flames roared up in a miniature twister, and threw off sparks in an expanding spiral shape that rose into the air. Jenny leaned back from the smoky assault, and then shifted her butt over in the sand, driving Michele up tight against Jake. "Smokey" Jenny said, and grinned at Jake mischievously. Jake wondered when casting spells on the wind had become part of her evil repertoire.

Jake examined the medal again. On one side there was a relief of a robed, haloed man with a storm tossed ship in the background. 'Saint Elmo' was inscribed on a miniature scroll framing the bottom of the scene.

Jake turned the medal over in his hand and leaned in close. There was an inscription there in tiny letters, but Jake's twelve-year-old eyes could easily make them out. He read it out loud.

To my Rose,
My Light,
My Life.

"What?" Jenny gasped, as she got up and pushed her way between Michele and Jake to get a look, her careful designs abandoned for the moment.

"To my Rose, my Light, my Life" Jake read it again. The medal seemed to grow warm, and vibrate slightly in his hand, and understanding washed over him with an almost audible whoosh in his ears.

"It's Rose Withers'!" he gasped. "It's Rose Withers' medal!" Jake looked around at their shocked, round-eyed faces. Another swirling gust reached into the flames sending spiraling sparks high into the night sky.

"Oh my God" Jenny hissed. "It *is* Rose's medal!" She paused as the realization sunk in fully. "Where exactly did you get it?" she asked when she could trust her voice again.

"It was buried in the sand where the little seal was laying. He must have dug it up when he made the little hole" Jake responded.

"Now you can tell Nate Withers!" Michele said.

"Huh?" Jake grunted.

"You can tell Nate Withers. Don't you see? You can tell Nate Withers what happened to Rose! This proves she never left! This shows she wasn't involved with whoever stole the lighthouse lens!" Michele exclaimed.

A slight smile crept onto Jake's face as he thought about that. Then a clouded expression pushed it away.

"What's the matter?" Michele asked him.

Jake looked at her and said, "This proves she never left the Gurnet, that's all. It shows she went over the cliff. It doesn't prove *how* she went over the cliff. It doesn't prove she was trying to save the people in the wreck. It doesn't prove she wasn't pushed over by whoever took the lens..." he said, his voice trailing off.

Their momentary feeling of triumph slipped away. They sat in silence pondering this setback, until Jenny spoke up. "You'll just have to tell him. You'll have to tell him what you saw," she said with a look of determination.

Jake shook his head slowly as he pictured the men in the white coats surrounding him. "He'll think I'm nuts" he said dejectedly.

"How do you know?" Jenny shot back.

"I know!" Jake replied, the frustration welling up again.

"You don't know that! Besides, all you can do is try" Jenny shot back. "Look, you've been looking for answers ever since you started having visions. Now you've got one right in your hand" she continued, her tone softer now. "You don't have all the answers, and you probably never will. All you can do is try,

197

and trust the answers that you do have. You have to tell him" she finished, squeezing his arm as she did so.

Jake wrestled with the idea, and he knew Jenny really believed it. He felt himself trying to believe it too, but he kept bumping up against the fear of exposing himself like that.

"Or you can just give him the medal and tell him you *think* she must have fell trying to help them" Nicky said. Jenny and Michele gave him a sour mind-your-own-business look. Nicky imitated their glares and shot it right back at them. Then turning to Jake, he said, "Look, you found her medal at the bottom of the cliff. He can't argue with that. It shows she went over. Now *you* know how she went over, but if you tell *him*, you're right, he *is* gonna think you're crazy" Nicky said.

"How do you know Dragon?" Jenny hissed.

"How do you know he won't?" Nicky shot back. "Besides, it don't matter!" He held up a hand when the girls started to protest. "It don't matter!" he shouted. "Look, if she went over the cliff, she wasn't involved. Period. It don't matter if she fell or she was pushed, she wasn't involved, see? She's gone, one way or the other." Nicky let that sink in. "So you give him the medal, Old Man Withers knows she wasn't involved, and he feels better. Then you say 'I think she was tryin' to help them', and maybe he believes you and feels even *better*. But maybe he don't believe it, and who cares? You already showed him she didn't take off on him. You already made him feel better, see? And you don't make him think your friggin' screws came loose!" he finished.

Jake smiled at the image of looses screws rattling around in his head. Nicky had a way of cutting through the crap. He wasn't one to be too trusting, Jake knew, and Jenny's advice about trusting the answers he had was too much for Nicky to sit through. Jake knew that Nicky wanted to help just as much as Jenny did; he just had a different way of looking at things. He cared less about making Nate Withers feel better than he did about seeing Jake not get hurt. And what he said made sense. Jake could just give the medal to Nate Withers. It *would* make him feel better. As far as what happened after, well he could play it by ear. He didn't have to figure it out right now.

"I'll give him the medal tomorrow" Jake said.

"Then what?" Michele asked.

"Then we'll see" Jake said. The girls tried another glare directed at Nicky, but it was wasted. He was staring into the fire, his face a stone mask, nothing more to say on the matter.

35
The Island

Tuesday morning was overcast, and the weather matched Jake's mood. The dull gray clouds seemed to press down on everything, and there wasn't a hint of wind. The air felt tropical and heavy, like a storm was coming.

Jake emerged from the shed followed by Bailey. He hesitated before going up to the cottage. He wasn't anxious to go see Nate Withers – after all, he'd never even talked to him before. Now he was going to show up with his dead wife's medal. He knew Jenny thought Nate was just a sad old man, but all the other kids thought he was creepy, and Jake wasn't anxious to find out which version was true. Part of him wished he had never found the medal, never had the visions, and he still didn't understand why all this was happening. Why him? He didn't even know Nate Withers. And what did the wreck of the Arnold have to do with anything? And what was going to happen when he found out? Was he going to have to get caught up in someone else's business, someone who he didn't even know? Was he really just a strong 'radio' picking up random signals that others couldn't? His mind started going in circles, and he forced it to stop. Just give him the medal, Jake thought, that's all. Just do that. He didn't need all the answers to just do that. But he wasn't going to do it alone, that was for sure. He thought about asking Nicky to go, and he knew that his friend would say yes, but the idea of he and Nicky facing Old Man Withers alone didn't ease the anxiety he felt.

Jake decided to ask his dad. He wouldn't have to reveal too much, he realized. He'd just tell him about the inscription on the medal he'd found, and ask him to take him to the island to return it to Nate Withers.

Jake was finishing his breakfast when he casually mentioned the medal he'd found and asked his father to bring him to return it to Mr. Withers. Brian looked the medal over and asked, "How do you know it's Rose Withers medal?"

Jake had a moment of panic, then recovered and said, "She's the only Rose I know of. Walter told me the story about her living up at the lighthouse, and I just figured..."

Brian rolled the medal in his fingers while he thought about Jake's answer. He was fairly sure Jake wasn't telling him everything, but he decided not to push him. Instead he said, "Maybe we should check with Walter. He might remember if Rose had a medal like this. After all, we wouldn't want to upset Mr. Withers if it's not hers." Jake agreed with that idea, and Brian, Jake and Bailey walked over to see Walter Guthrie.

Jake told Walter the story of finding the medal in the sand at the base of Gurnet cliff. Jenny hovered in the background to see how her grandfather would react. When Jake handed the medal to Walter, he looked visibly shaken. He grabbed hold of the kitchen chair next to him, and then sat down in it. He put on his glasses and read the inscription carefully. Then he took off his glasses and wiped a tear from his eye. Jenny stood behind him with her hand on his shoulder. Walter reached up and put a trembling hand over hers. "This belonged to Rose, alright" he said. He cleared his throat and composed himself. "Where did you say you got it?" he asked Jake.

"Down at the bottom of the cliff at the lighthouse. A little seal dug a hole there, and he must've dug up the medal" Jake told him.

"And you found it" Walter said, not really a question.

"Jake thought we should bring it to Nate Withers" Brian said.

"And Jake's right" Walter replied. "Nate will be glad to have it. I wouldn't mind going with you" Walter said, his bushy eyebrows rising up.

"That would be good" Brian answered.

"What do you say we pay a visit to my friend Nate?" Walter said, looking up at Jenny.

*

A short time later, Jake held his father's boat steady while Jenny helped Walter swing his legs over the side. When they

201

were all safely aboard, and with Bailey at lookout, Brian backed slowly away from shore. The water was like glass in the still air, with no boat traffic on this Tuesday morning. The lobster boats had gone out at dawn, and none would return until late afternoon. There were a dozen pleasure boats sitting quietly at their moorings along the length of the beach, content to admire their upside-down reflections and wait for the weekend. Their sterns all pointed toward the lighthouse with the outgoing tide. The only imperfections on the mirrored surface of the water were the occasional clumps of seaweed meandering out of the bay, and the wake trailing out behind them as they cruised slowly along the beach.

As they rounded the Head, Jake saw that the rip was barely a series of ripples ahead in the dead calm. Brian pointed to port where the harbormaster's Zodiac was nudging up against the bulge of Brown's Bank in the distance. "Looks like they're clearing the wreck you found" Brian commented. Jake looked and saw the blue flashing light on the inflatable. There was also a small barge with a boom lift and some large metal flotation buoys on deck, the kind normally used to float moorings out to be dropped in position. With everything else that had gone on, Jake had forgotten all about the Ande.

They rounded the point and Brian navigated down the channel between the marsh and the island. There wasn't much water in the bay, but the skiff didn't need much. They passed Jake's boat sitting in the mud at the edge of the marsh grass, and idled slowly through the narrow channel between the point in the marsh and the island. When they were through, Brian angled the boat toward the island where a few small boats were moored. The people on the island kept their boats on this sheltered side near the beach, safe from the northeast wind. Brian cut the engine and tilted it up as the skiff glided toward the shore. They disembarked, and Jake pushed the boat out a little and set the anchor.

They walked onshore and toward the woods, with Bailey leading the way, sniffing and snorting at the new smells here.

They'd have to walk across the island to reach Nate's house on the other side.

They walked into the trees and started down a well-worn path. The midges were thick in the still air in the shade, and they waved them away from their faces as they walked. The first thing they came to was the old family graveyard. What little conversation there was stopped as they walked by the weathered gravestones, with their inscriptions recalling lives ended much too soon in the hard days of colonial times. Even the birds seemed to respect the silence of the place.

They continued along a grass-covered path through the woods, and then the trees parted to reveal the circular clearing with Pulpit Rock hulking in the center. No matter how many times Jake saw the monolith, it still looked out of place. It was huge, rising fifteen feet out of the grass, and sprawling thirty feet in diameter in the center of the grassy clearing. There wasn't another rock even close to it in size anywhere on the island. It seemed like it was placed there by Providence in anticipation of the Pilgrims arrival in that stormy December of 1620. Bailey was the only one among them that was unimpressed by the huge rock, and she promptly trotted up, sniffed at the base, and then peed on the historic stone.

They walked around the edge of the clearing, and then followed Walter as he chose another path leading back into the trees. This path was less defined, and there was more undergrowth grasping at them from the edges. After a while, it widened slightly and Bailey nudged past to take up the lead. She trotted ahead, sniffing and exploring, her stubby tail flailing back and forth as she investigated the new territory. Suddenly she froze with her head down and the hair on her back standing in alarm. A low growl rose in her throat.

"What is it girl?" Jake whispered. He peered into the shadows ahead and his heart froze. Thirty yards down the path stood the huge coyote that Jake had seen from the boat. Just then Bailey shot down the path.

"Bailey!" Jake yelled and took off after her.

"Jake!" Brian bellowed as he started running after his son. "Jake, stop!" Brian commanded. Jake slowed and stopped halfway down, looking back and forth between his father and his dog, torn between obedience and concern. "Stay here!" Brian said as he came up beside him.

Bailey ran to within six feet of the animal and then stopped and hunched her back. They stood there, hair up, heads down, staring at each other. Then a strange thing happened. Bailey and the coyote tentatively stepped closer together, and then slowly circled. They started what looked like a familiar dance, as Brian and Jake crept closer. Soon, Bailey and the coyote were sniffing each other, their hair started to settle back down, and Bailey started to wag her tail tentatively. Jake was astounded.

"Shadow!" came a cry through the still air. The coyote's ears perked up, and he looked up the path. "Shadow!" came the cry again, and the animal started to trot up the path away from them.

"Bailey, come!" Brian called. Reluctantly, Bailey slunk back to them.

A minute later, an old man came walking down the shadowy path with the coyote following obediently at his heels. "Hello Walter" he said. "What brings you here?"

"That's *your* coyote?" Jake blurted.

Nate Withers smiled and looked down at the animal. Then he answered in a rusty voice that didn't sound like it got used too often.

"He's only part coyote, son. He's mostly shepherd, and he acts all dog. Name's Shadow. That your dog?" he asked, pointing at Bailey with a nod of his head.

"Yeah, Bailey. She's all boxer, she's just white" Jake said automatically, still looking in awe at Shadow.

"Well, I won't hold that against her" Nate mumbled. "She's a smart dog, son. She took the time to figure out it was another dog she was seeing. Most dogs just try to attack old Shadow, and they pay the price." Nate looked appreciatively at Bailey, then directly into Jake's eyes. Jake felt a little shiver as their eyes met, and then felt the echo of the overwhelming loneliness he'd sensed when they'd seen each other at the lighthouse cliff. Nate felt the connection too, and turned his eyes quickly away. "Things aren't always what they seem, and your dog understands that" Nate said in a voice that sounded like dried leaves. "Now I've met Bailey, but do you have a name son?" Nate asked, his eyes still averted.

"Yes sir, Jake Edison" he replied.

"This is Brian's son – you've met Brian" Walter said. Nate nodded at Brian. After a pause, Walter said, "We got something to talk about, Nate".

Nate looked at his friend, his face barely registering his curiosity. "Well, come on up to the house then" he said, waving at a cloud of sand fleas circling his head. "We'll get eaten alive standing here. Ain't a breath of wind today." Nate turned abruptly and started back up the path. Shadow trotted up past him with Bailey close behind, tail wagging. The others followed, waving the midges away as they went.

As they made their way through the narrow path, Jake started to feel apprehensive. All of a sudden he wasn't sure he was doing the right thing. The old man's loneliness was like a crushing weight. Jake didn't know how Nate was going to react when he saw the medal his late wife had once worn. Jake was afraid that the finality of the knowledge that his wife had perished that night would make the loneliness complete, crushing what was left of the old man's spirit. Jake didn't want to see that, or worse, feel it if that happened.

His uncertainty must have shown on his face because Jenny reached out and put a reassuring hand on his shoulder. She squeezed slightly, and nodded as if to say 'you can do this'. Jake forced himself to calm down.

They came out of the woods onto a small patch of well-kept lawn. Jake stopped and looked up to see this side of the old house on the island for the first time in his life. He'd seen the side facing the water a hundred times, but he and his friends had never ventured all the way through the dark woods to see the back of the old place. It was a whole new perspective. From the water, the house was nestling into the woods, as if trying to hide in the ever-present shadows that lived there. The effect gave the house a forbidding look. But from this side, the house was framed by the bright blue sky and the expanse of the harbor with the waves rippling and dancing. There was a small red sailboat with bright white sails gliding gently down the channel, and the scene looked like something on a magazine cover. 'Things aren't always what they seem' echoed through Jake's mind again.

The house itself was old, but well maintained. The weathered shingles were square and tight, and a few spots were slightly lighter where they had been replaced. The yellow trim was fading, but there was no sign of peeling so it had been painted in the not too distant past. Jake knew first hand how often the trim needed to be repainted when exposed to the weather on the ocean's edge.

Jake followed the group around the left side of the building, and he went up the stairs and entered the door into a small kitchen. "Make yourselves at home" Nate directed. He got three coffee cups out of the cabinet and set them down on the kitchen table in the center of the room. "Jenny, do you and your friend there drink coffee? Or I've got some cider in the fridge" he said.

"No thanks, I'm fine" Jenny said. Nate glanced at Jake.

"I'm not thirsty, thanks," Jake said. He took a seat at the table with the others.

Nate lit the gas burner under the coffee pot to warm it. He pulled out a chair and was about to sit, but then raised one finger as he remembered something and walked over to the small pantry on the far side of the kitchen. It was such a familiar gesture; Jake got an image in his head of Nate bustling back from the pantry with a plate of scones like the perfect host. He had to bite his tongue to keep from laughing, as his mind's eye put a ruffled apron on the imagined Nate, the hostess with the mostest.

Instead of a plate of scones, Nate ambled back and set a bottle of Irish whiskey next to Walter's coffee cup as he took his seat.

"If you insist," Walter said.

"I do" Nate replied. "You'll be a lot easier to talk to. Now, like I said, what brings you here?"

Walter smiled at his friend, he was about to respond, but then he stopped and tried to choose his words. The twinkle faded from his eyes, and his smile evaporated. His face grew somber as he thought about the reason for their visit.

Nate saw Walter's expression change, and he sat back in his chair and crossed his arms. He knew immediately that it was serious. After all the years they'd spent together, words were only a small part of how they communicated. He saw that his friend was struggling with how to deliver whatever news he had. After a few more moments, Nate said "Walter? Let's have it. What have you got to tell me?"

Walter poured a shot of whiskey into his cup, but rather than wait for the coffee he drank it down. He seemed to gather himself, then looked at Nate and said, "Well, it's not what I've got to tell you, it's more that Jake here has something to show

207

you. By the way, Jake's the one I gave that old boat to that you found" Walter said.

Jake felt a 'click' in his mind as this tidbit of information registered. *Nate had found the old boat?* Jake thought Walter had found it all this time. But Nate had found it? Was this unknown connection part of the reason that Jake had been drawn into events that had nothing to do with him, but had everything to do with Nate?

"I've seen you out in it" Nate said to Jake. "She's not leaking too bad?"

"No sir" Jake answered. "We fixed a bunch of leaks, but they've held up good" he said. He thought of the first trip he'd taken in it this year – the day he got the quahogs for bait that started the whole 'cycle' that Jake was so in tune with.

The cycle, as Jake thought of it, was that you used the boat to get the quahogs, you used the quahogs to catch the fish, you used the fish frames to get the lobsters...then another thought flashed through his mind.

This year, the cycle had a twist. He'd used the boat to get the clams, he'd used the clams to get the fish, and in the process he'd also gotten the old anchor. And the old anchor had a cycle all its own, didn't it? He'd used the anchor to see the Arnold, and on the Arnold he'd seen the green eyed sailor, and the sailor had tried to tell him something. *"I thought the Arnold was to be our redemption, and it may yet be"* he had said to Jake. They were words that Jake didn't understand yet, but they meant *something*, they led *somewhere*, like the bait to the fish, but Jake didn't yet know where.

"It's funny, but that old boat looks like the one that we lost on the night of the storm," Nate mused, "the one that Rose used to fish and clam in the bay. But that'd be too much of a coincidence.."

Jakes young mind didn't dismiss the idea so easily as the notion 'clicked' into place, but he agreed that it wasn't a coincidence. He pictured the Corposant, or St. Elmo's Fire, releasing a spark of its long pent-up energy on the day that Jake had gone clamming with Stevie, setting the cycle of events in motion.

The reality of those unlikely events prevented Jake from mustering the skepticism needed to ignore the 'coincidence'. Jake was marveling at how well this concept fit into the cycle, but Nate's next question brought him back.

"So what is it you've got to show me?" Nate asked.

Jake thought he felt a slight vibration in his pocket. He reached in and closed his hand around the St. Elmo medal. It felt warm to him. He reached out to Nate and the medal slipped out of his palm and dangled on the end of the fine silver chain, spinning and reflecting little bolts of sunlight around the room. It seemed to cast a spell on them, like a hypnotist's trinket, and time stopped for an instant. They sat frozen, staring at the spinning talisman.

Suddenly the coffee pot boiled over on the stove, breaking the spell. Jenny jumped up and shut off the burner. Then she took the pot and filled the cups around the table. Walter poured a shot of whiskey into his cup and then slid the bottle over to Nate. Nate poured a shot into his own cup with a shaky hand, then set the bottle down and reached out for the medal. He took it from Jake and stared at the image of St. Elmo. Then he turned it over, and taking a set of reading glasses from his pocket, he read the inscription.

To my Rose,
My Light.
My Life.

Nate clenched the medal in his hand and sagged in his chair. Walter reached out and put a hand on his shoulder and waited. Finally Nate looked up and whispered, "This belonged to my wife..." and he hung his head and began to sob.

*

When he got his composure back, Nate stood up and walked into the living room. The others followed him. Nate sat down in an old wingback chair by the fireplace and looked at the medal closely.

"I gave this to Rose on the day we were married" he said.

"Where did you get it?" he asked Jake.

"I found it at the bottom of Gurnet cliff" he answered. Then he told Nate about the baby seal that they had been feeding, and how he had found the medal in the sand where the seal had dug his little shelter behind the rock.

"All these years..." Nate said, staring at the medal. "All these years I've wondered..."

"Well now you know," Walter said. "She never left" he said, and he sat down in the other chair by the fireplace. He looked at Nate and said, "She never left. She went over the cliff that night." The question of how Rose fell that cursed night seemed to hang in the air between the two men, unasked, and unanswered.

Jake was standing near the wall looking at an old black and white photograph. In the photo, a very young Walter and Sharon were standing on the beach with Nate and the woman that had to be Rose. She was beautiful – they all were. They were young and strong, and their faces were filled with the optimism of things to come. Rose had piercing dark eyes that seemed to stare into Jake's soul across the chasm of time. Staring into those dark eyes, he said without any hesitation at all, "I think she fell trying to save the people on the rocks that night."

Nate looked at Jake, and their eyes met. Jake felt the connection again, the loneliness, the sorrow, the uncertainty, but it was muted now. It was fading.

Nate felt the connection too. He had felt it that day when they'd seen each other at the lighthouse, and earlier today when they'd met on the path. He felt it again now. There was something special about the boy, something that couldn't be explained adequately with the common words we had. Something uncommon, but not unknown to Nate. It was the same something that had caused Nate to see Rose's face reflected in the blade of the knife that he had held to the throat

210

of the Columbian stranger so many years ago. It was the same something that had caused him to hear, not imagine, but actually *hear* his wife's voice telling him that he wasn't a murderer.

It was something that couldn't be easily explained to those unfamiliar with it. An analogy popped into Nate's mind, and it seemed appropriate. It would be like trying to tell someone who had never had one what a banana tasted like, Nate thought. It tasted like a banana, but until you had one, you'd never really know what one tasted like, no matter how well described. Whatever that something was, Nate was suddenly sure that this boy knew about it too, he'd tasted it. Nate was sure that Jake *saw* things too. So instead of asking why Jake thought Rose died trying to save the people in the water, he simply said, "I think you're right, Jake".

Nate thought of all the years of uncertainty, all the whispered rumors. People who never even knew her had speculated that Rose was somehow involved in the theft of the Fresnel lens, and worse, that she'd run off on Nate. Those rumors had slowly but relentlessly worn away at Nate's soul like the waves on a seawall. It had gotten to the point where even he'd started to question whether Rose had truly left him. Even though he *knew* it couldn't be true, the question cut into his resolve every time it surfaced in his mind, and he felt a wave of guilt for even considering it. But no more. No more. Rose had never left. It didn't matter what the local gossip said, Rose had never left, and he *knew* it. The hints of doubt, and flashes of guilt were gone for good. He squeezed the medal in his hand and let out a long breath.

Jake felt relief roll off of Nate like the warmth from a woodstove. And he felt his own relief too. He'd agonized over how to explain what he'd known about Rose without sounding like a lunatic. He'd never even considered the possibility that Nate would just believe him. He'd never considered the possibility that Nate could know it too.

Jake's relief was short-lived. He turned from the black and white photo and his eyes found the next item on the wall. It was a framed oil painting, and it was much older than the black and white photo of the two happy couples on the beach.

The painting was a faded family portrait of a man and woman with a small child. They were wearing clothes like the ones Jake had seen in his history books, the kind they wore in colonial times. The woman sat with the boy in her lap, a slight smile on her lips. The man stood behind her with his hands on her shoulders, but he wasn't smiling. His face had a tortured look; it was both stern and sad at the same time. He had a piercing gaze that cut into Jake so sharply that his breath stopped. Jake felt like he would faint as he stared into the gaze of those green eyes, not for the first time. Jake had stared into those same green eyes as they had frozen over on the deck of a crippled privateer more than two hundred years ago.

Jake forced himself to breath again, as another audible 'click' echoed through his mind like a puzzle piece snapping into place. He forced his voice to stay neutral as he asked, "Who's this?" pointing at the man in the painting.

Nate looked up from his chair to the portrait on the wall. A cloud of sorrow seemed to pass briefly over his face as he looked at the man that Jake was pointing at. He looked at Jake and said, "That is Zachary Withers, Jake. He was my great-great-great-great grandfather, the first of the Withers family to come to America."

Jake had so many questions running through his head, and absolutely no idea how to ask them. He stared at the painting, trying to think of a nonchalant follow up. 'Was he a sailor?' or 'Did he die in a blizzard within sight of shore?' Nope, not cool. Jake put on his best poker face and asked, "When was that?"

Nate regarded him curiously, as if seeing right through the ruse. He sensed Jake's frantic curiosity, despite his attempts to hide it. He noticed that Jenny was also staring open-mouthed at Jake and his not-so-casual reaction to the painting. Nate felt that sense of 'something' again, and he decided to satisfy Jake's curiosity. After all, Jake had brought him the medal, with its long sought answers, and Nate felt like he owed the boy something.

Walter and Brian exchanged a questioning glance. They felt like they were missing something. They watched Jake and Jenny curiously as Nate answered.

"Zachary Withers came to America in 1771, five years before the Revolution. That painting was done in 1778 while the war was going on" Nate said. He saw that Jake was hanging on his every word, and Nate decided to elaborate. The story was part of the family history, passed down through the generations. It wasn't a story that Nate could ever recall repeating, but there was a good reason for that. As he looked at Jake, for some reason he felt like the time was right.

"He was a merchant sailor that came to the colonies on a supply ship from England. When he saw what they were building here, he decided to stay. There were opportunities that he couldn't get back in England, a chance to build a life. A chance to be free from the aristocracy and the tyranny. A chance to make something of himself. He settled down right here in Plymouth. He bought some land and began to farm. He started a family. Everything was fine until the war came" Nate said.

"Now Zachary believed in the cause of freedom. He had lived in England, and he knew first hand what it was like to be a subject of the king, how men worked their whole lives only to have what they'd earned be taken away to support the crown and the ruling class. He believed in independence for the colonies. The problem was, some of the locals didn't believe him. Some of the locals didn't trust anyone with a British accent, especially someone who had just come from there a few years before. Pretty soon there were rumors that he was a spy, or a traitor." Nate paused here and thought about how false rumors had affected his own life. He shook his head ruefully and went on.

"Life started to get hard for Zachary and his family, so he decided to join the fight. Now he'd already been sending most of his crops to support the Continental Army in the fight for freedom, but that didn't seem to matter. He decided to do something more visible, something that might change the way people looked at him and his family. He decided to go to war." Nate pointed at the family portrait hanging on his living room wall.

"His wife Anna insisted that they have that portrait done before he left. She said that if anything happened to him, she wanted his son to be able to see what kind of man his father was," Nate said.

Walter had gotten up and walked into the kitchen, and he came back in and handed Nate a tumbler with whiskey on ice. He had one for himself too, and he settled back in his chair opposite

Nate. Nate nodded his thanks, took a drink and went on with the story.

"Well, something did happen, and it didn't take long. Being a sailor and not a soldier, Zachary decided to sign on with a privateer sailing out of Boston. He said goodbye to his wife and son and rode north the week before Christmas in 1778. He signed on board with the crew of the General Arnold, a brig that was sailing south to re-supply Washington's army."

And Jake had met him on that fateful trip. He felt a profound sorrow as he recalled Zachary Withers freezing to death on the deck of that cursed ship, within sight of his hometown. A man trying to clear his family name of the false charge of treason, dying on a ship named after a real traitor. And he shivered violently as he recalled the words of the frozen sailor - *"I thought the Arnold was to be our redemption, and it may yet be"*.

Nate saw Jake's reaction and paused. "Do you know the story of the General Arnold?" he asked.

Jake nodded, his face pale. "Walter told us the story. That's horrible" he said, glancing at Jenny. She'd lost the color in her complexion also, and she looked numbly back at Jake.

"It *was* horrible" Nate said, "but such is the way of the world. Sometimes we get caught up in the currents of events that we have no control over," he said, speaking from experience. He took a sip of his whiskey as his words hung in the air. Nobody said anything, or knew what to say. The room was silent save for the tick-tock of the grandfather clock sitting in the corner, chronicling the seconds riding the waves of time.

Tick-tock, tick-tock, flew the seconds off the clock, an undercurrent to our lives, flowing endlessly. It was a sound that you could hear if you listened for it, but you never heard it if you forgot about it, and you could never *not* hear it if you tried, like on a sleepless night when you tried and tried to shut out the sound. Tick-tock, tick-tock, the clock persisted. Some in the room heard it, some did not, as each retreated into their own thoughts, reflecting on the events of two occasions long ago, and the discovery of Rose's medal that had brought *those* events into the light of *this* day, across the ocean of time.

Tick-tock, tick-tock – Jake didn't hear it, but the flow of time enveloped him nonetheless, and he was swept away once more. The images came fast and furious, like a life flashing before the eyes in the slow motion world of a car wreck.

Jake saw Zachary and Anna Withers with their young son, enduring the taunts of the townspeople in colonial Plymouth, and then Zachary was gone, leaving Anna and the child heartbroken. The scene changed as Jake was washed forward in time, and he saw Nathaniel and Rose Withers, and Rose was holding a baby (*a baby?* Jake's mind cried), and then Rose and the child were gone, and Nate stood alone, shattered, his spirit broken. Then Jake was flung back again, and he stood on the deck of the General Arnold, just as the anchor broke free and the ship heaved, throwing Jake forward again.. Now he was on his father's boat on a sunny, still day as the anchor from the fated Arnold was wrestled from its watery grave. The boat rocked under the strain of the anchor, and the ripples that rode out from the boat rocked Jake back in time, but only by a day.

He found himself at the base of Gurnet cliff, feeding the bluefish carcass to the injured seal with the white patch around his eye. A moment later, Jake was flying forward again. He had the birds eye view of the seagull as he glided away from the skiff with the shadow of the old seaweed covered anchor hanging below, and he floated along in the still blue sky following the expanding ripples caused by the resurrection of the old anchor. He followed the ripples out over the still water, arms straining, head flicking back and forth, following the little waves until they broke against the exposed sand of Brown's Bank. A dark blotch in the sand caught his sharp eye, a blotch exposed by the action of the ripples transferring the last of their energy by washing over the sand. He swooped down and landed, and he began tearing at the dark spot of seaweed, wrestling sea worms from the mass and swallowing them greedily, tearing and pecking and widening the hole in the sand. Then a wave washed over, pushing him forward again, not by even a day this time, but by only a tide. It was high tide now, and the bank was submerged. Jake could see the dark patch on the bank, the seaweed waving gently in the current. A crab was picking lazily at the weed, and then suddenly a dark shape shot through the water and snared the crab. It was the little seal with the white patch around his eye. He swallowed the crab, and then dove back at the seaweed patch, poking and searching for more food, digging at the sand, widening the hole. The seaweed danced back and forth in the enlarged hole, alternately exposing, and then covering the name ANDE on the wreck that was buried there. ANDE flashing like a strobe, now you see it, now you don't.

All at once, Jake was standing on dry ground. He was standing on Brown's Bank, and it was yesterday. He was standing next to his bucket and clamming fork, bending over to examine the wreck of the ANDE, covered in seaweed and buried in the bank. The wreck that had been disentombed by the ripples from the anchor of the General Arnold. Then Zachary's words came again - *"I thought the Arnold was to be our redemption, and it may yet be"*. "CLICK" echoed in Jake's mind, a giant piece falling into place. It was one puzzle, not two, and it was almost complete.

A loud knock at the door broke the spell, and Jake was back in the living room of the old house on the island. Jenny was standing next to him, pretending to examine the old portrait that Jake had been staring at, but she really was blocking Jake from the view of the others over by the fireplace. He'd been gone again, that was for sure, and Jenny had seen him go. She recognized the blank stare, and she had walked over to check on him while the adults sipped quietly at their drinks and rummaged through their thoughts.

She had been getting nervous that she might have to try to wake him, try to bring him back from wherever he'd gone, but she didn't want to alert the grown ups. But she also remembered how scared Jake was of getting trapped 'over there', and she was getting more scared herself the longer he was gone. Just when she thought she'd have to shake him awake, and then try

217

to explain it to the others, a loud knock on the door had brought Jake back. She whispered 'Are you okay?' as his eyes came back into focus. Jake nodded, and then turned away from the painting and looked toward the door at the front of the house.

Nate was just opening the door. An old man stood there, hat in hand. He was wearing a uniform.

Harry Corbett stepped into the living room when Nate opened the door. He was the only person Jake knew that Walter could call an old buzzard, and still sound credible. He was only a year older than Walter, but Walter liked to remind him of it whenever he got the chance. Walter liked to say that Harry had been the Harbormaster since the glacier had melted off the beach.

Harry looked around the room, a little taken aback by the crowd he saw there. It wasn't like Nate to have any company at all, much less a room full of people. "I didn't know you was havin' a party Nate" he barked. He looked around and his gaze settled on Walter sitting by the fireplace. "Ah jeez, if I did know I might not of come anyway," he said, flashing a crooked grin at Walter.

"You wouldn't have been invited" Walter replied, returning the grin. Harry reached out a grizzled paw, and they shook hands.

"Nice to see you, Walter. Been a while" Harry said.

"Good to see you too" Walter said brightly, "I thought sure you'd be dead by now." That drew a grunt of a chuckle from Harry.

Harry looked at Brian next, and extended his hand. "I'm glad you're here Brian" Harry said as the men shook hands. "Saves me a phone call. You're part of the reason I'm here to see old Nate" he said. "You and your boy there. Hello Jake" Harry said across the room. "Jenny" he said, nodding to her.

"Hi Mr. Corbett" they said in unison, and then shared an exasperated look that made the men chuckle.

"What reason is that?" Nate asked hesitantly. He was a little apprehensive now. He'd gone whole years without a single visitor, and now he had a whole houseful of them on a single day. He'd survived the first crop of them okay, and while it certainly wasn't a happy visit, they had brought him some peace of mind. Now old Harry Corbett was darkening his doorway. What the hell did he want?

"I brought some news," Harry said. "It could take a while to tell it though..." he said, looking down at the glass of whiskey Walter was holding.

"Well sit down then" Nate said with a wave of his hand, walking toward the kitchen to get some lubricant for Harry's tongue.

"Don't mind if I do" Harry said, and dropped his large frame down on the couch below the double windows that overlooked the bay.

"Care to join us, Brian?" Nate called from the kitchen.

"No thanks, I'll stick with the coffee" Brian called back.

A moment later Nate came back with the drink. "Now, try to keep it brief – I'm runnin' out of whiskey" he complained as he handed Harry his glass.

"Thanks, Nate. I'll do my best" he said, and took a swallow. He set his glass down on a coffee table made from an old lobster pot and a piece of glass, and then looked up at Brian. "You remember that old wreck you called in? The one your boy found?" Harry asked.

"Yeah, I do. It was only yesterday" Brian said, and laughed. Walter joined him, but Nate just shook his head and scowled. He didn't have enough whiskey for this, he thought dejectedly.

"You remember, boy?" Harry asked, looking at Jake.

"Sure. The Ande" Jake said. He looked at Nate's quizzical expression and explained. "I found an old lobster boat buried in Brown's Bank when we were sea clamming yesterday" Jake said.

"That's right. That's the one!" Harry beamed, like he'd finally caught up with the conversation that he had started himself. He lifted his glass and took another drink, smacking his lips as he set the glass precisely back down on the little ring of condensation on the coffee table. Nate watched this, and he felt like he was about to explode.

"Well what about it?" Nate roared.

Harry looked at Nate with total confusion, the look of someone who's lost. Then his expression cleared as he got his bearings. "Oh, well" he said, "I got a call yesterday about an old wreck that Jake'd found out on the bank." He looked hard at Nate, like this was some bit of fresh news and he wanted to see how he'd react. Nate stood there staring back blankly, trying not to bite the end of his tongue off. When Nate didn't say anything, Harry looked a little disappointed, but he pressed on.

"So I got a crew together from the marina, and we went out to get her this morning. I didn't want her floatin' free you know, creatin' a hazard to navigation and all" he said, glancing around the room to see if they understood the hazards that a free-floating wreck poses to navigation. Satisfied, he took another sip, set his glass down carefully on the wet bull's eye, and continued.

"Well, we got her up using a barge with a boom crane. She come up pretty good once we got her moving. She kinda slid out of the hole slick as could be. When she come free, we was all pretty surprised at how good o' shape she was in" Harry said. He was rolling now. "It was an old lobster boat. The cabin was mostly intact, and the bow was all there. Most of the damage to her was along the stern. That musta been the part that was sticking up when she first got buried" he surmised, pausing for another taste.

"What's this old wreck got to do with me?" Nate said, his impatience creeping into his voice.

"Nothin'" Harry said. "That's the good news, Nate. It's got nothing to do with you," he said with a note of triumph. He smiled broadly at Nate. When he saw the look of anger on Nate's face, he realized he had more explaining to do, and he went on hurriedly.

"See Nate, the cabin was intact, and there were some interestin' items in the cabin. Very interestin' items. One of them items was an old Fresnel lens, all packed up neatly in a couple of big sea trunks with blankets. The pieces are still intact, as a matter of fact," Harry said.

221

Nate felt like he'd been punched. All the air went out of him as the news sunk in. The Fresnel lens? From the lighthouse? Sitting in a wreck out on Brown's Bank all these years? Nate was in shock, speechless, and Walter was right there with him.

Harry didn't notice. He finished his drink, and decided to finish his story. "We also found something else in the cabin, or I should say some*one* else" he said. "We found the bones of the man that took that lens. Found him huddled up in the cabin with those old chests, but they stood up better than he did, let me tell you. Nothin but a pile of bones left to him now. Sorry bastard musta got caught in the storm that night, the same one that drove the Sea Witch up on the rocks at Gurnet, and killed all those folks. Seems the storm got the thief, too" Harry said, satisfied.

"Found somethin' else funny, too" Harry continued. "There was a couple of gas cans floating around in that cabin. And they still had a little gas in 'em."

Jake didn't understand. He had a gas can on his own boat. "What's funny about a couple of gas cans on a boat?" Jake asked.

Harry looked at Jake, mildly impressed at the question. "Well Jake, you're right. A couple of gas cans on your boat wouldn't be that odd. Wouldn't be strange at all, as a matter of fact. Funny thing is, that old lobster boat had a diesel engine. No good reason for a boat with a diesel engine to be haulin' gas around. There's a bad reason that I can think of, though. Gas is pretty good for lightin' fires, and there was a fire out there on the point that day the lens disappeared. Mighty convenient too, when you think about it. A fire on the point, everyone on the beach, includin' those up at the lighthouse rushin' out there to fight it, and the next thing you know, that old lens is missing..." Harry said, letting that scenario sink in.

The images of arson and theft, and storms and shipwrecks formed in all of their minds, all except Jake's mind of course. In Jake's mind, the echoing 'clicks' were the final pieces of a very long story falling into place. This story started in colonial times, with vicious rumors driving a family apart. The rumors caused an honorable man to be labeled as a traitor, and drove him to meet his fate on a cursed ship, a ship that was itself named after a traitor posing as an honorable man.

That honorable man's family had somehow forged ahead, continuing on until another shipwreck in the very same harbor almost two hundred years later had caused the same kind of evil rumors to ripple back to the surface, rumors about the very same family. But there was something else now, another set of ripples, fanning out and canceling the evil rumors, spreading from the anchor of the first wreck to finally unearth yet another wreck that held the truth. It was all one story, Jake realized. From the green-eyed sailor to Nate and Rose, from the General Arnold to the Sea Witch to the Ande, it was all one story and it was coming to an end. Jake had all the answers, and Nate would be free of the hated rumors. Nate had given the boat to Jake, and the little Corposant, St. Elmo's Fire, had started the cycle that led to the medal of St. Elmo, and to the anchor of the General Arnold, and ultimately to all the answers. Or most of the answers, Jake realized. He still had one question, and he asked it now.

"Who was the thief? Who owned the Ande?"

Harry scratched his chin and squinted. "Well, that's a question for the medical examiner, that is" he said. "We'll know for sure when he gets a chance to sort through the bones. But I got a pretty good idea. It's just like you asked Jake, sort of. Who owned that boat?" Harry asked rhetorically. "But it wasn't the Ande, Jake. That there is all that was left of the transom, see; A-N-D-E. But when she was whole, that transom read WANDERER, and I know who owned her, and so does Nate, and so does Walter" Harry finished, looking conspiratorially at the two men.

"Son of a bitch!" Walter mumbled. "Malcolm Higgs!"

"That's right, old Malcolm Higgs finally turns up again" Harry said darkly. "We thought we heard the last of him the night of the storm when he didn't come back to the dock. Town was a lot more peaceful without him tearin' it up every time he got drunk. Good riddance, we all said back then. Even his brother

223

Donnie didn't seem to miss him hanging around his garage swillin' beer and aggravatin' the customers while Donnie was tryin' to make a living."

"Malcolm was in the garage that day the week before the storm" Nate recalled. "He was there when that Columbian come up and asked me about the lens. That son of a bitch heard everything."

"Well, he didn't hear too much more after that, if it's any consolation" Walter said. "Here's to Malcolm Higgs, lobsterman in life, lobster bait in death" he toasted, clinked glasses with Nate and polished off the last of his drink.

"Like I said at the start, Nate, it's got nothing to do with you" Harry said into the silence that followed. Everyone in the room looked at him, and Harry squirmed a little in his seat. "I mean, well, it's like.." he stammered, and then he found the courage to get to the point. "Dammit, Nate, you know what I'm talkin' about! The rumors, the talk. Why there's plenty around here that've been blamin' you and Rose for what happened that night. You've heard 'em Walter!" Harry pleaded to his friend for support.

"I know, I've heard 'em too" Nate said.

"What I'm sayin' is, that's the end of it, it's got nothin' to do with you," Harry continued, "There ain't any more room for talk. Those that've been flappin' their yaps can just eat their words now. Dontcha see? It's the end of all that bull shit!" he bawled. He leaned toward Nate with his palms out and said earnestly, "This clears the family name. *That's* what I came to tell you."

Harry hoisted himself off the couch and stood for a moment to get his legs under him.

"Harry?" Nate said. Harry looked at him. "Harry, thanks. Thanks for comin' by" Nate said as he stood and shook hands again. "Don't be a stranger" he said as the harbormaster turned to leave.

"Now that I know you're entertainin', I'll stop by more often" Harry said, and he went out the door. Nate watched him lurch down the slope to the water's edge and start barking orders at the baby faced assistant harbormaster waiting in the Zodiac. Nate shut the door, a slight smile on his lips.

Walter was just coming in from the kitchen. He poured the last of the whiskey into the two glasses and handed one to Nate. "You're gonna need more whiskey" he said and settled back down in the chair by the fireplace.

"I take it you're stayin' a bit longer?" Nate asked sarcastically.

"Story's not over yet" Walter said matter-of-factly. He looked at Nate, and their expressions flashed a range of emotions. Jenny had seen them do this before. The two of them were carrying on a conversation without a single word being spoken. Walter's look was urging, Nate's a question, Walter's said you-know-what-I-mean, Nate's said are-you-crazy?, Walter's softening, pleading.

Finally, Walter said, "Nate, it's time for the whole of it. It's time for the truth."

Nate looked horrified. "But.."

"You heard Harry, Nate. This clears the family name" Walter persisted. His piercing blue eyes had none of their usual mirth now. His laser glare held Nate as still as a butterfly on a pin. "It's time to tell her" he said.

Nate hung his head and sighed. The gesture could have been one of defeat, but Jake swore he felt relief washing over him, flowing from Nate, a feeling like a great weight being lifted, like a cast being removed from a freshly healed limb, binding ropes being torn free. It was a feeling of apprehension, then surrender, then utter freedom all rolled up into one satisfying swoosh, like a fresh sea breeze pouring through an open window. It was the last time Jake would connect like that with Nate Withers, but forever after, whenever he would experience the liberation of surrender, Jake would think of this moment.

"Tell who what?" Jenny demanded, losing patience, unable to deny her curiosity any longer. Walter and Nate shared one more look at her outburst, and they began to chuckle quietly. "Tell who what?" she practically shouted at her grandfather, not amused by their laughter.

Walter feigned a look of trepidation and held his hands up as if to ward off an attack. From behind his defense he said "Hold on, hold on!" Then he lowered his arms and looked seriously at Nate. "It's time," he said.

Nate nodded almost imperceptibly. He walked over to a bookcase against the far wall and pulled out an old leather bound photo album. He sat down on the couch and began flipping through the pages. "There's a bit more to the story," Nate said. He found the photo he was looking for and opened the album for them to see. In the picture, a youthful Nate stood next to Rose, his young wife. Their faces were bliss, pure and simple. And Rose was holding a newborn baby.

'Click'. Jake leaned over to see better, and the image was already familiar.

Jenny looked at the picture, confusion, then comprehension, and then wonder parading across her countenance. "You had a baby?" she exclaimed.

Nate nodded. "We did," he said, his eyes beginning to fill, and a single tear rolling down one leathery cheek. He wiped his eyes with the sleeve of his chambray shirt, and took a drink before he continued.

"Rose and I had a baby boy in 1960" he said, his eyes taking on the far away look of one peering back through time. "He was born just after Labor Day. We named him Zachary" Nate said, focusing again on the portrait hanging on the wall, then shifting his gaze to Walter, and finally settling on Jenny. Jenny shifted nervously, starting to look uneasy, looking to Walter for direction. Walter sat stone-faced, swirling his whiskey glass and watching the ripples in the amber liquid.

Nate took a deep breath, then exhaled. He sat up straighter in his chair, and continued in a stronger voice. "Well, it was only a couple of weeks later that Rose was killed trying to save those folks on the ship" he said. He glanced at Jake and there was gratitude in the look.

"I was in town that day, as you know, and Rose and the baby were alone at the lighthouse when the fire started out on Western Point. Walter, you know this part better than me.."

Walter nodded still staring into his glass then took up the story. "Rose came down the beach riding with old Jack Seward, God rest his soul. Jack had been at his cottage on the Gurnet, and Rose took the baby and got him when she saw the smoke. Jack dropped Rose off at our cottage and went to help, and she came and banged on the door to let me and Sharon know there was a fire. There weren't many others on the beach at the time, being after Labor Day. Rose left the baby with Sharon, and she and I went over to the point to lend a hand. Of course Sharon offered to go instead, but Rose said that Nate was in town, and she was going in his stead. Part of being a keeper's wife, she said. Well, when we got there, the Devonshire place was burnin' full out. We started a bucket brigade, and did what we could, but after a while there was nothin' to do but keep the flames from spreadin' into the dune grass. After a few hours, it started to rain. It pretty much put the fire out before the wind came up, thank God."

"Well, anyway, it was getting dark now, things were under control, and Rose said she needed to get back. We rode back out to the beach, and the first thing she says is that the lighthouse is dark. I offered to drive her up there, but she says no, she can take care of it, and I should go help Sharon with the baby" Walter smiled, shaking his head at the memory. "She meant it too. She knew that old light as well as Nate, and she was proud of it. She said she'd get the light straightened out, and she'd come back for Zach. I knew better than to argue with a woman

227

whose mind is made up, so I hopped out and went to help with
Zach. Rose took my truck up to the lighthouse, and I went in
and got the fire stoked up in the wood stove so Zach would be
warm. The storm was really taking off now, and tide was
coming hard. Pretty soon it was full dark and blowin' a gale.
The water was lappin' at the dunes out front, and we knew Rose
wasn't gonna make it back 'til the tide and storm surge settled
back. I looked up toward the lighthouse and couldn't see
anything, but I'm tellin' you, it was so black and stormy, I
doubt I could of seen it if it was lit" Walter said, not for the first
time. He looked at Nate who nodded, agreeing with Walter's
claim, again, not for the first time.

Walter took a drink and quietly said, "That was the last time I
saw her. Rose never came back for the baby."

Nate cleared his throat and took over for Walter. "None of us
saw her again," he said, "at least not in person." Nate glanced at
Jake, and there was a conspiratorial look that shocked him. He
knew! Nate *knew* that Jake had seen Rose. Jake stopped
breathing for an instant, but Nate looked away and went on with
the story.

Brian noticed the look that Nate and Jake had shared, but he
didn't mention it later. He did recall it at times, though, as Jake
continued to surprise him in the coming years.

"Well, you know what happened next" Nate said. "Rose was
gone, and my life was shattered" he said matter of factly. He
paused here collecting his thoughts.

Jenny finally asked, "What happened to the baby?"

"That's actually what I started tellin' about" Nate replied. This
drew a chuckle from Walter. Nate said, "You gotta understand,
this is 1960 we're talkin' about. You gotta understand that, see?
It was different then – there weren't any day care centers, and
nannies were for the rich, see? And besides, children needed
mothers. We weren't that confused about things back then.
Children needed mothers. They needed fathers too, don't get me
wrong, but if a child could only have one, he needed a mother."
Walter nodded silent agreement at Nate's statement.

228

"Here was a newborn child that had just lost his mother. And his father is in the Coast Guard, liable to be shipped off anywhere at the whim of the gover'ment, if they don't decide to throw him in the brig first, of course. That's no life for a child" Nate said. "I had a sister livin' out in Westfield. Her husband was a logger, and they had a nice home, a nice life. Long story short, my sister took Zach in. I got transferred, and while I was away, I had time to think. Lots of time to think. I knew it would be better for Zach if he had a real family, and of course, my sister loved him as her own by now. So we agreed, and she adopted him. Zach grew up in Westfield, happy as a clam. He never knew he was adopted, and we never figured a good reason to tell him. Called me uncle Nate his whole life." Nate smiled at the memories. The effect it had on his face was profound. Jake could see the outline of the strong young man Nate had once been in the broadly smiling face. But as quick as it came, it disappeared. A cloud replaced the shine on Nate's countenance.

"He had a good life, too. I'd go visit him, and occasionally, he'd visit me. We'd fish and sail in the bay here" Nate said with a sweeping gesture out the window at the blue water. The sun was breaking through the overcast now, with glints of light dancing across the wave tops in the freshening breeze. Shadow and Bailey bolted past the window chasing a rabbit they'd spooked from the bushes, oblivious to the people watching through the window.

"Zach fell in love with the ocean during his time here. So when he was eighteen, he up and joined the Navy. Said he wanted to get out of Westfield, wanted to see the world, wanted to sail the oceans" Nate said. "My sister wasn't thrilled, but I gotta say, I was proud of the boy" Nate said, shaking his head slowly.

"Well, suffice it to say that he loved the Navy. Spent eighteen years in the service of our country, and never regretted a minute of it - until he fell in love, that is." Nate and Walter both drank the last of their drinks and set the glasses down.

"My sister and her husband had passed on while Zach was in the service, so when he got leave, he started coming around to visit me. Many's the time I thought about tellin' him the truth, tellin' him he was my son. But the thing was, everything was good. He had a good life, and I had his company when he was home. I figured it was better to just leave things be for now. I figured it was better to keep him from bein' called the son of a thief, or the son of a murderer, or all the other things folks have been whisperin' all these years. Oh, I figured I tell him eventually, but not then. I figured there was time," Nate said, "but I figured wrong."

"Zach was killed on an aircraft carrier in an accidental detonation while preparing a fighter jet for a mission. I never got to tell him the truth" Nate whispered. "He had planned to get married, and I told the woman he loved how he died, but I never told her the truth of who he was either, for the same reasons I didn't tell Zach. I never told her the truth 'cause I didn't want to tarnish the memory of the man she loved."

Nate gave Walter a questioning look. Walter nodded.

"Well it turns out the woman he loved was pregnant. She had a daughter. And I never told her what happened to her father, or who her father was" Nate said, looking at Jenny. "I never told her until now" he finished.

Jenny's face went white. Her eyes went round, and her mouth mimicked them. She looked from Nate Withers to her grandfather, back and forth, and no words would come. Walter got up from his chair and walked over and hugged Jenny, held her.

Nate said, "Jenny, my son Zachary was your father."

Walter held her closer and said, "And Nate is your other grandfather."

A whirlwind of images flew through Jenny's mind, seemingly disconnected scenes that suddenly made sense. Jenny's birthday was in July. She *always* came to the beach in July and celebrated her birthday with her mom and her grandparents. And now she realized, Nate was *always* there, always seemed to be visiting Walter. And he always seemed to act surprised that it was her birthday, but he always seemed to have some small gift to give her when he found out the occasion was special. One year, he'd given her a fistful of one-dollar coins he claimed he got as change out of a machine when he bought stamps. One year, he handed her a bunch of two-dollar bills, with a similar story. Said he had no use for funny money. Thinking of it now, Nate did a lot of shopping and letter writing for a guy who never left the island and kept to himself. One year he had given Jenny a framed panoramic photo of the beach taken from the top of the lighthouse. He'd claimed he found it cleaning out an upstairs room, and was going to give it to Sharon until he found out it was Jenny's birthday. She still had the photo hanging over her bed at home. She'd look at it on cold winter nights and wish she were at the beach, sitting around the fire with her friends. She loved that photo; the one Nate had given her. The one her grandfather had given her, she thought.

'Click". The final piece snapped into the imaginary puzzle in Jake's mind, but not really. As his mind's eye struggled to arrange all the pieces he had found this day, Jake saw a complete picture take shape. But the thing was, there were no clean edges. While the picture was a whole one, there were no flat sides to the pieces on the edges; there was no straight border to this puzzle. There was always room to add more pieces, room to build larger and more complete pictures, room to expand, like the ever-expanding ripples from an anchor tossed into a calm ocean on a sunny day.

Nate held out the photo album to Jenny. "Would you like to get to know your father?" he asked.

Some say that when you love someone they become a part of you. Here was the man that had loved her father the most. Jenny nodded and reached out for the book.

Walter let her go to Nate. He looked at Jake and Brian and said, "I believe we have some catching up to do. I'm sure Nate will give us a lift back to the beach later."

Brian nodded, and he and Jake quietly slipped out the door.

231

40
Answers

On the ride back, Bailey kept watch as usual while Jake sat on the bow facing the center console where his father stood steering the boat. Brian had lots of questions, but seeing his contemplative mood, decided not to ask them of Jake just yet. He could see Jake was still working things out, he could read it in his eyes. Jake had always been thoughtful, not content with the 'what', but wanting to know the 'why' of things. Brian decided the questions could wait, and he let his mind drift elsewhere.

Jake sat on the bow, rocking gently back and forth as his father made a continuous series of course corrections in response to the influences of the current. Jake watched the wheel go back and forth, back and forth, always adjusting, always responding. He thought back to the day when he'd helped his father repair the roof, and the conversation they'd had. The energy never going away, but lying just below the surface, the ripples that formed the waves that formed the tidal waves, building and building, until finally satisfied, they settled back down to form a sheet of glass on the ocean's surface, waiting patiently to return when the time was right. He thought of the events that had built and built over the last week, the visions of Rose and Zachary Withers, and the questions that followed, the storminess in his mind as he prepared to meet Nate, and then the answers that followed when he least expected them, and finally the peace he was feeling now, sitting on the bow, watching the wheel go back and forth, back and forth.

Suddenly Jake asked Brian a question, as if he'd been following along in Jake's mind. "Dad, do you think people make ripples too?"

On another day, it may have seemed an odd question to Brian, but not today. Not after he'd seen the events that had unfolded, the answers that had been revealed. Brian understood the question, recalling the same rooftop conversation that Jake was remembering. He too had been running the events of the last few days through his own mind, letting his thoughts drift as the engine hummed behind him, feeling the sun on his face, letting his hands steer the boat without interference from conscious thought. Brian had been thinking about recent events also - the riptide that Nicky had got caught in, and his own father's words returning to him, not for the first time - *'Don't fight it! You can't beat it. Go with it!'*

On this day, the question made perfect sense to Brian. He answered simply, "I'm sure they do Jake."

Jake grew quiet again, and he watched the wheel go back and forth, back and forth. Life was kind of like that, he thought: an endless series of course corrections. No trip followed a straight line. It was only when you tried to force the tiller that you truly got lost. Each journey required a leap of faith, a belief that just doing the next right thing would bring you closer to your destination.

Jake remembered how he had agonized last night over what to say to Nate Withers. And he recalled Jenny's words then - 'You don't have all the answers, and you probably never will. All you can do is try, and trust the answers that you do have.'

He was thinking about these words as his father brought the boat close to shore to drop him on the beach. Jake walked through the surf and was met by Michele at the water's edge.

"What happened?" she asked.

"It's a long story" Jake said, and then without hesitation, "Do you want to go for a walk?"

Michele nodded.

From the Author

This is my first attempt at writing fiction. I hope you enjoy it, and I apologize if it's a little rough around the edges, but you are what you write, I think.

I always wanted to attempt a novel, and one day I finally decided to give it a try. I knew it would be a story about the beach and there'd be some fishing involved. Other than that, I wasn't sure where it would go. But the longest journey begins with the first step, and I was determined to take it.

The only preparation I made was to read Stephen King's book 'On Writing' before beginning. In it he states that he usually doesn't know his stories until he has immersed himself in the project. That was good enough for me. If you're considering writing, I highly recommend that you read his book.

As I was working on this book, my extended family continued to deal with the loss of Lori Dragonetti. She battled with cancer at the end of her young life, but that never stopped her. Even while she was sick, she used her energy to give hope to others fighting the same battle, and hope to all of us that know her.

Her efforts continue today. Her friends, 'Lori's Angels', raise thousands of dollars each year for the fight against breast cancer. I believe that life is energy, and if our lives can be measured by the good that we do, Lori still has more energy than I'll ever have. As I said, I knew many of the events that would take place in the story, but I now know that the events that occurred while I was writing this book influenced what the story was really about. Lori showed me what I was writing about.

One event that occurs in the book is the recovery of the anchor from the 'General Arnold'. This particular scene was born from some personal experience, and I had always intended to include it if I ever did write a book.

Curiously, about a dozen years ago, while fishing for flounder with my son Greg, my brother David, and a few cousins, we recovered a huge old anchor from the seabed in the vicinity of Gurnet Light. Less than two weeks later, I happened across the story of the real 'General Arnold' while reading Edward Rowe Snow's book 'Storms and Shipwrecks of New England'. I think it may be a coincidence, but young Jake might argue the point.

Now I'd like to say a few words of thanks.

I'd like to thank my readers who struggled through the drafts and provided valuable feedback. You know who you are - Peter, Penny, David, Chris, Mike and Mike.

I'd like to thank my good friend Warren, who has always been generous with his wisdom, his wit, his hospitality, and his friendship.

Speaking of friends, I'd like to thank my brothers Tommy, David, Michael and Jimmy for allowing me to write about the relationships among teenage boys with a dose of honesty. Even though they may give you a hard time occasionally, when things get dicey, your true friends always have your back.

And finally, I offer a special thanks to my wife Sherry. Her constant, quiet support was instrumental in my being able to complete this book. She never once laughed, never once gave me a reason why someone with no experience couldn't write a novel. I spent hours and hours working on this project when I could have been doing something more 'productive', but she never once complained.

Thank you Sherry, I'm looking forward to the next thirty years.

Peter Endicott
December 5, 2010

LaVergne, TN USA
13 March 2011
219933LV00004B/63/P